CATHERINE WIMPENEY w
Manchester. *Her Sister's Shadow* is her debut
leaving Marple High School Catherine worked as a mental
health nurse. In 1991 she completed a degree in Psychology
and subsequently qualified as a Psychotherapist. She has
now retired from therapy and currently works in the family
business of Lightning Protection. Her writing keeps her
connected to the field of mental health and Catherine is
drawn to reading and writing in the moody psychological
suspense genre.

HER SISTER'S SHADOW

CATHERINE WIMPENEY

NORTHODOX PRESS

Northodox Press Ltd
Maiden Greve, Malton,
North Yorkshire, YO17 7BE

This edition 2021

1
First published in Great Britain by
Northodox Press Ltd 2021

ISBN: 978-1-8383430-5-7

This book is set in Sabon LT Std

To my mum Theresa Daulby, who would recite Shakespeare to me while she prepared dinner.

This novel contains themes of mental health, suicide, medication, and domestic abuse. If you have been affected by any of these issues the organizations listed can provide help and advice.

Samaritans Helpline: 08457909090
(freephone, 24 hours a day, seven days a week)
Website: www.samaritans.org

National Domestic Abuse Helpline: 08082000247
(freephone, 24 hours a day, seven days a week)
Website: www.nationaldahelpline.org.uk

Get Self-help: Cognitive Behaviour Therapy Resources
Website: www.getselfhelp.co.uk

"Every four minutes someone in the UK tries to take their own life; every 90 minutes someone in the UK succeeds. People who attempt suicide but survive are grateful to have survived and regret their original decision. 9 out of 10 people who attempt suicide and survive will not die from suicide in the future."

Taken from the suicide-prevention charity
The Rose Paterson Trust
Website: www.rosepatersontrust.com

Prologue

Kay

Drawing on my vanilla vape, I brood; there isn't the same satisfaction as there is with a normal cig. I miss the snap of the lighter, the hum of the flame as it burns oxygen and the first dizzying inhalation. You can crush a cigarette out in an ashtray, flick it away nonchalantly, or throw it on the floor and twist your foot in an act of finality: all intensely gratifying actions. Mood can be interpreted just by watching someone put a cigarette out.

I watch as the rising sun hits the slope of the War Museum roof and hints at a lovely summer day. The sand martins and willow warblers have arrived, and swoop and dip over the black water of the Manchester Ship Canal. Lycra-clad joggers huff and spit as they run along its banks.

The first yellow trams arrive and disgorge the baristas and hotel staff, followed by the execs, actors, and office workers. Lights come on, doors open, coffee machines steam, and the grassed areas slowly fill with break-time escapees and visitors. I feel a sudden urge to shatter this innocent scene. I want to scream, to confess, anything to relieve the weight of guilt which squats like a slab of granite on my chest.

I take a seat outside Catena and order an Americano. The waitress asks if I want milk with it. Her ignorance irritates me; she should know an Americano is always served black.

Chapter One

Kay

The investigation room buzzes with activity as I weave through the back-to-back desks, most are occupied by detective's intent on their computer screens, cups of coffee or bottled water close at hand. Their phones ring intermittently, like robins marking territories.

Jackets are discarded over chair backs as the heat from the ardent sun bores through slatted blinds. Odours of cup-a-soup and cucumber linger in the air.

A detective propels her chair a short distance across the blue-carpeted floor and passes a sheet of paper to her colleague, Detective Ashida Asante.

'These are the numbers,' I hear her say.

She looks up as I dodge past. Detective Constable Alison Cromer, one of the newer recruits, on the fast-track route from university.

'Oh, sorry, ma'am,' she says.

I wonder what she sees when she addresses me.

One of the phones stops ringing.

I make an attempt at approachability, but in truth I don't want to be approached.

'Afternoon,' I answer. 'Are those the numbers for the Assad mobile trace?'

It's a case I'm Senior Investigating Officer for, death by

dangerous driving. The investigation has uncovered a previous connection between the victim and the driver, which leads me to believe it was either deliberate or planned.'

'Yes, ma'am.'

'OK.' I walk backwards for a few seconds, such a good act, casual, in control. 'Can you give me an update at three this afternoon?'

'Yes, ma'am.'

'Great,' I turn and face front again.

'Hey,' DI Matt Anderson calls from across the room.

Matt and I were in training together; but I was promoted to DCI over a year ago.

Don't even bother asking if I slept my way to the middle. I didn't so much as flutter an eyelash. I used to wonder whether I should be insulted, because I'd never been propositioned in an inappropriate, Weinsteiny way. There wasn't a 'hashtag me neither' movement, so I'd just moved on.

My promotion hasn't affected our working partnership or Matt's penchant for acting like my big brother.

'You look like shit,' he says in his strong Salford accent, following me into my office.

I run my hands through my hair and try to hide the tremor.

'I slept in a doorway.'

'Which one?'

'Waitrose.'

He nods. 'Class.'

Landing heavily in my chair I exhale.

'You still not sleeping?'

I never know how to handle these probing questions.

'Why don't you stay at ours one night? Caro would love it; she asks about you all the time.'

'Look, Matt, I love you all, you know that, but just now, at night, I need to get up, move around. I'm restless.'

'Well, how about dinner next week?'

Cornered. Fuck. I nod.

Matt heads for the door, then stops. 'Listen, you know when you're restless at night, phone me. Really. I've told you, day or night. As Homer Simpson said, *me casa es su cazi.*' Thanking Matt, I check my watch. He's well-meaning. But as if I would call him when I can't sleep? He's a married man. I know Caro well, she's always been nice to me, but it's because I understand the boundary.

The following day is the summation of a long and drawn out court case. The jury retire and we wait for the outcome. When it comes, we aren't disappointed. Gary Brunswick is found guilty of kidnap and murder. The judge describes him as a dangerous man and sentences him to a whole life order. She says, '*it is wholly appropriate that I pass this sentence because of the danger you represent to the public.*' I resist the urge to high five Matt or give the judge a double thumbs up.

Watching as Brunswick is led away, I've a vague sense of something. Foreboding sounds too dramatic; it's something nesting, waiting to hatch. I'm distracted by it so much that when I exit the court, I walk straight towards the waiting cameras. A few flash tantalizingly in my direction and a dozen questions are thrown at me. I'm almost lured onto the rocks, but then Matt's hand is on my arm and he gently steers me away.

Superintendent Barbara Dean is close behind. She approaches with confidence and begins her statement; it's clearly her show. Anyway, my mother once told me I had a face more suited to radio.

As we drive back to headquarters, Matt says, 'We did a great job, pardner. You and I will clean up this town.'

'The only way I'm cleaning up this town is through a community order,' I reply.

Matt laughs. It's a good, throaty laugh. 'You'd probably meet a better class of people.'

Matt's expression changes, distracted by a driver coming towards us on the opposite side of the road. 'Fuck, was that idiot on his phone?' He follows the car through his rear-view mirror. 'Fucking unbelievable. I know him, he's that McGill, McGrath character, whatever his name is.'

I turn, but only catch a glimpse of a man in aviators at the wheel of a black four-by-four.

'The one who gave Brunswick an alibi, said he was working for him,' Matt explains.

I remember, a sly looking guy with close-set eyes. He'd provided the alibi which meant Brunswick was free to torture and kill a young boy called David Foster. A quiver of loathing shoots through me.

David's father, Mark Foster, crazed by grief, had pleaded with me more than once, 'Just give me five minutes alone with Brunswick.' I've heard it many times over the years, from both fathers and mothers. I get it. But Mark Foster's had been the only request I've ever seriously considered.

'He should have been prosecuted for perverting the course of justice,' I say, though it sounds laughable, a 'very naughty boy' slap on the wrist. 'Brunswick should have been hanged, along with the creep who alibied him.'

'Too right,' agrees Matt. 'That bastard knows some influential people.'

'Fucking egg and butter man.'

Matt frowns, 'What does that even mean?'

'Ah you know, small time guy, acting like a big shot. You don't want to go after him, clean up this town?'

'What? Nah? Another day won't make a difference.'

Typical Matt, loading the bullets but leaving the safety catch on.

'Y'know,' I say. 'Quentin Crisp said he never cleaned his house. He said that after three years the dust settled on everything and you couldn't tell.'

Matt shakes his head. 'Dirty bastard. Is he the one works in records?'

'Yeah, that Quentin Crisp.'

Matt looks at me. 'What?'

He pulls into the car park of the main building. 'You still on for tonight?' he asks, as he deftly parks up.

'Sure, looking forward to it,' I lie, feeling a flip of dread at the thought of the overload of sympathy from Caro.

'Pity, Caro's making a moussaka, and I don't usually like to share.'

As we enter the investigation room, Matt claps his hands in congratulations. A few members of the team join in; one whoops.

'Well done, everyone,' I add. 'Great team effort. The drinks are on Matt.'

Ashida shouts, 'Champagne all round.'

'Order a bottle of their very best Cava,' Matt jokes.

It's nice to see them in good spirits. I've pushed them hard. But I cannot shake the feeling of being an imposter. I have used the case as a diversion.

At four pm, Matt leaves to join the rest of the team for a drink at The Angel, but I decline, and tell him I'll see him at his house at seven. I approved the early finish and the celebration, but it's too soon for me. The averted gazes and dropped voices have increased, it seems, over the last few months. I'm tired of the sudden change in atmosphere whenever I enter a room.

I pack my briefcase, pull my jacket from the back of the chair, and picture the night ahead. I've not eaten all day and can feel the emptiness. Jangling food receptors, begging for an injection of carbs. I'd planned a binge, but then remembered dinner with Matt and Caro, and their six-year-old daughter, Lucy.

I've promised to provide an updated report to Barbara before I leave. Turning right out of the dim corridor towards her office, I can make out lowered voices. Instinctively, I slow my step and approach. The door is slightly ajar; inside Matt leans over the desk, he and Barbara intent on an open file.

'You think?' I hear Barbara ask.

Matt replies but his head is turned away, so I only catch the word 'annual.' They don't notice me. I feel a tightening in my throat. What am I witnessing? Something? Nothing? It feels momentous, life changing. They are close. Matt is clearly a confidante, a part of the inner circle. How have I not seen it before now?

As I retreat, I pass a waste bin. I drop the report into it in disgust and walk away. Then I think better of it, spin on my heels, and retrieve the file before leaving.

While we've been stewing inside the courtroom, outside the pavements have warmed and the bars in Spinningfields and along Deansgate are crammed with the pink-necked masses. The smell of al fresco food is tantalizing on the warm evening air. Manoeuvring my car through the traffic, I feel envy for all the party people. The tiny doll girls overdressed in barely-there outfits. How do they do it with their crammed social lives, and appearance of wealth? I've never managed it; I like to keep them separate. I compartmentalise. I keep my social life separate from work life, only my compartment for socializing is akin to an Ikea flat pack. My work life balance is a seesaw, glued to the ground at the work end.

I picture Matt and Barbara, discussing. Discussing *what?* They looked like conspirators. Matt had supposedly left the building.

I slam my brakes on at a pedestrian crossing. 'Shit.'

When everyone has passed, I set off again, mindful, less white-knuckle grip on the steering wheel, foot lighter on the accelerator. I pull onto my driveway, a neat two-storey with a racing green front door. This was once a welcoming space, but now I feel like the house doesn't remember me. The lounge walls are a deep shade of blue, which looked great in the *House and Garden* magazine; it spoke to me. It still speaks to me, but now it shouts, 'Hello, you lonely bastard.'

The house smells good though, which compensates for the emptiness. I like a diffuser in each room. My mum once said I had a very fussy nose. I guess she was right. Aromas are important to me, but I don't want the smell of a sweet shop or funeral home; I like a masculine smell. Cigar smoke for the living room, strong roasted coffee for the kitchen, and patchouli for the bedrooms.

Throwing my jacket and bag on the chair, I switch the lamps and the TV on, then go through to the kitchen to flick the kettle on. All these mundane actions help me to plant my flag, reclaim a sense of home.

The kitchen is probably my favourite. A black marble counter covers the dove grey shaker-style cabinets. I put it together myself, except for the marble top. I did all the tiling and painting too, saved a fortune. Impressed my dad. He laid a spirit level on top of the cupboards, a faint high-pitched whistle hidden within the deep timbre of his wheezing. When the bubble settled dead centre, he nodded in appreciation and told me I'd always been more of a son than a daughter. Which to him was the biggest compliment he could bestow on me.

I look towards the kitchen cupboards and then frown at the large wall clock. I'm expected at Matt's at seven. It's going to be a rush.

It's a balmy evening, and for the first time this year I've decided to wear a dress. I source most of my clothes online. I'm six feet tall and usually buy a size eighteen. I have unfashionably large ankles, which makes it challenging to find comfortable winter boots. Summer is a much easier time in the shoe department, but a complete ball ache for anything in the clothing one.

'You'll have to do,' I say. Considering myself in the mirror. A fashion editor would describe my outfit as an easy office-to-party look. 'For respectability at the office, just cover the straps and décolletage with a cardigan, or a jumper, or a monk's habit. Discard the cardi in the evening, add a sparkly necklace, and red lipstick, and *voila*, total transformation.'

Pulling my M&S sandals from the bottom of the wardrobe, I'm already perspiring. I rummage around again and eventually locate a beige evening bag and turn away from my reflection, unimpressed. Don't get me wrong, I don't hate my body, but neither do I find myself attractive. I view my form like a Tibetan monk might, or a life artist, interesting in its aesthetic and functionality, but not a thing to be ravished. Not anymore, anyway. Not in that way. No, too many scars, too much pain. Sometimes I experience a sexual twang, or twinge, a sense memory. But I ignore it. In my experience, cultivating desire only brings heartache.

Slicking a little Pink Sherbet over my lips, I press them together. I spray dry shampoo into my damp roots, then order a taxi. Halfway to Matt's, I instruct the driver to turn around and take me back. I write and rewrite a short apology text to Matt, begging him to forgive the short notice and apologizing to Caro. I say I'm not feeling well, then I turn my phone off and just hope he doesn't get it into his head to come around.

Back in the house my slippers make a satisfying slapping noise on the kitchen tiles. Reaching up, I open the large cupboard and remove various packets and cartons in a well-worn ceremony. A large bag of marshmallows, a box of Mr. Kipling French Fancies, a packet of Yum-Yums, a small bottle of chocolate milk, a bag of chocolate buttons, and four Freddo's bars. This has been my plan all along. Who've I been kidding?

Half an hour later I screw up the empty bags and push them into the kitchen bin. There's no one to hide them from anymore, but the empty wrappers are evidence I can do without.

Retracing my actions in reverse order, I turn off the lamps.

Upstairs, I briefly consider making myself sick, but I hate the smell and the taste of vomit. Instead I wash my face and brush my teeth, all the while avoiding my reflection.

In bed I feel fat and disgusted with myself. All my thoughts consumed with shame. I haven't thought about Helen, or Jack, or David Foster since the first mouthful of my binge. I pray fervently for sleep without nightmares, vowing only to eat salad and fruit tomorrow.

The impact of landing with a smack onto cold concrete reverberates up through the memory foam. I wake up, screaming, the recollection bloody and raw, like the gap left by a rotten tooth that's just been pulled. The damp sheet is entwined around me like a vine and it takes me a moment to extract myself. The edges of the dream fade but the fear remains, gripping my insides.

The bathroom tiles are cold on my bare feet. What if I'm still asleep? I concentrate on the pattern on the floor tiles. What can I do to establish I'm awake? Cry? Cut myself? Phone someone? Who? I run the shower and sit under it. Grabbing a towel from the side of the bath, I bury my face and sob as if no one is listening.

Chapter Two

Kay

Mhander Assad is sitting across from me. His solicitor beside him and Matt beside me. We've agreed Matt will ask the questions. He's still annoyed with me and doesn't know I saw him in his secret meeting with Barbara.

Assad and his solicitor are looking at me expectantly. Matt pushes his chair back, nodding at me to follow him. Outside he leans his arm against the door and whispers, 'What's going on with you?'

I just stare at him. I've no idea what he's talking about.

'You were supposed to start the questioning. We agreed I'm just the back up. I'm unfamiliar with all the nuances of the case.'

I'm shocked at his level of annoyance and I've no recollection of the discussion he claims we had.

'Did you just say nuances?' I ask. This is Matt after all.

He stares at me and shakes his head with an expression I've seen him use on Lucy.

'Is this your attempt to better yourself, to get higher up the arses of the brass? You'll be saying *au fait* next.' Ignoring his puzzled expression, I carry on. 'Firstly, I would appreciate it if you addressed me properly, *Detective Inspector*. And we agreed that you would do the talking,' I say with more conviction than I feel. 'You're just as up to date on the *nuances* as I am.' I hiss, 'If this is about last night-'

'What?' He looks even more puzzled. The furrow in his brow could probably grip something in its deep crease. 'Why would I be? It was moussaka, *ma'am.*'

I ignore the sarcasm for now. 'I saw you with Barbara Dean.'

I watch the crease clear as it dawns on him.

'Look, Kay, you need to... maybe...' He can't look at me anymore. 'You're not... y'know?'

I think I'm going to punch him, the self-serving, condescending prick. I bring myself up to my full height and he steps away.

'I'll speak to you later.' I open the door to the room and re-enter.

Matt catches it just before it swings closed and follows me in.

'My apologies,' I say. 'I just needed to clarify something with my colleague. Shall we recommence?'

I try and focus my thoughts as I take the lead. Assad is shifty all the way through the interview. He's trying to act cool, but his cover behaviours signal deceit. He almost killed a man named Dinesh Bibi. Witnesses say he seemed to deliberately change course in his car, and head for Dinesh as he was crossing the road. We've discovered a tentative link, in that they both attend the same mosque, but that's about all. We're hoping Dinesh will regain consciousness and fill in the gaps. But for now, Assad is playing his cards close to his chest. I grow exasperated but I think I hide my annoyance well. It's misplaced; I should be bollocking Matt.

Eventually, Matt and I leave the room, unspeaking. *He lied to me* keeps going around in my head. *Why didn't he tell me he'd met with Barbara? Why had he made out he was leaving for home?*

My phone rings. It's Barbara Dean; she asks to see me in the afternoon. With stomach dropping in dread, I reply, 'Of course.'

At two o'clock I make my way to Barbara's office. Worry about the meeting pecking at my insides, like a carrion crow on roadkill. Barbara's speaking on the phone and seated behind her desk when I knock at her open door. She waves me in and finishes the call, gesturing for me to take a seat. She's every inch the commanding officer, immaculate in her uniform. Short, stylish brown hair with a scattering of grey.

'How are you, Kay?'

Compared to what? I think. It's what my dad said to a nurse in the hospice when she'd asked him the same question, she'd laughed. It was Dad's joke. I should let it rest with him.

'Getting there,' I reply.

'Good. I just want to say you did some great work on the Brunswick case.'

'It was a team effort.'

'Look, I don't know how to be any other way than direct, so here it is. I'm a little concerned about you.'

My heart does an emergency stop. Barbara's kind grey eyes, scrutinise me.

'Meaning?' I try not to sound defensive, but it flows out, natural as spring water. 'Has Matt said something?'

She glances to her right, a micro-movement, and avoidant. I'm certain it was Matt.

'It's what I've observed-'

Like when?

'-I think your concentration.' Her eyes travel over me. 'You look like you've slept in your clothes.'

I look down. I'm wearing the same thing as yesterday, and OK, the day before, but it's a fucking suit. I didn't hang it up, fair enough, but it's not dirty. I wonder if I should make the 'I slept in a doorway' joke but decide against it. I reach up, straighten my hair and tug at my jacket. 'But I've just put Brunswick away for life. You just said it was good work. I got his confession. Does that sound like someone you should be concerned about?'

Barbara pulls a bottom drawer out and reaches in. 'You are an excellent detective and I want to keep it that way.'

She places a blue folder on the table. 'I've had a couple of notifications from Joanne Green.'

I frown, feigning ignorance, though I know exactly who Joanne Green is.

'She informs me you failed to attend your appointments again.'

A million replies swamp my brain, but I'm so stunned I can't catch hold of one.

'Sorry.'

'Kay.'

'Barbara, I'm sorry, I am, but honestly, I'm doing fine.'

Barbara leans forward and clasps her hands together, a friendly expression on her face. 'After what happened I think you probably needed more time. We have a duty of care, and now would be a good time, with the case done and dusted. Why don't you just make the most of the therapy sessions? They're completely confidential, you know. We don't chat about you over our hummus wraps.'

'No, Barbara, I know. But why would I want to confide in some twenty-five-year-old with a college certificate and a probable obsession with the Kardashians?'

'That's offensive, Kay, and unlike you, so I'll give you a pass.'

I feel like an idiot. I remind myself I'm a detective chief inspector and not in the headmistress's office. But Barbara's right, and her straight talking has always been one of the things I've admired most about her.

'But to answer your question, because HR said so.'

Ah, that would be Melissa Dawson, the woman who sucks the human out of human resources.

'It was a condition of your administrative leave, Kay. Unfortunately, you missed appointments on-' checking her blue folder '-eight occasions.'

No! I'm about to protest. Barbara raises her hand and interjects. 'Also, for your information, Jo Green has a Masters in

16

psychotherapy, and she's at least forty.'

Bloody hell. I thought it was just coppers who looked younger. 'I apologise, and you're right. I don't like talking about it, to anyone.'

Her tone softens. 'I know, and it's totally understandable. You've been through hell, but you know you have to be responsible for your own mental as well as physical health.'

That blue file again. 'Your next appointment is on the twenty-sixth. I'm recommending to occupational health you take some time off. That way you'll be free to attend.'

The feeling is there again, blocking my windpipe. I force it back down. 'The Assad case needs my attention.'

'Exactly,' she says. 'It requires your *full* attention.'

The insinuation isn't lost on me.

'You can continue with it, obviously, but I've assigned DI Anderson to cover in your absence.'

And there it is. Matt hasn't even mentioned it. He's had plenty of opportunities. The realisation that everything has already been arranged before I'd even set foot into her office makes me feel naive. The whole conversation has been a *fait accompli.*

'How's Ellie?' She asks.

I look up at the mention of my niece. Helen's daughter. Barbara met her at Helen's funeral and often asks after her.

'Good, yeah, getting there. It takes time.'

'Well, you need time now. Go to the cottage, you used to love it there-'

I wonder what she knows.

'-Have a proper break and a rest, do some grieving. Meet up with Ellie.'

'I don't need time off to grieve. I can multitask. I need to work, y'know, I need something to focus on.' I try.

'Kay, a break is a good thing, not a punishment. And-'

'OK,' I say, cutting her off. I stand up, suddenly aware of the creases in my suit. I pull the jacket closed and button it up. It strains across my bust and stomach and I hold myself in.

'You can come and talk to me if you need help with anything. My door is always open, except when it's closed.' She comes from around her desk and walks me to the door. 'Wales isn't it? Your cottage?'

I nod. 'Scotland, but close enough.'

Returning to my office I pull my jacket off. The sleeves stick to my arms, and I have a small paddy as I struggle with it. When it's finally off and I can breathe again, I sit for a moment, wishing that I'd taped the conversation, wondering if Barbara did.

She had said a condition of my return to work, almost a year ago now, was that I attended therapy. I'd attended two, OK, one session, the assessment. Since then things had been fine, so why now? Why am I suddenly being encouraged to take some time out? I look at the qualifications and commendations that adorn my wall, and they stare back as if to say, figure it out, detective.

I notice my leg is shaking, up and down like a piston. I place a hand on my thigh to steady it. Eventually it slows and stops.

I see Matt through the glass partition wall with his back to me, speaking on the phone. He swivels his chair around and our eyes lock. His expression freezes. I don't blink. I imagine I can travel through his gaze, through his orbital receptors and into his brain, moving to the hypothalamus and amygdala. I read his pity. I know guilt when I see it. He looks away and the link is cut.

Chapter Three

Kay

Monday morning comes, and everything feels unfamiliar, my actions laboured. Following the meeting with Barbara I seethed for a while, then returned to her office and informed her that I would take my leave starting immediately. Unruffled, she'd agreed. I'd expected a little resistance, so that I could at least remain indignant and appear to be in control of the situation. Instead, I left feeling deflated and wished I'd slept on it, (as if I would have slept) before acting so rashly.

Shortly after I got home, I received a text from Joanne Green, offering me an appointment for this morning.

★ ★ ★

Dr. Joanne Green sits opposite me in her tidy cream therapy room. Her dark red hair cut into a trendy asymmetrical style, different from when I last saw her. I couldn't be arsed with the maintenance of such a cut. She still looks younger than forty. You can't trust your eyes nowadays. Botox isn't helpful for eye witness statements.

Joanne's wearing a black cotton dress and wedge sandals with red gel toenails to match her fingernails. She's wearing a wedding ring but no other jewellery; nothing to see here, move along. Eyes a bluey green, hard to decide in this light.

She's about five foot six and sits with a straight back.

Certificates adorn the wall behind her, British Psychological Society stands out with Joanne's name etched in an elegant looping font. The print is too small to decipher anything else. On her desk is a small laptop, several pens and a professional journal. I spot a small rectangular picture, its face turned away. I have a strong urge to lean over and look at it. What's in that photograph that makes Dr. Green want it on her desk? What would it reveal about her?

Months ago, in the assessment, Joanne explained the model of cognitive behavioural therapy to me. She's drawn it out again on a flip chart, a circle with arrows moving from the trigger through to thoughts, feelings, physical symptoms, and behaviour. *Whatever.*

'On the second question. Do you feel bad about yourself - or that you are a failure or have let yourself or your family down? You've ticked number four, *all of the time.*'

'Yes,' I reply.

'And how do those feelings manifest?'

'How do you mean?'

It's warm in the room, like the throat catching heat of a dry sauna. I lick my lips and taste old coffee. I can hear the passing traffic, and the faint whiff of petrol fumes floats through the open window. A church bell peals in the distance and I check my watch; it's bang on eleven.

'What image or memory came to you when you think about the question?'

Joanne has the habit of looking at my forehead and not my eyes when she asks a question. I imagine a yellow post-it-note there with 'traitor' written on it, resisting the temptation to reach up and check.

'Well, I imagine everyone who ends up in this chair feels they've let themselves down.'

'So, asking for help means you've let yourself or your family

20

down?'

'Yes.'

'You don't want to be here?'

'No.'

'I see.'

She considers me as I look around her office. 'Can you elaborate?'

Elaborate on nothing? I know I'm being a bitch and obstructive.

'Look, Jane,' I say.

'*Joanne.*'

'Joanne. The way I deal with things is not to dwell too much. The only things I tend to dwell on for any period are the cases I investigate. I use all my-' I make a patronizing inverted commas sign '-dwelling for that. I've run out of it by the time I get home.'

'Have you heard of the curse of the strong?'

'Oh, for fuss sake.' I shake my head and look towards the window. 'Sorry,' I say. 'I didn't actually swear, though.'

'It's OK. The curse of the strong refers to people who believe it's a sign of weakness to ask for help, or to admit to mental health problems.'

'Okay, it's not that. It's just I don't like being on the other side, answering questions.'

'Do you want to talk about the death of your sister?' she asks, addressing my forehead.

The session finishes and I agree to keep a thought diary. Joanne advises me to consider anti-depressants. I say I can manage that, and immediately forget about it and leave. I wonder whether she has my GP notes from when I was a child. When I was around twelve, I started to worry about world affairs and constantly sought reassurance that everything would be OK. I sat close to the television and absorbed world disasters and tragedy, as though each story was a Saturday matinee cliff hanger. It worried my mum, and it drove Helen to distraction because there was only one television in the house then.

My school had provided sessions with an educational psychologist. When she asked me what I thought the problem was, I had no means to describe the fear which consumed me like a flesh-eating bug. All I could say was I was afraid of what would happen next.

The diagnosis had been generalised anxiety disorder. I'd been prescribed a low dose of medication. Watching the news was forbidden, and my father, who eventually returned home permanently, was given strict instructions to stop reassuring me. I recovered, but I always knew when I grew up, I would apply for a post where 'making the world a better place' was in the job description.

Putting a shit like Brunswick away for the remainder of his natural certainly fulfils my career goals. Acknowledging the department can manage without me for a few weeks is another matter.

I drive away feeling the thing inside me has moved up during the session and taken up permanent residence. If I open my mouth wide enough, I'll see its head poking out.

I stop at Waitrose and buy a couple of reduced-price sandwiches. I briefly check the use-by dates on a box of fresh cream cakes, then throw them into the trolley. Why would anyone need to put a use-by date on a box of cream cakes? They'll be lucky if they make it home. Finally, I chuck in a bottle of chocolate milk, kitchen roll and some floor cleaner, then make my way to the self-service check-out. For some reason the floor cleaner won't register, and I need an assistant to come and authorise it. For fuck's sake, it would be easier to smuggle crystal meth over the Mexican border. The cashier gives me a cursory glance. I feel like showing her my badge. She sanctions the bleach with an authoritative air. Those cashiers don't miss a trick. I could do with a few of them on my team.

After unloading the shopping into the boot of my car, I walk briskly over the road to Marks and Spencer. A box of chocolate biscuits, two small cartons of rice pudding, a loaf of bread, a packet of lemon Yum-Yums, tea bags, tampons and a roll of bin liners later, I'm done. Evening ahead sorted.

Chapter Four

—

Kay

It seems I'm on a sleep treadmill, which generates energy for vivid dreams and nightmares. I invariably awake exhausted, frightened. Lumbering downstairs, I flick the kettle on and see I've written 'black bin liners' on the kitchen whiteboard as a reminder. I rub it clean with a piece of kitchen roll and scrawl FUCK YOU on it in big black letters.

Maintain a structure, Joanne said. So I've spent the last few days attempting to clear my house of unwanted stuff. I've sorted clothes I no longer wear into piles for the charity shop and clothes I intend to slim into; I've transferred the second pile to the spare bedroom wardrobe. I pause mid-sort and lie down.

When I awake, some of the clothes I've sorted for the charity shop seem a lot more appealing, and I end up putting them back in the wardrobe. What can I tell you? It's an imperfect system.

Ellie called for a catch-up. Since Helen's death she's taken it upon herself to phone me every week. I should really be stepping up to the mark for her, but she has Nate and her dad to look out for her, and I do have a very demanding job. Or I did. I told her about my imposed leave. I was grateful to her for being outraged on my behalf. She invited me to stay with her and Nate for a few days in York. A 'cheeky holiday' she called it. In truth, I've been avoiding her and don't want her to see the guilt in my face.

'I've got some stuff to catch up on here. I'll be fine.'

'Are you sure, Aunty Kay? I could come there and spend a few days with you. You don't sound great.'

'No, thanks.' She wouldn't feel like that if she knew. 'I'm just exhausted.'

'Aunty Kay, are you crying? Do you want me to come?'

'No, no, thank you, my love. I'm not crying,' I say, surprised to find that I am. 'I think I have the flu. I'll take some Lem-Sip.'

'Have you seen Dad?'

At the mention of Jack, her dad, I feel immediately guilty and answer too quickly, 'No. Why?'

'He said he was going to call to see how you were.'

'No, no, Ellie, I don't need him to check on me, please tell him. You and your dad should be looking after each other. I'm fine.'

'We *all* need to look after *each other*. You included.'

The sympathy draws fresh tears, and I stay quiet as I cover my nose and mouth with a tissue.

After a moment Ellie says, 'It's OK to cry, you know. Just get some rest and I'll phone you later.'

The call ends and I flop back on the bed, sniffing the tears back. Then I pull the covers over my head and stay there for the rest of the day and through the night.

Arms flailing, I feel the pull of gravity on my insides. I know I need to wake up. Gasping, sweating, aware I'm gripping the sheets, I sit up.

The relief of waking is immense, but I feel somehow bereft, like a mother whose new-born has been snatched from her arms. Facing me on the wall is a photograph of all of us, me, Helen, Mum and Dad. I should move it. It provokes such poignant memories, but I'm the only one of us left to remember. I need to break this mood and get some fresh air. I climb out of bed and shuffle into the bathroom, shower and dress.

Downstairs, I make myself a strong black coffee in my retro thermos, a present from Ellie. Finally, I step outside and take a deep breath.

It's a fine sunrise; the first yellow rays of morning dust the sky with the promise of the day to come. Scanning the Manchester skyline, I count eight cranes grouped closely together in the distance, their lofty red necks tilted towards each other as if in conference.

As I sip my coffee, the shell of a building under construction draws my eye. The steel hoarding reads MCGRATH BUILDING SERVICES. I recognise the name, but I can't place it. Through a small gap in the panels I spy a digger, its silent, empty bucket like a pelican's pouch waiting to scoop up the cracked, weed-strewn earth.

I have that primitive animal sense of knowing I'm being observed and snap my head up sharply. All my senses alert and attuned to movement. The air around me stills. From high above, I can vaguely discern a dark shape. My jaw tingles. I feel a coldness creep through my sinews. Riveted to the spot.

The shape retreats into the shadow again. I feel disconnected from my surroundings and tell myself I've imagined it. I start to walk away, but turn back at the sound of falling rubble. It hits the ground and a cloud of dust erupts, like a genie summoned.

Shielding my eyes, I peer up again. There's definitely something or someone up there.

I walk along the perimeter of the building; searching for an opening, then push against the partition until I feel it give. I look up again and count the levels, so I know which floor I'm aiming for. Brick dust crunches under my feet as I take the exposed stairs. Each level is numbered with red paint. I'm alert, wary. Arriving at level five, I can see the door has been pushed slightly ajar. In all my years as a detective, in all the dangerous situations I've had to go into, I can swear my heart has never beaten so hard. There is such a bad vibe to this whole situation, what Matt would call a spider sense. Listening to it has probably saved my life on a couple of occasions.

Cautiously stepping through the opening, I can see a woman with her back to me.

'Helen?' The word leaves my lips before I can stop it.

She turns.

Not Helen, obviously.

The woman looks to be in her early thirties. Purple crescents frame her dark eyes. She has shoulder-length brown hair and is wearing a black leather jacket with a long black dress, a bit Goth. I look down and notice her bare feet.

There's a resignation in her expression.

I stand very still as the air settles.

'Hey. I'm Kay.'

'Please don't come closer,' the woman says.

Her voice is weary but I heed the warning in it.

'For every step you take towards me I'll take one back.'

I curse myself for not phoning the emergency services, but I couldn't be sure whether I was hallucinating. I'd told myself it just couldn't be real and for a moment I wonder if I'm still trapped in a nightmare.

'OK,' I say, my training kicking in. 'I'm going to sit. If that's all right?'

She pauses, gives a slight nod of her head.

Lowering myself to the ground, I realise I'm vain enough to want to do it with some degree of grace.

'I'll probably need your help to get back up, though.' Jesus Christ. Hilarious.

No reaction.

'Can you tell me your name?'

'It's Ava,' she replies flatly, lifting her head.

Memories flash before me. I curse myself for having looked up, for giving a shit.

I see myself stand up and walk back down the stairs, away from the building without looking back. It's what I should do. People kill themselves: fact.

But I stay put.

'Are you alone, Ava?'

She nods.

'Can you talk to me, tell me what brought you to this?'

'And why would I do that?' she asks.

Yes, why?

'Do you think I haven't spoken to people? Do you think that this was my first option?' she turns her back again.

My thoughts dry up with my saliva. This woman, Ava, emanates a profound sense of defeat. I can hear it in her, see it in her eyes and the movements of her body.

The realisation I'm the only thing standing in the way of her imminent death hits me.

Has fate brought me here? I wonder.

'Give me a chance?' I say.

'Why would you care?'

Because it cripples the ones you leave behind. The misery is purgatory, hell on earth.

'Try me. I'm not perfect, but I might be able to help.'

'There are no answers. No one can help me.'

'Is it money?'

She shakes her head. I want her to stop in case the movement throws her off balance.

An image comes: *hair, soaked red, rivulets mixed with the dust and grit on the concrete.*

'My ex-husband,' she says quietly. 'He finds me every time. It's like he's planted a tracker in my head. I can't escape him.'

'Have you tried the refuge?'

She sighs. 'Yes, yes, it's no use. Look, please can you leave? This is private.'

'Do you have children?' I ask, hoping to build a connection, playing for time.

She smiles. I know smiling means nothing; she could be whistling *Dixie* and still jump.

'A son, Josh. He's gone.'

Shit. Wrong question. Quick. Change direction.

'Wait.' Hands up, submissive. 'I'm a detective. I could help.' I'm ad-libbing, but I've got her attention. 'I have my ID in my pocket.' Slowly standing, I pull my ID out. 'I'm Detective Chief Inspector Kay Harris.'

She blinks, slowly. 'What's that, a magic wand?'

Shit. I realise I may've just compounded her belief that no one can help. I know she needs a place of safety, a safe house; maybe I could..?

An idea like a single cell begins to form and multiply. Within seconds it seems possible. 'I've a place in Scotland. You could stay there, and I could pull some strings, do things you couldn't do on your own.' It sounds strange saying it, a bit weird.

Silence.

'There'd be no strings attached. No conditions.' Even weirder?

'And why would you do that?'

Fair question.

'Because I can. Because, well, it's a long story, but I'm telling you the truth. You could be free of *him*. I could help.'

I step towards her.

'No, *you* can't,' she whispers, and steps back.

Caution abandoned, I rush forward. Caught off guard, Ava recoils, though I manage to curl an arm around her waist. I pull her away from the edge, clumsily. She screams at me as we fall onto the concrete and I land on my back, winded. Twisting around, frantic, I see she's landed on her side, a foot away from me. I scramble towards her with the feeling I'm moving through my nightmare. I reach her as she slowly pulls herself up. Heart still thudding, I check if she's hurt. Her jacket appears to have protected her arms from any serious injury; apart from a scrape on her ankle, she appears fine.

'Where are your shoes?' I ask.

Chapter Five

—

Kay

Our parents bought Tay Cottage when Helen was fourteen and I was eight. Helen hated coming here, away from her normal routine. I was just happy to have the family together and my sister to myself. That was before Mum got ill and Dad was lost to us for a time.

It's a double-fronted white cottage. The etched stone lintel over the front door proclaims that it was built in eighteen seventy-six. The rooms are decorated to Mum's taste, favouring deep jewel colours, velvet fabrics and cushions were always a feature. Dad used to complain there were too many, but I sided with Mum. In the evenings when the fire was lit, Mum would pile cushions up at one end of the settee and lean back, feet up. She'd signal to me and Helen and we'd clamber up and somehow interweave with her, like a pride of lions. I'd never felt so safe.

Downstairs is a small porch where the inner door opens into a wide lounge. On the right as you go in is a large eight-seater dining table, hardly ever used nowadays because everyone prefers to eat in the kitchen.

To the left, a large sofa faces the fire, with another sofa turned sideways to the fire and an armchair to the right. Behind it is the entrance to the large farmhouse kitchen. Two large carved newel posts, just to the right of the fireplace frame the bottom of the staircase. Four stairs up there's a small landing where the staircase turns back on itself. Two bedrooms and the family bathroom on the first floor, then the attic room.

The attic used to be Helen's room; it has an en-suite. I was so envious of her. Mum and Dad said it gave her the space she needed. The two small skylight windows can only be opened an inch. Ava sleeps there and I stay in the bedroom on the first floor, my old room.

Not for the first time I question my motives for bringing Ava here. I admit I'm confused; I'm not sure if I've stepped outside of an ethical, professional boundary. Surely, if I'm on leave, it's up to me who I bring here. I tell myself I'm just helping another human being. Also, I've noticed a strange atmosphere in the cottage. I'm still having vivid nightmares; seems I've brought my ghosts with me.

'I used to play white noise on my iPhone to help me go to sleep. It sounded just like this, the river and the trees,' Ava tells me, as we walk through a thistle field on the ridge overlooking the loch. She tilts her head and listens. The shadows under her eyes remain and I know she's not sleeping well. Her hair blows flat against her head, reminding me of a blackbird's wings.

'Glen Lyon was once described by Sir Walter Scott as the longest, loneliest, and loveliest glen in Scotland,' I tell her.

She nods. 'I can see why you thought it would be safe here.'

It's the first time either of us has addressed the reason we're here. So far we've made polite small talk while manoeuvring our way around the cottage, and getting accustomed to sharing the space.

'Do you feel safe?' I ask.

It's a moment before she answers. 'Do you?'

'Me?'

'I could be a danger to you, if he finds me.'

In truth I've never even considered this. The cottage is

remote, and her ex wouldn't have any reason to look here.

'No,' I answer truthfully. 'But what about you? Why did you trust me, a stranger?'

She exhales and shrugs. There's a whole lot in that gesture.

'You don't know me either,' she says. 'You've gone out on a limb for me. I could be a mass murderer.'

My turn to shrug; it's infectious. 'But if you were a murderer...' I pause and wonder if I'm going too far.

'Yes?' she challenges, eyebrow raised.

'You would have killed him, your ex, and not turned on yourself. I think I would have...' I see her expression and my words trail off.

'You're a copper, trained. I can see you doing that, no problem. I bet you can look after yourself.'

'True,' I nod. I think about Matt and his betrayal. I could have punched him in the face, twice a day, quite happily for it.

Droplets land heavily on my waterproof jacket. 'Come on,' I say. 'The rain's very wet around here.'

The evening air has chilled the house, and I light a fire in the living room while Ava runs a bath. The family bathroom is located on the first floor. I climb halfway up the stairs and listen out for splashing water and call out, 'Ava?'

There's a moment of tense silence before she replies, 'I'm fine.'

Returning to the living room, I check my phone. Two messages. I'm surprised to see one is from Matt. I listen.

'Hey, I'm just giving you an update on the case. We're interviewing Assad's girlfriend today. She's just got back off holiday.' There's an awkward pause. *'Anyway, hope you have a good rest.'* I hear Caro's voice in the background. *'Caro says hi. Just ma-'* then the connection fails. I decide not to phone him back. He can stew for a bit.

Then the next message begins and I need to sit down. It's Jack, the familiar, deep intonation. There's no humour in it, but there's warmth and regret. It's a short message. '*Please, can we talk?*'

I pace, not wanting to think. Does he know I'm here? I think about the time we've spent here, all those days and nights. When childhood memory was overwritten with a new story. One which included Jack, and love, and betrayal.

I'm startled when Ava enters, white towel wrapped around her head like a fifties film star. I walk quickly into the kitchen and grip the edge of the Belfast sink. Ava follows. I move to the fridge and pretend to search for something.

'Do you want any help?' she asks.

I mumble, 'Thanks, no.'

She returns to the living room without a sound.

'Stir fry okay for you?' I call after her.

We eat at the long wooden kitchen table. I pour a glass of red wine for myself then offer some to Ava.

'Just a drop. Alcohol is a central nervous system depressant, you know.'

'I'll drink to that,' I say and pour a small amount into her glass. We clink them together and Ava takes a delicate sip while picking at her food. I, on the other hand, down half of my glass in a matter of seconds. I could knock the whole lot back, but restrain myself, I watch as she moves her food around the plate.

'Don't worry, if you don't like it, I won't be offended. Cooking was never my forte. I'm better at cake.'

She looks up. 'No, it's really good, it is. It's just that I have no appetite.'

'Not a problem.'

The wine is having the desired effect. I scoop our plates up and put them on the draining board, Ava watching.

'What happened to you, Kay?'

'What do you mean?'

'Well, you look distracted. Is it on account of me?'

An image comes. Helen. They have lessened in frequency

over the last couple of months, but when they come, they strike like a volley from a fast bowler. The room tips slightly, as though the house is adrift on the loch. I grip the back of the chair to steady myself before replying.

'No. How can it be?'

'Well, like I said. Hasn't it occurred to you that my ex might come looking for me? He's found me before; he'll find me again. He's like the robot who chases Arnold Schwarzenegger.'

'Ava, no one knows you're here.' I can see the doubt in her eyes. 'Look, I said I would help and I will.'

'How?'

'I'll come up with a plan, I'm a detective, and I know stuff, got certificates and everything. Just lie low here, and don't kill yourself.' I sound patronizing. It's the wine, I've not had enough of it. I pour myself another glass.

'Why there?' I want to know. 'If you don't want to answer it's...'

'No, it's fine. I know, it's not exactly the Golden Gate Bridge is it? I was hardly going to be immortalised. It's one of Adrian's. It's his company, McGrath Construction.'

That name again.

'It seemed apt. It's a stalled project. The client ran out of funds, and I know of old that Adrian would never put a security guard on until there was something on site worth nicking.'

I nod. We're quiet for a moment, each lost in our own minds.

'What changed your mind, on the ledge?' I ask tentatively.

'What makes you think I did? After all, *you* pulled me back.'

'I suppose I'm asking are you sorry I stopped you?'

'Well, he's still out there. The reason I decided to kill myself hasn't gone away.'

I can see my reflection in the black of the kitchen window. I lower the blind and feel her watching me, waiting for me to do something.

Chapter Six

Kay

Helen is with me. I'm so happy because I want to tell her something. I keep missing the chance. I reach out and my fingertips brush hers. Then we're free-falling. The wind whips and buffets us as our coat tails flail about like thrashing wings. She falls through a bank of clouds and disappears.

I sit up in bed and look around, feeling like I've walked in on a conversation which has stopped abruptly. Grief is a wound, and each time I dream of my sister, the scab is ripped off and the wound is re-opened.

I quietly open the bedroom door in my t-shirt and jogging bottoms. The worn wooden stairs creak and groan under foot, like the irked old bones of the house. There's a noise coming from Ava's room. I turn around and impose myself again on the aged wood. The door to the attic is slightly ajar and I can vaguely make out Ava's shape in the bed. I'm aware how weird it will look if she suddenly wakes up, but she seems to be dreaming. I can't quite catch what she's saying. It might be '*Let me go.*'

The words almost a whisper and spoken so pitifully they send a shiver right through me. A cold finger of fear traces its way up my spine. I can smell rose and jasmine, Helen's perfume. A primitive instinct tells me she's standing just beside me. My eyes water, breathing rapid and shallow. Very slowly, I turn.

The space beside me is empty. My muscles loosen, I hang my head and sigh. Gently I turn to head downstairs.

Scouring the cupboards, I can find only crackers and some cheese. It's been two days since my last binge. I've not been able to leave Ava on her own, so there's no binge food in the house. I cut four slices of bread from a large tin loaf and toast them.

I remember we have an old bottle of brandy in the pantry, Jack's favourite brand. My hand shakes as I pour. Embers from the fire still glow in the hearth, and as I lie down on the old worn settee, the mug of brandy balanced on my chest, an image of Jack catches me unaware. Tears slide down my face and onto the cushions. I search for the TV remote and distraction.

I wake up at five a.m., head fuggy and brandy brained, as Jack used to call it. Spirits have never agreed with me and I've never learned. Donning walking boots and a waterproof, I go for an early walk around Loch Tay.

The last time I saw it this early was the previous April. The banks swollen by the melting snows of the surrounding mountains. Some of the roads to and from Stirling were closed. I didn't mind. It gave Ellie and me valuable time together. We'd discussed selling the cottage, even if I was loath to let it go. Still, we'd sorted through Helen's things. Emotional was an understatement. We reminisced, looking at family photographs, laughing and crying at the same time. Ellie asked if I'd found her mum's journal. I told her I hadn't, unsure whether she believed me. She hadn't pushed further.

I watch the mist clear over the loch, revealing a water colour palette of blues and greens, the perfect perspective of mountains in the distance with small white boats bobbing in the foreground. Crossbills add to the dawn chorus with a *glipp* and *tupp*, their very own Scottish accent.

I open Helen's journal.

September 27th

I'm not on a one to one any more, which is an improvement. They just check up on me every fifteen minutes now.

Mike, the psychologist said he thought I was making progress. How would he know? Anyone can act as if they're getting better, once they learn what to say and do. Edward Semper, the mass murderer, was pronounced completely rehabilitated by his psychiatrist, while he had the body of his latest victim in the boot of his car.

I miss Jack and I miss home. I know he's busy at work, but I can't help wishing he could make it here more often.

Ellie's been a few times. She said she thought I'd put a bit of weight on. I never thought I'd be pleased to hear those words! Kay's been too, though I know she's just started work on a big case. She has a lot of responsibility, she's always carried a lot of responsibility, even as a child. I still feel guilty about that. I wasn't there for her when Mum was ill. I was too busy with Uni and coping with my own stuff.

I really don't think I can recover here, there's nothing to do. Apparently they used to have art and pottery classes and a film club, all part of the occupational therapy programme. Alas, one of the staff nurses told me all the funding was taken away and given to the eye department. There's no way to spin it, mental health just isn't sexy enough, the eyes have it.

I keep going over the same stuff. I know I've not been easy, but Jack knew when we got together that I'd been treated for depression for many years. I told him you never really recover from depression. He always said it didn't matter, some of the most amazing people have depression, I was in good company.

The thing is when you admit to it makes you vulnerable. People take advantage of it; Jack did. If anything was wrong between us it was always blamed on my 'moods'. He never took responsibility. Sometimes he's a shit. I'm so hurt by what he said. I know what he wants from me, but I'll never give it to him.

Feeling like a voyeur I snap the journal shut. It's clearly not for my eyes. It's for her husband. He should really have it. But there are things I need to know first, to protect everyone.

Ava is still asleep when I return to the cottage. In the kitchen, I rip chunks of bread from the remainder of the loaf and shove it into my mouth. I'm so thirsty I drink straight from a bottle of milk which dribbles down my neck as I mulch the food together. Not an attractive look. Searching the cupboards, I find a packet of crackers and empty them onto the counter top, then cover each with butter and crunch greedily. The crumbs cling to my jumper until my chest resembles a mud-cracked landscape. It isn't a very satisfying binge but it does the trick for now.

Needing a distraction, I switch the computer on and access Holmes 2 the police database where all the witness statements and interviews, and numerous other documents are recorded. I request all available data on Adrian McGrath. The records department will assume it's a new case I'm working on. There are copious photographs of McGrath on Facebook. I have a sudden flash of recognition. I know him: he's the man in the black four-by-four, the butter and egg man. Gary Brunswick's fake alibi.

Fuck.

I click again. Various selfies. Adrian with a football team, at the gym, a black-tie gala, smiling into the camera as though he's somebody. One in particular catches my attention, Adrian with Gary Brunswick, the man who murdered David Foster. They look cosy. Brunswick, a good foot taller than McGrath, has one arm slung across McGrath's shoulder. Buddies in an 'I've got your back' kind of way. For a nanosecond I envy them.

Bastard.

I realise Ava may be right. She may not only be in danger from herself, but also from outside forces. I already know McGrath has powerful allies. I wonder how I can keep her safe while taking the actions needed. I can't be in two places at once, and I can't exactly lock her in the cellar.

Noises from above. Ava is awake. I close the laptop and put the kettle on, still reeling from the discovery that the crook on Facebook is the man who made it possible for Brunswick to be free to murder a child. The same person who drove Ava to want to kill herself.

Water splashes from the spout as I slam the kettle down on its base.

'Morning,' Ava says, entering the kitchen.

'Morning.' I wipe the spilled water away and try to calm myself.

'You OK?' Ava asks.

'Yeah, sure, never better.' I turn and bare my teeth in a forced smile, hoping it will trick my nervous system into standing down. 'I was thinking we could go into town if you'd like. There are a couple of nice cafes and a cinema, we could see what's on? It'll do us both good to get out of here.'

She frowns.

'Here.' I pull a pink brimmed sun hat from the coat rack. Then I root around in the kitchen drawer for an old pair of sunglasses. They've been in the drawer for many years and even though we've had a few clear-outs the sunglasses have always survived the cull. It's one of those satisfying 'I knew they would come in handy one day' moments.

A small dimple appears on Ava's cheek, and for a moment I glimpse her as the untroubled young woman she should be.

'I'm not sure about the hat, it could draw attention for the wrong reasons.'

'Well, forget the hat. I can look after us both. It might not be a terrible thing if you're spotted. It'll send the message out that you have your own personal bodyguard with you, and a cop at that.'

Chapter Seven

Adrian

Adrian replaced the phone in the receiver and stared at it for a moment. It was an original GPO 706 telephone with a 1960s rotary dial in two-tone green. Identical to the one they had in his grandparents' house. He loved the authentic ring tone and the feel of the receiver in his hand, the solid black numbers, and the sound of the turning dial. So he'd had it updated and installed in his office.

His grandparents' had moved from Old Trafford to Marple in 1963. During the 80's he'd spent more time with them than with his mum, who had a small flat in Reddish. His dad, Vance, had abandoned them both when Adrian was six years old, to pursue work in South Africa. Adrian had heard Grandma and Grandad comment, when they thought he was engrossed in *Danger Mouse*, that their daughter even struggled to keep the wolf *at* the door. He'd often wondered what they meant but knew instinctively if he asked, Grandma would answer, 'never you mind,' and Grandad would follow up with a question about homework. Grandma and Grandad worked as a team, like velociraptors.

By the time he was ten years old they were living with his grandparents permanently and his mum had started her nurse training. Adrian recalled it as a happy time. A peace had descended on them like a comfort blanket. Arguments between his mum and his grandparents were rare and Adrian no longer felt the breath blocking anticipation of having to choose sides when a disagreement erupted.

One night, after returning from a late shift his mum had complained of bad pains in her stomach and was taken to hospital by ambulance. Adrian recalled the green telephone in the hallway ringing and his Grandma answering it with her customary, 'Marple 6782.' He'd watched from the top of the stairs as she'd listened before replacing the handset very carefully into the cradle with both hands. When she turned around Adrian saw an expression on her face he'd never seen before. Her features were distorted so badly he was afraid she'd injured herself. They told him the following day that his mum had died from blood poisoning, or sepsis as Adrian later came to understand it.

Adrian was a small thin child who had gone relatively unnoticed at school. Up until the age of twelve he had tentatively attached himself to friendship groups but never had anyone who he could call his best mate. After his mums' funeral some slow burn bullying from a lad named Si, about his being brought up by old people, finally ignited. One Monday afternoon when school had finished Si had shouted after him, asking if he ever took his gran to the toilet. To Si's utter shock, Adrian had dropped his school bag and turned around. Oblivious to the scrum of red cheeked, grey socked lads on the periphery, egging them on, his rage broke the surface like a bulldozer. It ended with a broken nose for Si and threatened expulsion for Adrian.

Due to his extenuating circumstances Adrian was allowed to stay on. When things had settled down he discovered a small group of lads who seemed eager to be his friend, one of them being Si. They would carry out 'favours,' like stealing aftershave or porn mags. Nothing too challenging. It was more about completing the task than the value of the item. Adrian was loathed to bring any further trouble to his grandparents' door, so the first, second and third rule was never to dob anyone in, especially him.

By the time he was twenty-five his grandparents had died leaving him their sole beneficiary. Taking the same group of friends with him he set up a firm which offered local, cost effective building work. He soon had three work gangs and started tendering for the bigger developments around Manchester. He'd seduce quantity surveyors with a low quote. Later, with an apologetic tone, he'd hike up the price, citing additional unforeseen costs. His small business grew. He opened a gym and supported local housing projects. He refined his accent. Where his Mancunian friends still over emphasised their vowels, he flattened his. He expressed the 't' sound in words such as site and right. Last year he'd opened an Apprenticeship Training Centre called 'Ground Up' and had won a prestigious Business of the Year award. He thought he was the man his mum would have been proud of, while still cultivating associations with people who would have stolen the wool from his grandmas' crochet needle. He told himself he was living on the right side of wrong rather than the wrong side of right.

He retrieved a mobile phone from the desk drawer, selected a number and listened. It was answered on the second ring.

'Well?' Adrian asked, curtly.

Polyps in his nose always made Si sound like he was coming down with a cold. Adrian wondered why he'd never had them sorted. The bigger issue, on the job he'd been tasked with, was that it made him easily identifiable. He had clear instructions to keep a low visibility and under no circumstances should he speak to anyone.

'No sign as yet,' Si said, pronouncing sign as 'side'

'None?'

'Sorry. I could ask?'

'Don't.' Adrian answered, cutting Si off, his fist balling reflexively. 'Just. Keep your mouth shut, your head down and keep following.' He put the phone down and exhaled. He wanted Ava to know he had all the control, and she had none. All Si had to do was follow her and report on her movements. If you could describe it as movement. She went from her flat to the scummy shop she worked in, then back to her flat. Stretford to L.A, Lower Ancoats. It always made him laugh.

Chapter Eight

Kay

Aberfeldy has a nice high street, a few gift shops and plenty of places to eat. The air has warmed but there is a refreshing breeze, good for keeping the midges away. We call at the old cinema. *The Greatest Showman* is on the bill, but Ava says she isn't in the mood for anything emotional.

'No, I get ya,' I say.

I avoid comedies too nowadays. They're all right if you like laughing.

We weave in and out and politely step on and off pavements to accommodate other tourists, who smile and nod their thanks. I've always trusted my instincts, but somehow I can't settle on anything. My mind races, then seems to stand still; I can't pin a thought down. Am I misinterpreting what people are thinking? Or am I mind reading?

Back at the car, we put our bits of shopping in the boot, then head to The Watermill for some lunch. The food has always been good there.

The teashop is filled with an assortment of older women in their summer cropped trousers and loose pastel cotton tops, and men in various polo shirts and shorts, their swollen, hairy-toed feet shoved into Birkenstocks. All becomes clear when I spot a sign proclaiming "*fifty per cent off all food for pensioners on Mondays*." I'm envious. When I was younger,

I'd imagined by thirty I'd have met a half-decent man, and that the half which wasn't decent wasn't a serial killer. Someone to travel the world with, sharpening our wits on each other, like a couple in a Billy Wilder play, adoring and nit-picking in equal measure.

I'm forty now and the dream is rice paper thin. I've dragged it with me, over the rocks of adolescence and the ragged edges of my twenties and early thirties, my comfort blanket. But I've wasted too much time, invested unwisely, and got little return for my stake. If this dream of mine were a horse, I would have to shoot it.

We peruse the menu, then I order quiche for both of us, with a portion of chips to share.

'It's nice in here,' Ava says. 'Did you come here with Helen?'

I stop. I know for certain I have never mentioned my sister to Ava.

The couple at the next table look over at me, concern in their expressions. I must have turned white.

Unperturbed, Ava continues. 'You don't sleep well, Kay. You have nightmares, and the sound travels.'

I sit back, there are so many possible responses.

'You don't have to talk about her, it's fine.'

My phone rings. Ellie. Standing clumsily, I pull the tablecloth with me, then realise and release it. I signal to Ava that I'm nipping outside to take the call. Then I walk around the corner of the building, away from the main thoroughfare.

'Hey.'

'Aunty Kay, where are you?'

'Why?' I ask.

A beat of silence.

'I mean are you outside?'

'Oh, sorry, yeah, I'm just shopping.'

A blond-haired man catches my eye, conspicuous in black suit trousers amongst the legions in their summer frippery. He walks over to an ice cream vendor. A dark-haired woman in a grey dress greets him. She's holding the hand of a little boy aged around five. Grinning, the man hoists the child onto his shoulders. The woman hands the boy his ice cream and he laughs then she places a light blue baseball cap on the man's head. There's something so touching and intimate in this scene.

'I was thinking of coming up for a few days. I'm off from next Monday.'

'Oh, yeah?' I say, as thoughts queue up and bump against each other. Has someone been talking to her, I wonder? Who? Tectonic plates shift again, a sensation of the familiar becoming unfamiliar.

'Well, I'm not sure where I'll be next week. I've got some business stuff to sort out.'

'Oh, I thought you said-'

'I'm okay you know. You don't have to worry about me.'

'I know, sure, but. I don't know if I am.'

Her comment floors me. With so much happening I've just assumed she's fine; she's got Nate.

'I just thought we could go to the cottage, do some fishing?'

I look around, expecting to see Ellie over the road, holding her mobile and watching me, knowing all along I'm already at the cottage, trying to trick me. 'Do you think we cleared Mum's stuff out too soon?' she asks.

'No. Maybe. I don't know. Why, do you?'

'I don't know... It's just...'

The empty air is loaded. Have I done the wrong thing again?

'Look, love, you're right. Why don't you come the week after? We can have a good talk. I'll stock up on pizza, ice cream, and jelly.'

'Erm, I'm a touch more sophisticated now, remember.'

'Oh, sorry, yeah. Plant-based food. Yay.'

'You can knock yourself out with all that refined shit.'

'Don't worry, I'll stock up on spinach and tofu, and we can watch a David Attenborough doc.'

This raises a laugh and the tension dissipates.

'OK. I better go anyway, back to the grind. I'll give you a call to sort out the dates and stuff.'

We say our goodbyes and I return to the restaurant. The food is just being served. The waitress smiles kindly as I take my seat.

'That was Ellie, my niece.'

The waitress overhears. 'Ah, are you waiting for someone?' she asks. 'Only I can hold on?'

'Oh, no, just keep it coming, it's fine. Thank you.'

'How is she?' Ava asks.

'Good.' I nod.

'I'm sorry if I spoke out of turn before,' Ava says. 'You know, about Helen. I assume she's your sister? There's a nice photograph of you on the kitchen dresser, the three of you.'

The waitress passes to serve another table. When she moves out of earshot Ava says, 'You don't have to talk about her, if you don't want to.'

I put my knife and fork down and they clink loudly against the plate. I make an apologetic gesture.

'I completely understand. You don't know me. But maybe if you talk about what's troubling you, you'd sleep better.'

'Yeah,' I say, counting money out, adding under my breath. 'Maybe we both would.'

I pay the bill and leave a good tip. As we walk back towards the car Ava stops to look in a shop window. She points at something and says, 'Don't look around now but there's a man. He's staring. I'm sure he was behind us when we left the cafe.'

I see his reflection through the shop window. He's on the pavement opposite. He's focused on me, though, not Ava. I don't immediately recognise him, but he could be someone I've arrested in the past.

'Do you recognise him?' I ask her.

'I'm not sure, but Adrian knows a lot of people. I wouldn't necessarily know them.'

'Let's go to the car, see what he does.'

We walk quickly. I turn as we reach the car park; he's only a few feet behind us. He stops and nonchalantly gazes into a shop window.

'Stay here,' I tell Ava.

I reach him in a few quick strides. The man looks up, pale grey eyes widened in surprise.

'Can I help you?' I demand.

Holding his arms up, he shrinks away as if he expects to be struck. 'What did I do?' he asks, in a thin, weedy voice.

People passing by slow down and watch. One young boy trips off the edge of the narrow pavement.

'Watch where you're going, Ryan,' a woman, presumably Ryan's proud mother, says in a shrill voice.

'Do I know you?' I'm being careful not to touch him, but the passing shoppers leave very little room to manoeuvre.

'No,' the man says. 'I don't know you.'

'Are you following us?'

He looks even more confused. 'Look, I don't know you. I'm not following you. I'm parked in the car park.' He points.

I look him up and down, then straight into his eyes. 'OK, look, I'm sorry. It just felt like you were watching us.'

Lowering his guarded pose, he shakes his head. 'I'm a tourist. I'm watching everybody and nobody in particular.' He stands straighter, his tone less defensive. 'It's you who's watching,' he mutters. Then he scuttles away towards the car park, leaving me standing, mystified.

'It's you who's watching?' What the fuck?

'I think I need a refund on the undercover training,' I say to Ava, as I drive us back to the cottage. 'First rule, never let anyone notice you noticing.'

I glance at her as I drive and realise it jars me to have her in the car. I'm not sure why. Not for the first time I wonder, *what the fuck am I doing?*

'I've been noticing for years,' Ava says. 'Moving and noticing.'

'It would have been harder with children?' I say absently, then remember what she'd said about losing her child. 'I'm sorry, I forgot.'

She turns her head away and looks out of the window.

I change the subject. 'I did a search on McGrath construction.'

'I thought you would. And what did you discover?'

'Plenty on LinkedIn and Facebook, loads of pics, especially in the gym. He's a bit up himself.' I feel it's better not to mention Adrian's child-killer buddy.

'What are you planning to do?' she asks.

'Nothing too permanent. Best you don't know, plausible deniability and all that.'

'When?' she asks.

'Soon,' I reply.

I don't know why I don't say it out loud, but all the time I'm wondering, does Ava still want to kill herself? And how do I keep her safe?

Chapter Nine

Kay

It feels cool inside the cottage. Even though it's July and the sun's shining, the warmth doesn't seem to permeate the walls. Ellie complains it's cold in the winter, but because the fires aren't lit and the heating isn't on, it's even colder in the summer. I'm inclined to agree, and as the sun takes a final curtain call, I lay some wood and coal in the hearth. I watch the first tendrils of smoke curl up the chimney. The flames flutter like tiny orange flags, casting flickering light across the pink rose wallpaper. I feel I'm watching through a Victorian zoetrope. It calms me, and I breathe out and sink back into the worn armchair. I picture Helen at the window seat, snuggled up in a blanket with a mug of hot chocolate, and oversized tartan socks on her feet. She preferred the cottage in the winter, especially when it snowed.

We were trapped here one year, when I was about ten. The roads were treacherous, and impassable. It hadn't fazed Mum one bit. She appeared to thrive on it. She lit candles in the morning, and made stews and pies, and pulled all the board games out of the cupboard. Helen teamed up with Mum against me and Dad. Mum being the only one trusted to keep score.

Even at that young age, I picked up on the tension. I could sense Mum's irritation at Dad, who constantly checked the forecasts and listened to traffic updates. When the snow finally began to melt, she looked at him like he'd caused the thaw deliberately, with his own body heat. The atmosphere was colder in the car on the drive home than it had ever been in the cottage.

I pick the journal up from the small side table and turn it over in my hands, touching the cover with the flat of my palm. I sit for a moment like a clairvoyant, trying to feel her energy through the maroon moleskin.

September 30th

My medication has been changed again; they've added something to help my agitation. It's impossible not to be agitated in here. There's a woman on the ward, Josie; the patients call her 'Miss Havisham' behind her back. She was jilted on her wedding day. She threw petrol over herself, then lit a match and went up in flames. She wears a plastic mask over her face now. I think it's to retain moisture. I don't know why she's here. She's probably completely harmless, but she scares the shit out of me.

I think I'll be going home for an overnight stay this weekend and I'm looking forward to it, I think. I'm just nervous everyone will fuss around me and be terribly polite.

Kay came today. I'd asked her to bring some shoes for me, as we're the same size. God bless Kay, she brought me her very best shoes. I tried them on; it was weird to feel them on my feet again when I've only worn slippers for a while.

Kay is buzzing with this new case she's working on. It's funny, it was always me who wanted the career. I said I'd never have kids. Kay was the one who talked about marrying George Michael when he was in Wham. Then it was Boy George. Her radar's always been slightly off. I wish she could find someone. Still, she's happy in her job. She looks good, glowing. We're like the portrait of Dorian Grey: I rot in here while Kay blooms.

I tried to phone Jack, but his phone keeps going to messages and I don't want to disturb him again if he's asleep. I think of him, alone in our house. I imagine I'm there with him, holding him. I miss him.

I'll see him tomorrow at the ward round. I'm feeling tired now but as soon as I shut this book, I'll be wide awake again. I might go in the day room and watch something. Depends who's in there.

I shut the journal. Helen wrote so kindly about me, in a manner she never expressed to my face. I suppose it's much easier to write it than to *be* it.

I remember the time she's referring to. I was at the cottage with Jack. Although neither of us said it out loud, we were each playing a role. We were young lovers, living an alternative life, neither wanting to break the illusion. What an idiot I was; still am. Helen needed me, and I wasn't there for her.

Once, when I was five or six years old – I think Helen had gone on holiday with the school – I made a den in the front room at home. I covered it with old blankets. The door was a tablecloth you had to lift to enter. Mum plugged little lights in and pinned them carefully to the fabric. I thought they were fairies. I ate all my meals in there that day and wanted to sleep there, but Dad put his foot down and sent me to sleep in my bed. In the morning the blankets had been tidied away and the lights folded back into their box. I cried and cried. Mum tried to explain she needed the tablecloth because Aunty Ruth, who'd 'lost her confidence in Tenerife' was coming. But I was inconsolable. Eventually they put it back together again. Aunty Ruth didn't seem to care there wasn't a tablecloth if I was out of the way. I became invisible after a while, happily playing with my dolls, watching the shadows of the grown-ups through the fabric.

My den remained there for the entire week. Sometimes, I still think about it. Not so much the den, but the feeling. I hadn't felt it again, until that weekend with Jack. For a time we both believed we could make it work. But again, I woke up to find it had all been tidied away, my glimmering sanctuary, my safe harbour, gone, destroyed.

There's creaking on the stairs and Ava appears, her dark hair like a tangle of black ribbons. I feel a sudden drumming in my chest, which just as quickly abates. I've been so engrossed.

Ava squints at me. 'You OK?'

'You made me jump.'

She enters. 'There's a joke in there somewhere.'

'Oh, sorry.'

She takes the chair opposite. 'Were you going to burn it?'

'No. I was just...'

Ava leans over and slides the fireguard back into place. I don't remember moving it.

'When are you going to tell me?' she asks.

'Tell you what?'

'Why you helped me? You said it was complicated.'

'It is.'

'Uncomplicate it. The more you hide a problem, the more you add to it. Tell me what happened to your sister?'

Replies lodge in my throat.

'You're hoping that by helping me, you'll make up for not being able to help her. Is that it?'

'I don't want to talk about it.'

'You're torturing yourself with it.'

'Yes, you're right,' I answer. 'Yes, I did help you to make up for what happened to my sister. It was all about me after all.'

'Well, I'm glad I was there for you,' she says, sarcastically.

'Apart from anything else, it was obviously the right thing

to do, because you're still here.'

'I'm still here because you made me a promise.'

'Promises are for deathbeds,' I reply.

'Well, you can take me to mine now. I should go.' She stands up.

'Wait, sit down,' I urge. I need to think.

'Look, I have nightmares every night. I'm back to square one. Don't think for a minute he won't find me here. He's a man with connections. He probably knows exactly where I am.'

I run my hands through my hair.

'You have trouble taking action, don't you?' she says.

'I take life-saving action every day of my life.'

'I mean in your personal life. Do you have any idea what it took for me that day?' She sits down and covers her face with her hands. 'What level of resolution? I just can't go through it again.'

Suddenly she's up. She pushes past me and flings the front door open.

'Wait!' I shout. Fuck.

I follow her out. She's running towards the loch. The water's high and the waves are boisterous. It's a cold morning. There's rain in the air and dark grey clouds move over the mountain peaks.

I can see the determination in her stride, and the slope of the hill aids her momentum. I run to catch her up. I'm two metres behind her, but my limbs feel heavy and slow, my boots like lead weights. She reaches the stony banks and the pebbles crunch loudly under her feet. I reach out for her, fingers elongated. A flashback to the building site. Something feels wrong. Something in my periphery is warning me, like the pure high pitched 'see' of a hawk's alarm call, signalling danger. I stop.

Ava stops too. She turns to look at me as though she has read my mind. Slowly she sinks to her knees on the gravelly shore.

'I can't go back to that,' she cries. 'And I can't wait forever, in this, this purgatory.'

I'm distracted by the image. I try to zero in, it's important. But it's like trying to see the road through a steamed-up windscreen. It dissolves completely as we both turn at the sound of a whistle. A woman walking her Labrador.

Ava gets up and we watch. The woman leans forward against the wind, boots crunching on the stony shoreline. The dog runs gleefully towards me, lolling tongue and golden smile. I feel the power behind its muscular body as it jumps up and places two wet paws on my jacket.

'Juno, get down,' the woman shouts. I notice her strong Scottish accent.

Slobber drips from the dog's jowls. Its coat feels damp and waxy, and it smells like an old barn, but I don't mind. It's a relief, to feel the connection with this living, breathing, joyous animal.

'Good boy,' I say, rubbing its head.

'Sorry, she's really still a wee pup at heart.'

'No, it's OK.'

I study the woman. She's about the same age as me, though not as tall. She's wearing a waterproof jacket. Short blonde hair sticks out from under a cream bucket hat. She has a healthy carefree look about her.

'Come here, ye terror.' The woman clips the lead back onto the dog. 'So full of energy, I just have to let her run it off.'

'It's the perfect place for it.'

Ava joins us.

'You up at the cottage?' the woman asks.

Ava gives a warning signal with her eyes.

'Erm, yeah, just for a few days. Sorting a few things.'

'You selling?'

'Well...'

'We've noticed it's always empty nowadays. Used to be people here regularly.'

'Yes, well, life gets busy. Things change,' I answer casually.

'Of course. It's a beautiful house,' she says as the dog strains energetically against the lead. 'Well, good luck with it.' She waves a gloved hand as she walks away. After a short distance she stoops to untie the dog's lead and it bounds ahead. 'Go on girl.'

The words carry back on the wind as I watch her walk into the distance. I've been vaguely aware of Ava walking back to the cottage. I catch up with her on the driveway.

'Hey.'

She turns. 'You said too much.'

'Come on, I've been coming here for years, she probably knows exactly…'

'And in all those years, have you ever met that woman?' She pushes the door open and I follow her in. 'Sorry, Kay, I'm just paranoid.'

'So paranoid that you felt safe enough to go into Aberfeldy, without the hat and sunglasses?'

She falters. 'I was concerned, yes, but if you want the truth, I was a bit creeped out.'

'By?' I don't want to give her time to think of a lie. The quicker the questions the less time to think.

She sinks onto the settee and the cushions lean in on her. 'I thought they were Helen's. I thought for a minute-' She sighs and looks away.

'What? Come on.'

'You were pretending I was your sister, trying to make me into Helen. Which is why I'm here, isn't it?'

I force a laugh, as though the Chief Constable has just cracked a bad joke.

'All the way through the town, without any kind of disguise, then we bump into one woman on the beach and you're suddenly Lord Longford.'

'Who?'

God, what are they teaching kids in school these days? 'Lord – look, it doesn't matter. We both need to keep calm.'

'Agreed.'

Taking a seat on the arm of the sofa, I pull my boots off. 'Nice dog though,' I say, propping them on the shoe rack to dry. 'I'll put the kettle on.'

In the kitchen I look out of the window, to the beauty of the mountains. Green is supposed to be a soothing colour. I try to fill my eyes with it, while my brain battles against rest.

What I'm certain of is that Ava remains impulsive. I realised it when she ran out. Whether I'm trying to help her because of what happened to Helen is irrelevant. She's here now, in my care. What would be the point of all of this if she just went right ahead and topped herself? How would I explain it?

As I fill the teapot my phone pings: an automated reminder from Joanne Green. I have another appointment tomorrow afternoon. I'd forgotten all about it. Shit. I run through all the outcomes of not attending and wonder if I can rearrange.

Returning to the lounge with the coffee and a plate of digestives, I see Ava has made up the fire. The room's too hot. Before I take my seat opposite her, I pull my jumper over my head and self-consciously yank my t-shirt down to cover my muffin top. I feel like Shrek in comparison to Ava's waif-like frame.

'Tell me about Adrian,' I say, patting my hair down.

'OK. Where to start? He's greedy, a bully, and a misogynist. He admires himself, hates to lose, can't deal with criticism, can give it but can't take it.'

'Hmm. Any bad points?' I ask, dipping a biscuit into my coffee. Timing is crucial; too long and the biscuit ends up as sludge in the bottom of the cup. Just right and coffee-soaked confection melts on your tongue.

Ava offers a weak smile.

'He doesn't have any criminal record,' I say. It isn't a

question; I've checked the database.

'No, he always keeps his hands spotlessly clean.'

'Meaning he gets others to do his dirty work?'

'What? No, he likes a manicure.'

Heat rises up my neck and I move on quickly. 'OK, so I either find him at the gym, or at a nail bar.'

'Ha-ha, about sums him up.'

The conversation is energizing. I'm in my comfort zone; this is what I do. Ava looks impressed, probably relieved I'm formulating a plan instead of just lounging around aimlessly, passing time.

'Sounds narcissistic.'

'Yes.'

'Seriously, Ava, I've never asked. Did he ever hit you?'

Clenching her hands around her calves, she rocks.

'He would push me, y'know?' She turns her head away. 'He'd force himself on me. It was physical and emotional. Taunting, name-calling, showing me up in front of friends, so I never knew top from bottom. Then I found out I was pregnant. It was the catalyst. I went to my first refuge. He found me, promised he'd change, blah blah blah. Five times is the average, you know for abused women to return to their abusers. I'm ashamed to say I never pressed charges, and I went back.'

Rising from the chair, she throws a large log on the fire. Slow flames flicker from underneath it. She sits down again.

'And the baby?'

'Josh. I lost him.'

The through draught catches, and with a low roar the fire blazes to life again.

The memory of Geraldine Foster identifying the body of her murdered son comes to me. Her beautiful boy had been tortured by Brunswick for hours before his heart finally saved him by stopping.

The loathing I feel for McGrath is a tangible thing. When I picture him, my whole body seems to expand. It makes a pleasant change from self-loathing, which makes me want to curl in on myself.

When Ava has gone to bed, I open the laptop and enter my password into the database again. It still bothers me McGrath walked away from the first investigation into Gary Brunswick, without a blot on his reputation, despite Brunswick eventually being found guilty. I cast my mind back to the case. I don't have to cast far. I'm wading anyway.

Ten-year-old David Foster went missing the week before Christmas. He told his mum he was going to his mate's house down the road. The next time she laid eyes on him was to identify his body.

Detectives will tell you that some cases stay with you. They are as significant in your life as graduation, your wedding day, or the birth of your first child. They don't make it to the family album, but they are there, in the glassine paper which separates each page. Inhumanity exists just beyond the range of the camera.

I'd never been so driven, so determined to take apart a case and smash into the ground the degenerate crud who had abducted and murdered David.

In the early part of the investigation we looked at all the family members, then friends then associates. Religiously applying the ABC principle of detective work. Assume nothing Believe no-one and Check everything. Which was how we came across Brunswick. He was a coach with the under twelves youth club David played for. He'd been employed by McGrath for many years as a site manager and had then moved over to work in the apprenticeship training centre called 'The Ground Up'. He'd allegedly been in a meeting with McGrath around the time David had been abducted.

I looked at Brunswick once and for reasons I can't explain, I looked again. He had opportunity. He lived close to David. He had contact with him through the football team. His car had been captured in the vicinity en-route to and from work.

I interviewed the football team and their parents. One of the mothers told me after David had gone missing that her son had told her Brunswick had asked him if he could take a photograph of him for the team magazine. He said Brunswick made him feel like he couldn't say no. She described Brunswick as an 'odd fish.'

That shred of doubt was all I needed to conduct a more focused search on Brunswick. It led us to David, but it was too late to save him.

Too late for us all.

Even though I've an innate dread of anything to do with IT, the search gives me a sense of connection. I feel more grounded than I have since I left Manchester. The stored information feels like a living thing. It waits for the right questions. Sometimes it withholds, leading to frustrating and time-consuming dead ends, story of my life. Sometimes it coughs up information like a regurgitating gull.

I search the database quickly, following my previous lines of investigation. After Brunswick was arrested, we discovered he'd forged his FA Level 2 football coaching certificate and other documents, which had given him kudos with the team manager. He'd obviously studied coaching otherwise he'd have been ousted months earlier. But the football manager had described him as a competent coach who was popular with the team and parents. The documents are there along with a photograph of the team. It's unposed, natural, they're celebrating, all doing a thumbs up sign. David Foster is peering around the side of another boy like he's just realised the camera is on them. Gary Brunswick is at the back, smiling.

By two in the morning I have pages of notes. Most of them are scribbles but I've caught the thread of something which should have been followed up at the time. Normally I'd be able to issue 'actions' which the team would follow up. But this is different. Barbara will lose her shit if she discovers that I'm still working when I'm supposed to be taking time out. I put the request in anyway. I'll be back at work in two weeks and will be able to pick up the thread then. I stand on stiff legs. The fire's out and the room has chilled around me. The house is telling me that's enough for now.

I search around for my phone and see a missed call from Barbara and another text from Matt, asking if I'm OK. There's nothing else from Jack.

I climb into bed and before I switch the bedside lamp off, I look around the room. There's a photograph of me, Mum and Helen on the beach. Mum and I are looking into the camera, but Helen's looking away. She looks thoughtful, rather than happy.

I recall the whispered conversations. Mum and Dad instructing me not to 'mither' her, she was going through a 'difficult patch', 'needed space', and patience.

Much later, I found out Helen had depression. I think even at eight, I would've had the capacity to grasp that she was sad. But no one bothered to explain. That's when the division between Helen and me began. We never really recovered. I learned not to talk about stuff. Helen thought I wasn't interested.

She seemed to improve when she went to university, but within a few months of her starting, Mum became ill, and Dad, well, Dad couldn't cope. I remember Mum lying in bed, wasting away, and Dad disappearing for days on end, leaving me, thirteen years old, to deal with helping Mum to the toilet, to dress, to eat. Only a handful of teachers at school knew. Everyone just assumed my dad, good ole Jim, was keeping the family together and looking after his sick wife.

Aunty Ruth's confidence was apparently depleted to such an extent that even when her sister-in-law was dying, she couldn't make the fifteen-minute drive to help us out. Eventually, social services were alerted, and Mum had a professional palliative care package put in place. But I was still the only one there some nights.

Helen's journal lies on my bedside table. I pick it up.

October 1st.

I've just come out of my session. I told the psychologist about the disastrous weekend and why I came back early. I think it's hilarious that I didn't have anywhere else to turn.

God, it was embarrassing, to tell my psychologist that my husband has been shagging someone while I'm in here. Locked up like fucking Mrs Rochester.

He asked me who it is that Jack's shagging. My words, not his, obviously. He used clinical words like 'adultery' and 'unfaithful'. They don't do it justice. I've had my heart ripped out and put on a stake for all to see. I had to tell him that I have no idea, that Jack wouldn't tell me. He said it was no one I knew, so it was irrelevant. I didn't have the energy for it. I'll find out one way or another.

How could he do this to me while I'm in here? While I'm going through this? God, I hate him so much right now.

I can't read any more. My heart is in my throat. Helen told me she'd found out about his affair, but to see it written down is another matter. Her words spit at me from the page like molten metal.

There's an aching in the base of my back. I ease myself onto my side and turn the lamp off. I feel a gentle waft of air on my face and smell Helen's perfume. I put my head under the covers and lie very still, waiting for her to haunt me.

Chapter Ten

Kay

Terrible cramping pain wakens me, and I know I've started my period. I wonder why it still surprises me. Why, after twenty-eight years, I don't recognise the symptoms. I become irritable, and argumentative. I suppose it's because women aren't supposed to admit to this nowadays. It's not part of the sisterhood to admit you have fucking terrible pain and can hardly walk sometimes. Or confess that the pain can make you irrational and snappy.

I go to the bathroom and sort myself out. Searching for my hot water bottle, I recall I last saw it in the cupboard under the sink. The cramps are nauseatingly strong. I hunch over as I creep downstairs. Eventually I find it. As I'm filling it, I remember the strong painkillers I stored away last time I was here. I feel almost jubilant when I find them in the kitchen drawer. Co-codamol. They'll do the trick nicely. Thank you, universe. As I'm closing the drawer, something catches my eye, an item I'd all but forgotten about. I put it in my pocket and return to bed.

As the hot water bottle and the tablet begin to take effect, I listen to the sounds from outside. An owl hoots somewhere in the distance. I want to hoot back to it, to let it know it's not alone. Then I fall asleep.

The bed dips behind me as someone climbs in.

Jack is here. My body swells with desire, plumping, softening. I turn to him, but I'm trapped by the sheets. It's impossible for me to move. My heartbeat is rapid. I'm very afraid.

I open my mouth to speak but the words won't come out. My mouth feels stretched, my face distorted with effort, but still nothing comes. I'm paralysed, petrified. Some primitive instinct tells me to close my eyes, to go back to sleep. I try to calm my breathing and relax. Relief sweeps through me as I'm able to move, but it's a momentary illusion. I'm still trapped. Something's holding me in place. Is it Ava?

I stop fighting and surrender, lying there waiting, more afraid than I've ever been. Incredibly, I must have fallen back to sleep. I wake and immediately turn. There is no one there. Exhausted, I sit up, not trusting what I see or feel. I could still be trapped in a nightmare by some wicked jester.

Unnerved, I switch the bedside lamp on and scan the corners of the room. Helen's journal is about to slide from the bed. I catch it, then lean back and continue reading from where I left off.

Divorce Jack? Why would he expect me to be so noble? Only death will part us. Maybe he should kill me and put us both out of our misery? He can clearly handle guilt. I seem to be able to handle very little. Distress intolerance they call it, inability to regulate my emotions. Can you imagine what divorce would do to someone like me? It would destroy me. And if he tries to leave me, I'll kill myself. Just saying.

I shut the journal and attempt to clear the jumble in my head. I try to remember when I last slept properly. It's been a while; it takes some effort to try to recall what happened yesterday. Life has become so disorganised. I need to stamp some certainty on it, take decisive action, gather all the fragments and put them together.

As dawn breaks, I get up and shower. Hot water pelts my body, cascading over and around me, like the tumbling currents of the river Affric. The runnels traipse a hundred different routes over my skin as I lift my face into the flow. I stand for a moment, hands leaning against the wall, savouring the warmth as it seeps into my muscles. I run through my plan.

I've always been an upstanding cop. I admit I've used some alternative sources to acquire useful information, but I've never falsified anything. My job has been my saviour, the only thing I've ever been good at. It's the thing which preserves my sanity. I'm not going to blow it all over a shit like McGrath, but sometimes you must use your position *creatively*.

I reach blindly for the shower gel and squeeze a globule into my hand, then quickly splash it onto my body, rubbing underneath my arms.

A heady wreath of rose and jasmine. Helen is here. I gasp and inhale warm water. Slippery, panicked hands on the tap, turn it the wrong way, and the water is suddenly freezing. Leaping out of the shower, I grasp the plastic curtain, snap, snap. The rings are yanked from their moorings, and I fall forward awkwardly, righting myself as my feet find the safe dry land of the bathroom rug.

Disorientated, I turn full circle, my breath rasping, water dripping from my eyelashes. I look up, expecting to see Helen's reflection in the bathroom mirror, or some cryptic message spelled out in the condensation.

Water continues to splash noisily into the shower base. Reaching through the torrent, I turn the dial until it stops and only a few cold rivulets weave their way down the wall tiles.

A tipped bottle drips its slimy contents onto the steel shower pole. Rose and jasmine body wash, Helen's favourite. It stands next to my coconut shower cream. A laugh bursts unexpectedly out of me, so marked is my relief. There are no ghostly presences or portents. The perfume has been emanating from here, Helen's shower gel.

It's a pretty bottle, expensive looking, Ellie has obviously left it for her own use, or to remind her of her mum. Leaning forward, I lift it to my nose and inhale. Then I return it to the shelf and wipe the shower down with a towel and reconnect the shower curtain before wrapping myself in my bathrobe.

I catch my reflection. Brown hair, wavy now with the spray from the shower. I've dark rings under my eyes. I look shattered, hardly the picture of health Helen described.

Downstairs, I make a small tray of food up for Ava. I find an empty plastic bottle and fill it with water and shove it into my cardigan pocket.

The attic room's cold. Placing the tray on the side table, I see Ava is turned to face the wall, her tiny frame hardly noticeable under the quilt. I check the windows are closed and feel the radiator is on. Ava stirs. I nudge her.

'Ava.'

She turns, squinting.

'I've brought you a pot of tea and some food. There's some fruit and this.' I pull the bottle of water from my pocket.

She half sits up, still cocooned in the quilt. 'I'll be back tonight,' I say.

I leave the room and pull the door closed, then reach into my pocket and retrieve the key I found amongst the bits and bobs in the kitchen drawer. I insert it quietly into the lock, feel resistance, and then the barrel softly yields.

Chapter Eleven

Matt

Matt's seated at his desk when Detective Constable Alison Cromer approaches.

'Sir, I think you might be interested in this. I've been scrolling through Companies House and I came across Mandher Assad.' She leans forward and hands him a print-out.

His desk phone rings and he ignores it. Frowning, he scours the page. He spots the information the detective is referring to and his expression clears.

'Bloody hell, they had a business together.'

'Yes, in 2008, and it looks like Dinesh ripped Mandher off. It says here that Mandher resigned as director, then Dinesh changed the name of the company. I think they forced him out somehow.'

'OK, great work,' Matt says. 'Do you want to question him with me?'

'Don't mind if I do,' Alison replies. 'By the way, did you get the info DCI Harris requested?'

For a moment Matt is nonplussed. The phone is still ringing. Signalling for Alison to stay, he answers it. He listens for a moment, then, 'Yes, ma'am, I'll get onto it.'

He sighs as he replaces the receiver. 'You mean Kay Harris? Our Kay?'

Alison nods.

'Is she back?' He scans the room.

Alison shakes her head. 'No, it's information she requested on someone called Adrian McGrath.'

'McGrath, McGrath.'

'I wasn't sure what to do with it.' Her voice dips. 'I mean, is she working from home?'

Matt stands and waves his hand in a dismissive gesture. 'No, no, she's... it's just a hunch she had before she went off. Don't mention it to anyone, OK? I'll look at it. Just pass anything else she asks for on to me.'

'Sure thing. I mean yes, sir.'

Chapter Twelve

—

Kay

Wednesday morning

Clouds the colour of pigeon wings stretch above me as I take the slip road onto the M74. According to the sat nav, arrival time in Manchester will be around midday. My appointment is at one thirty. It's a shitty time really but the traffic shouldn't be too bad on a Wednesday afternoon. I should make it back around seven this evening. Ava will be fine until then. I've taken more painkillers, but I feel the dragging pain and know I'll need to stop at the services. My jeans cut into me and I have to undo the button. The zip unfurls under its own steam. I feel the tension in my shoulders and lower them, rotating my head a little to loosen up. Jesus, I wish my life could go back to how it was. I doubt that can ever happen now.

Groping around on the passenger seat, I locate my bottle of water. The plastic crackles in my grip as I swig its tepid contents. Humming a nameless tune to exercise my vocal cords, I activate the hands free and call Ellie. The phone goes straight to messages.

'Hi.' I hear the croak in my voice and take another sip. 'It's me, just letting you know I'm doing fine, getting everything sorted for next week. Speak soon.'

My next call is to Matt. He picks up on the first ring.

'Hi.'

I try to read his mood through that single word. 'Hi. I saw your missed call. Just letting you know I've not dropped off the edge of the earth.'

'Well, I've been, y'know, worried.'

'Yeah, sure. Anyway. I was just letting you know.'

I'm about to press 'end call' but he continues. 'More of a picture's emerging with the case. Looks like Assad was ripped off by his business partner and his wife.'

His voice becomes distant, as if he's turned his head away. I imagine him in Barbara's office, signalling to her that I'm on the line. 'Then one day, there he was, crossing the road in front of him, and – bam.' He delivers the final word with some force and I jump. 'The consultant is saying he should make a full recovery.'

'Listen,' I say. 'I should have said. I'm sorry about not coming for dinner. Caro's moussaka.'

'No, I was out of order. Just call me *Zorba the Geek*.'

I feel tears starting. 'OK, yeah. Right, I'd better go. I'll see you.'

'Don't jump down my throat, Kay, but did you request some information about Adrian McGrath?'

Damn! He's definitely in Barbara's office; he's setting me up again.

'Kay?'

'Who?'

'Adrian McGrath. The guy who...'

'Oh, yeah, I'd forgotten I'd even asked for it. It was with you saying he'd perjured himself, a loose end so to speak. It can wait.'

'You moonlighting Kay?'

I feel the change in dynamic between us. I've always suspected Matt would be a pain in the arse if he were the one with the superior rank.

'What? No, just keeping it ticking over.'

'You seen Ellie?'

My hands tighten on the wheel. 'Why, has she phoned?'

'No.'

I say that I've another call coming in and cut him off.

Chapter Thirteen

Kay

Fifteen minutes late. I'm buzzed up to Dr Joanne Green's office and take a seat in the waiting room. I phoned ahead and left a message saying I was stuck in traffic. Still, with my history of attendance, she'll see my late arrival as shoddiness, unaware I've just driven for nearly six hours to get here. At least I'm showing willing, and it should keep HR and Barbara Dean off my back for another week.

I pull one of the paper cups from the stack, fill it with water from the dispenser, then down two more Co-codamol. Joanne appears in the doorway, and does a double take, probably because she wasn't expecting me to turn up.

When we're seated, she goes through the usual stuff about confidentiality and risk.

'If you tell me you are suicidal, or you know of someone who is...' She goes on and ends with... 'I'm duty bound to report it.'

I've the weirdest feeling she knows about Ava. I've done it myself in questioning, it's a standard interrogation technique to gauge how suspects lie, or tell the truth. I picture Ava locked in the attic.

'Why would I know of anyone who is suicidal?' I ask.

Addressing my forehead as usual, she replies, 'I'm not saying you do, I'm just outlining confidentiality. I start every session this way.'

It makes sense, but still, it's convenient.

My head still feels full of grey cloud, a building storm. Standing too quickly, I cover up the dizziness by putting a hand on the window ledge. 'Do you mind?' I ask, as I struggle with the catch. If Joanne knows I have Ava locked in the cottage, she could be setting me up. I scan the car park, but don't see any sign of Matt, or anything suspicious.

I feel Joanne's eyes on me, then I sit down, relieved to feel some air on my face.

'You look tired, Kay.' She tilts her head to the side with a kindly expression she must have learned at therapy school.

'I'm. I've just come on. I've a lot of pain. I'm dosed up on shit.'

I pull a large, bulky cushion from behind me and look at her. She gives no indication what I should do with it. I tag her as someone with no respect for soft furnishings and lay it gently on the carpet. Then I stretch my legs out, crossing one over the other. The room is still too warm.

'We talked a little about Helen last time. Do you want to continue where we left off?' she asks.

'If you like.'

'You said last time you blamed yourself?'

'Yes.'

'Can you elaborate?'

I take a deep breath in then exhale. 'I wasn't there for her.'

'You have a highly demanding job. Wouldn't she have understood?'

'Suppose.'

'What about the day she died?'

Blood mingled with grit.

'Have you ever spoken to anyone about it?'

'Yeah, obviously, I had to speak to work. I spoke to Matt and Barbara Dean.'

'On a personal level, have you talked about how difficult

it was?'

A bloom of black ink spreads across the memory. 'Erm, no. I don't need to.'

'You're still not sleeping though? Having nightmares, reliving it?'

I lean forward again. I'm so hot.

'Can you talk me through the day she died?'

I try the Jedi mind trick. 'There's nothing to talk you through.'

'Start in the morning. As I recall, you were in Manchester.'

I think I might vomit. I ask for water and reach out to steady myself on the desk, but it seems to move and I'm falling forward. I see the detail in the blue carpet, as it rises up towards me. Then there is a blank.

I'm staring at the top of Joanne Green's head. I notice her grey roots and think she must be older than I first assumed. Then I remember: Barbara said Joanne's in her forties.

I'm on the floor of her therapy room. The cushion is under my head, almost exactly where I put it, ha, serendipity. Joanne is leaning over me, holding my wrist, checking my pulse. Either that, or she's giving me the last rites.

My head throbs.

Slowly I sit up, Joanne puts the cushion behind my back and I lean against the chair. She hands me water and I sip it gratefully.

'What've you taken today?' she asks.

I run through a montage of myself, popping pills into my mouth, from waking in the night up until now. Christ, I'm an idiot.

I almost lie, but I'm not together enough to do it convincingly. Besides, I just counted them out on my fingers, like a five-year-old.

'Eight co-codamol, I think.'

'Since?'

'Three this morning.'

Joanne leans on the desk to lever herself up. 'OK, don't take any more of those until after three o'clock tomorrow morning.'

Picking my notes up, she scribbles something, probably recommending home help, or supported housing.

'If you need something, take ibuprofen, but nothing with paracetamol.'

'Roger that.' I nod and start to rise.

Her buzzer sounds, but it may just be in my head. Joanne approaches the door and speaks through the intercom, then turns back to me.

'I've phoned for an ambulance, Kay. I'm sorry, I can't let you drive.'

'What? No, I can't.' I protest, as a man in green paramedic overalls enters.

I'm so dizzy I fall back onto the chair.

'You just need a check-up, make sure you're OK,' the paramedic is saying. 'I'm John,' he adds, and smiles. He's handsome, has a forty-ish Paul Newman look about him.

'I bet people faint all the time when you turn up.' I think I must have said this out loud, because he smiles again, eyes crinkling up at the edges. Then he puts the blood pressure cuff on my arm.

'OK,' he says when he's finished. 'Your BP and pulse are a bit low, I think we need to keep you under observation.'

Another paramedic appears, and my protests fall upon deaf ears as they help me down the stairs and into the ambulance.

When I arrive at the hospital I'm wheeled into an examination cubicle, and a green patterned curtain is pulled around me. Let me tell you, a curtain isn't as effective as a good old-fashioned wall, or four of them to be more precise. I learn everything about the lady in the next bed, who is called Kitty and has a suspected hip fracture. Her bowels are regular and the last time she ate was at eleven o'clock, just before she fell. After half an hour of Kitty's history, I almost feel like I know her.

I'm so relieved when the doctor arrives. I tell her I'm much better. All I can think of is Ava, locked in the attic.

'I'm fine now. Please can I sign myself out?'

The doctor makes some notes and does my blood pressure again.

'What tablets did you take exactly?' she asks.

I explain about my painful periods again, and overdid it on the co-codamol.

'Any suicidal thoughts?'

Now I get it. They're thinking of admitting me to a psychiatric ward. Shit. I try to control my speech, so she can't hear my panic. It's like trying to sound sober when you're pissed.

'No, absolutely not. Look, doctor, I wasn't in a therapy session for suicidal thoughts.'

'You were in a therapy session?'

Me and my big mouth.

'Yeah, it was the therapist who called the paramedic. She was duty bound. If I hadn't been there, I would have just gone home for a lie down.'

Four hours later they discharge me. I go to the reception desk to order a taxi.

'Oh, Miss Harris, you don't need a taxi, there's someone here to take you home.'

I turn and see Jack walking towards me.

'Kay.' He waves, looking concerned. 'Sorry, Joanne Green phoned me. Apparently I was the only one she could get hold of in your contacts.'

Oh, shit. Could this day get any more stressful?

Chapter Fourteen

Kay

Outside I take some refreshing breaths of air as Jack guides me across the road and towards his car. I experience such a feeling of familiarity, I just want to lean into him, to feel his body heat. To carry on as if nothing has happened.

The car smells of him, sandalwood and spice. He places my leather holdall at my feet. God, I'd forgotten the kindness, the caring. His hair has gone slightly grey at the temples. I feel like I missed the turning of a season.

He leans across me to fasten my seat belt. I block him and reach for it myself. I want to feast on him but can hardly look at him. I know everything and nothing about him. His open-neck check blue shirt and dark blue jeans are clothes I'm not familiar with, and I'm reminded that he exists without me. Even his wristwatch is unfamiliar. I imagine how I must look to him. I reach up and pull my hand through my hair as he manoeuvres the car out of the car park.

'Can you take me to Sale, please, to get my car?'

'What happened, Kay?' Brown eyes try to lock onto mine. I take evasive action.

'I fainted,' I laugh.

He looks concerned.

'Don't be,' I say out loud.

'Don't be what?'

'Oh, sorry, I thought you said... You looked concerned, but I'm OK.'

'Are you ill? You've lost weight.'

'I've just stopped eating small children.'

'It wasn't your fault, you know.'

Typical, no foreplay, just straight down to it.

'No? I'm her sister.'

'Kay.' He tries to take my hand, but I make it limp, so he places his back on the steering wheel. 'I could look after you.'

I could easily succumb and live suspended in a viscera of denial.

'Yeah, Ellie would love that.'

'Ellie loves you.'

He doesn't get it. Are all adulterous men so thick? 'Yes, but she wouldn't love *us*.'

'I think she'd get used to it.'

'Jack, she would be devastated. She blames herself already.'

'For what?'

'Don't you talk to your daughter? For always backing off, for never visiting. How do you not know this?'

'We are all to blame,' he says.

I look at the car's digital clock. It's five thirty. Ava.

The only conversation between us for the next ten minutes is the directions I give him to the therapy rooms.

Relief floods through me when I see my car.

'Just here,' I say.

'I was supposed to take you home,' Jack says. 'Are you OK to drive?'

Undoing my seat belt and grabbing my bag, I open the car door. 'Thanks, Jack, but I'm fine really, and this was a terrible idea.'

The slamming of the door cuts him off mid-sentence. I can still faintly hear him. I feel his eyes follow me as I cross the road, fumbling around in my bag for keys. As I reach the other side, I lift my head, and see his car reverse into the road and take off. He doesn't look back.

Within the confines of my car, I allow the feeling in. No matter how I push it down, the pain I can't locate resurfaces. It's like I'm playing Whac-a-Mole with grief, guilt, and desire. I pummel one and the other pops up. Covering my face with my hands, I cry out something. It sounds like *why?* But I can't identify the word. Clutching my stomach, I rock back and forth. Christ, I miss Jack. I should be missing Helen, I'm so sorry Helen. I'll be back with you in a minute, and I promise you I'm suffering, but I need this.

In this minute, I miss Jack. I miss him. I miss him. I miss him. Love isn't safe.

Chapter Fifteen

***

Kay

I drive for two hours without a break, then decide to stop at the service station for the loo. I grab a take-out coffee and a few things from the food shop. My phone rings: an unknown number. I let it go to answerphone, then listen to the message.

Hello, Kay, it's Joanne Green here. I'm just phoning to make sure you got home OK. Could you ring me, please, to let me know? You can call me on this-

There's a pause. Could it be she's talking to someone else about me?

Sorry, the buzzer just went. Call me day or night. I'm in clinic this evening until half nine. We need to set up a follow-up session, this week if possible. I'll phone tomorrow with some dates and we can take it from there. Bye.

I debate whether to call her. I debate everything nowadays. Used to be a time when I was so certain. She'd said her door buzzer had just gone, so it's probable she has a client with her now.

'See, Dad, police school wasn't a complete waste, was it?' I say out loud, as I return the call on hands-free. Joanne's answerphone comes on. Something is going my way.

She's very professional sounding on the answerphone. I wonder what she's like when she's pissed. I leave a brief message telling her I feel much better and thanking her for her concern.

'Now fuck off,' I say when the call has ended.

My cramps have abated, and I feel less dizzy. Back in the car, both my bladder and the traffic are lighter. It's a fine night. Time to think about Jack. I've longed to see him again, but I'm honest enough to know I can never be with him again. Even for those few moments with him in the car, I knew it was impossible for us. That Jack could even suggest us being together is bizarre.

'Why isn't he a guilty cripple like me? Has he received divine intervention and thrown away his emotional crutches?' I'm talking out loud to myself again. Talking to yourself is more like listening than speaking. I think it's helpful.

I catch my reflection in the rear-view mirror. I'm as pale as a thirsty vampire.

In the dark, the house looks old and wise, a holder of secrets. I feel a mixture of relief and apprehension as I let myself in, noting the lounge is as I left it, cold ash in the grate, and empty coffee cup on the stone mantelpiece. All is quiet as I climb the stairs. As I pass my bedroom, I retrieve the key from my bathrobe pocket. I unlock the door to the attic room, half expecting to see Ava pacing, tearing her hair out with hunger. She's sitting calmly on the bed, a book opened in her lap.

'Hi,' I say. I'm wary she might spring up and try to get past me.

'Why did you lock the door?'

Still holding the door handle, I reply, 'I'm going to make some tea and toast. I'll be back up and then we'll talk.'

Back downstairs, I unpack the shopping I bought from the service station. I'm pleased with myself; locking Ava in her room is proving beneficial in several ways. Now I can binge without the worry of her walking in on me, doughnut in flagrante.

When I return to the attic room with refreshments, I don't bother locking the door. The front and back door are locked and secure anyway, and Ava seems remarkably calm, just a little bemused, which is fair enough.

'It's not ideal, but it's for your own safety,' I say as I take a bite of toast.

I notice the watercolour on the wall behind her. Mum bought it from an antique shop on the high street, signed by a local artist. It depicts the early morning mist, descending like white gauze over the loch, blurring the lines between mountains and water.

Ava looks at me for a moment before speaking. 'I don't know what I expected but I definitely didn't see this coming.'

I look away, stare into my mug. 'No, me neither.'

'I'm interested to hear how you justify it? Kidnapping.'

I shake my head. 'If only you knew.'

She mimics me. 'If only you knew. If only I knew what?'

I rise, feeling the guilt bursting from me. Ochre rivulets of tea run down the wall where I've thrown the mug.

'If you knew me! If you knew about me!' I shout. I see the scorn in her face and rush from the room, slamming the door behind me. Downstairs, I throw myself onto the worn settee and hold a cushion to my face. My breath warms the fabric, the backflow of air dampens my cheeks. My head's in a vice. I understand why physicians might have drilled holes in the skull of mad patients to relieve pressure.

I suddenly remember I haven't locked the bedroom door, but Ava hasn't followed. I don't really blame her. Quietly I retrace my steps. The door's closed. I stand at it, listening.

'Ava.'

I hear the springs on the old bed. Keeping hold of the

handle I peer through the keyhole. From this angle I can only see the pale green wall opposite.

'Ava.'

'Yes?' Her voice is thin. Is she crying?

'I'm sorry,' I say. Then I insert the key and lock the door.

Three missed calls from Ellie, two from Jack. I also have an e-mail from Barbara, which I'm reluctant to open. I recall the time after Helen's funeral, when no one mentioned her name, or asked me how I was doing. They just assumed I was fine. They left me to it. Now, when I want to be left alone, they're all in my face.

I send Ellie a text.

Hi El, all's fine, just keeping busy. Don't worry about me. I'll call you about coming up. XX

I send a similar one to Matt, without the kisses.

Lying in bed with a hot-water bottle on my stomach, I wonder what to do about Barbara. I check my watch; nearly midnight. She'll be asleep now. I risk dialling and breathe a sigh of relief as it goes straight to answerphone.

'Hi, Barbara, sorry for the late hour, I've been keeping busy decorating and the time has just-'

'Hello, Kay.'

Fuck.

'Oh, Barbara, sorry, I just realised the time.'

'Not a problem. I keep very late hours these days.'

'I saw your e-mail, just thought I'd touch base.'

'I was just asking how you were doing.'

Hmmm, coincidence that she e-mails me on the day I see Joanne Green. 'I'm good, yeah.'

'Decorating?'

'Yeah, and grieving. Decorating and grieving.'

'Oh, yes, of course. How's it going?'

'Oh, y'know, lots of talking, crying, regret, guilt about the poor choices I made.'

'It sounds like the time off might have helped you work through things.'

'Oh, no, sorry, I was talking about the decorating. It's a nightmare.' I laugh at my own joke but there's a silence on the other end. I find that I don't care. My grief is mine, the closest, most familiar thing I have. The only thing I have. I don't want to chat with her about it, hummus wraps or not.

'Oh, I see. So, are you decorating the cottage, or are you still at home?'

Detectives never take a fucking day off. I'm insulted she's checking my story. Aren't I allowed to lie in my free time?

'No, I mean yes. Sorry, Barbara. I need to go, you know, have a personal life.'

I end the call then feel ashamed. It had been a mistake to phone her. I consider phoning her back to apologise but decide it's best to leave it until tomorrow.

Chapter Sixteen

——

Kay

Helen is flesh and blood again, standing in front of me in the queue in M&S. The relief is indescribable. I can reach out and touch her, ask if her camel coat is new. She says it was a present for Bonfire Night. I tell her I like her new shoes, but she's near to the checkout now and doesn't quite hear me. Then I move to a different queue and she's over on the other side of the shop. My trolley is piled high with cakes and biscuits, and I'm desperately trying to get through the checkout before Helen leaves. I realise I've wasted time. I don't have her mobile number, or her address, and I've no way of getting in touch with her again. I run, pushing my trolley ahead of me but other shoppers block my way and I lose sight of her. I weave in and out, eventually reaching the carpark and see her getting into a bright blue car. I continue pushing the leaden trolley, but the wheels are wobbly and I keep getting stuck. I move closer.

'Helen, Helen.'

What I have to say is bursting out of me. This time I won't blow it.

She sees me and winds down the car window. Small pieces of paper billow out, flapping and twirling. When finally they settle, I wake up.

I want to go back. I've read that if you keep your head still when you wake up, it's possible to return to your dream. I try, but all I see are the blurred shapes and lines on the back of my eyelids.

Sitting up in the cold bedroom, I experience the loss all over again. It's a torture in my head, through my body. I gather the bedspread around me and go downstairs. Digging around in my jacket pocket, I find my vape pen and check the battery. Quietly opening the front door, I move outside, inhaling deeply on the vanilla and cinnamon. Across the bay, lights from the town form a glowing seam, like flowing lava dividing the sky from the loch. Stars glimmer, glint, die and are reborn. There is so much beauty out here, especially when there's nothing to see.

I stand in the doorway, wanting to scream into the emptiness. Instead, I draw on my vape and blow the fine mist out into the air. Despite the beauty of the night, I decide it's too bloody cold and return inside.

Stepping from foot to foot on the cold kitchen tiles, I wait for the kettle to boil. Minutes later, back in bed with a mug of cocoa, feet resting on the hot water bottle, I open Helen's diary.

December 1

Mr Rachid came onto the ward today. I had a review with him. I said the right things and I behaved impeccably. I'm still on the section but I'm off the one to one and back on fifteen-minute obs. They're short-staffed so it's better for them too.

Hopefully, no one else in my family will ever know the indignity of having to leave the bathroom door open while they bathe or use the loo. Mind you, I remember when we first got married, I had to persuade Jack that it really wasn't romantic to use the toilet while I was in the bath.

Interestingly it was during that meeting with Mr Rachid

that I realised my marriage, my life was over. Mr Rachid isn't the most handsome doctor, neither is he young, he must be in his sixties now and he's happily married. No, the reason I knew that we were done was because of the lovely blue jacket he was wearing.

I wonder if Jack recalls the last time we went to the cottage?

Well, he left his blue jacket there. I remember it particularly because we almost stopped to go back for it. Jack said it was fine to leave it there because he'd have something nice to wear when we went back.

I'm wondering where this is going. I have a bad feeling.

It was lovely to see Kay on Friday, she's so thoughtful. She bought me some truffles by Iain Burnett. The guy's known as the Highland Chocolatier. She said she hadn't seen Jack at all. I thought he must have been keeping a low profile because of his shame. I saw it as a good sign.

I know the time she's referring to. Jack and I had returned from the cottage and decided not to see each other for a while, to let the dust settle and allow Helen time to recover. How noble of us. The guilt was crippling, but it wasn't as painful as giving Jack up, even if it was for his wife, my sister. I know, right.

Helen had told me she'd discovered Jack was having an affair. She didn't know it was with me, obviously. I was under the impression they were going to give it another go. Part of me was happy for her. I knew she'd be devastated if she found out. I remember swearing to myself that she never would, and I'd make it up to her somehow, be a better sister.

My eyes feel sore and heavy, but I continue reading.

I also asked Jack, very innocently, if he had seen or spoken to Kay. He was adamant that he hadn't. He protested too much. He wore the blue jacket yesterday when he came to visit. So, if he hasn't been to the cottage and Ellie hasn't been, the only other person who could have given it to him is Kay. Everything fell into place. I've been such an idiot. It's so obvious why he wouldn't tell me who it was. He was protecting Kay. Kay is the other woman.

The words don't immediately sink in, I read them again. Horrified, I cover my mouth with a hand. I stand, pacing back and forth.

'Helen, no, no, no.'

Seizing the journal, I go over the last paragraph again, before tearing at the pages, ripping them from the spine. It's harder than it seems. I see snippets of sentences, *other woman*, random words, *chocolatier*, as dismembered sections falls to the floor.

I lower myself to sit amongst the ragged sheets like a nesting cuckoo, spent, depleted. Just before she died, Helen knew I'd deceived her, in the most cowardly, underhanded, and unforgivable way.

At Helen's inquest the coroner asked if anyone knew the whereabouts of her journal. We all suspected the hospital staff had disposed of it, to cover up negligence. Then Ellie and I came to the cottage to begin the clear-out. There was a card from the post office, saying they had tried to deliver something. It was the journal, addressed to me. She meant for me to know the pain I'd caused, to know what propelled her on, in her last hours.

It's taken weeks for me to gather the courage to open it. I've almost destroyed it on a few occasions. Once I threw it in the kitchen bin, but took it out again when I needed to throw tea leaves in. It seemed disrespectful. The thing is, I knew there was going to be something devastating in it. Why else would she have sent it to me? Other than to persecute me. Even from the grave, she's still using emotional blackmail.

My chest hurts, tears have dried on my face, and those which still fall feel thick and glutinous. I've never felt so alone and wretched, so consumed by self-loathing. I pull myself up onto the bed and lie across it, clutching the tattered journal.

I would give anything to just have one more minute with my sister. To tell her how sorry I am.

I find myself outside Ava's bedroom, I knock gently. I've no idea of the time.

'Ava?'

Silence.

'Ava?'

I hear something.

I reach inside my pocket for the key but it's not there. I slide down the door, still clutching the journal. 'Ava, I don't know if you're listening, but I need to tell you something. You were right. This is all about me. I did a terrible thing, and I thought if I helped you I would feel better.'

I hear movement now. Then I feel the pressure on the other side of the door. Ava is there.

'I can hear you,' she says. I've the impression she's kneeling on the other side.

'My sister, Helen.' My voice catches. My face feels wet. 'I loved her, worshipped her when I was small. But she was always distant, always so troubled. I could never find a way, so I gave up.'

I stop for a minute and breathe.

'It felt like a special invitation to an exclusive club if Helen included me in anything. But she was also cold. Any wrong comment and she'd shut down, turn away. She became ill. I knew she wanted more children, but it never happened for her. She got depressed and just lay in bed. We were really worried about her. Then she was admitted to a psychiatric ward, on a section. I got close to her husband, Jack. We had a thing.'

My nose is running and my face is itchy with tears. I pull

my t-shirt up to wipe it.

'I was working that day. On my way back from a meeting, a call came through about someone jumping, a suicide, in Manchester city centre. I arrived at the scene. The uniforms were already there. A woman had killed herself. She'd jumped from the eighth floor of a car park.' I turn to face the door and cover my face.

The perimeter has been established with blockade tape, but people are pushing against it, inquisitive, concerned. I force my way through, holding my badge up, ready to take charge.

Behind the protective screen I see rivulets of red, mingled with grit, a face destroyed so badly, unrecognisable. From the clothing it's clearly a woman. The hair is soaked red, it could be any colour. Then I see the blue shoes. I bought the exact pair in the sale at Russell and Bromley, but they pinched a little so I gave them to Helen. I shout something; voices echo around me. Backing away blindly, I bump into an officer, who catches me as my legs buckle.

Chapter Seventeen

Kay

Thursday

The dawn chorus wakes me. Hair is stuck to my face, my eyes feel swollen and mouth gluey. I push myself up and feel the pain in my back from crashing out in a weird position. I recall waking up outside Ava's room and shuffling back to my own room, but I've no idea what time it was. I wonder if she'll remember everything I said.

The journal is open on the bed, ragged pages exposed. I close it and shove it under my pillow.

After showering, I leave my hair to dry. I can't remember the last time I looked at my reflection. I'm afraid to look in case I'm transparent. My clothes are piled in a heap on the bedroom floor. As I pick them up, scraps of paper flutter to the floor like confetti, reminding me of my tantrum last night.

Downstairs I find the Sellotape and begin to piece the ripped pages together.

I tidy the kitchen a little, but soon get bored. There is a stash of binge food in the cupboards but I'm not feeling the urge. Sitting at the kitchen table, I think again about my deception, and I'm surprised by fresh tears.

It suddenly occurs to me that all isn't lost, there may be some redemption. With a mug of tea in hand I climb the stairs and knock lightly on Ava's door before unlocking it and entering. Placing her tea on the side table I notice how cold the room is again. I think she keeps turning the radiator off. She's cheap on the upkeep, I'll give her that. My mum would have loved her.

When I turn back a feel a jolt of shock. Ava is sitting up in the bed, wide awake.

'You look like shit,' she says.

'I slept in a doorway.' It's true this time.

She picks up the mug of tea and leans back.

'You need to get some fresh air. Get up and get dressed,' I tell her.

She stops and looks at me, a distrustful expression on her face. I don't blame her. I've been a bit psycho.

'I thought it was the right thing at the time, to keep you safe. I'm sorry.' As a sign of my sincerity, I place the key on the night table beside her. 'I'll see you downstairs.'

When Ava eventually emerges, I've laid the Scrabble board out and I'm counting out my tiles. I'm embarrassed by my outpouring the night before, kneeling by her bedroom door like a confessional. You can take the girl out of the church, but you can't take the church out of the girl.

'It's absolutely chucking it down outside, so I thought we could have a game,' I say.

She comes to the table and kneels. 'My God,' she says. 'It's been years since I've played.'

'Grab yourself a drink and prepare to be thrashed.'

She disappears into the kitchen and returns with a glass of water.

We play for the best part of an hour, but my concentration wanders and I feel restless. I throw my letters in and concede the game.

'You played a blinder with that opener,' I say. Ava placed SQUEEZY down and scored an amazing hundred and twenty-six on her first go. It's been a useful way to defuse the atmosphere, but each time I've looked across at her I've felt a gnawing guilt for locking her in.

'I need to apologise,' I say.

'A hundred and fifty isn't that bad a score,' she answers.

I smile. 'No, really. I'm very sorry.'

'Well, it sounds like you've had a rough time too.'

'Yeah.'

'What a pair we are.' She leans over and takes my hand in hers. 'You should stop blaming yourself. You're actually a good person. Who else would have tried to help me like this, put themselves in such danger?'

'You still believe he'll find you?'

'Not him personally. It'll be his cronies who come.'

'All this way? Are you sure?'

She picks eight letters up from the board and lays them out across the top eight squares. They spell out POSITIVE.

Chapter Eighteen

Jack

The River Irwell simmered below him as Jack crossed the Italian designed Calatrava Trinity Bridge. Built in 1995, the bridge spanned the boundary between Salford and Manchester. On approach it had always reminded Jack of the iconic Concorde plane on take-off. The metal suspension wires swooped above like skeleton wings luring the eye up along the 41meter pylon of smooth carved silver. Footfall echoed around him as people hurried or strolled, for business or pleasure, pin stripes or gingham. Jack would normally be at his office now. He'd started his business in lightning protection when he was twenty and now had ten crews of engineers working for him.

Today Greg, his capable second in command, was overseeing everything while Jack had taken some time out after a call from Ellie. He stopped for a moment and rested his foot on one of the lower rungs and looked over the guard rail. A brightly plumed male goosander dipped its long bill into the water and up tailed for a minute. He noticed a few more along the banks and recalled hearing the Irwell had once been described as *'that melancholy stream'* due to the level of poisons dumped into it from the various dye houses and bleach yards which once lined its banks.

With the closing of the mills and the expansion of the city, the river had been cleaned up and re-stocked. The wildlife seemed to be happy enough with this arrangement, he thought. He pushed away from the rail and walked on past House of Frazer on Deansgate, joining a small group at the lights. Checking his watch as he crossed, cutting wide to get ahead of the crowd. Even so, Ellie had arrived before him. He spotted her in a far corner booth of Piccolinos', her favourite restaurant.

The waiter guided him to their table through an elegant room of marble and copper with accents of powder blue upholstery. It was a busy afternoon. The clink of cutlery and aromas of fillet steak being served to a nearby table wafted around him. Italian mood music played in the background. Ellie rose, phone in hand.

'Sorry love,' he said, then kissed her cheek.

'Never mind dad, late is the new early,' she answered with a smile.

'So it is. How's things?' He asked, manoeuvring himself into the booth.

'Good, yeah.'

Standard answer from daughter to dad.

Since her mum's death Ellie had developed a grey wash to her complexion and she'd lost weight. Jack was relieved to see she had more colour in her face and her cheeks appeared fuller since he'd seen her a month ago. Ellie was the opposite of her mum. Where Helen had been dark haired, Ellie was blonde. Helen hazel eyed, Ellie's blue. Ellie's humour was gentle, rounded, compared to her mum's cuttlefish sharp wit.

The waitress arrived and placed cutlery wrapped in white cotton napkins on the table and took their drinks orders. Jack watched as one of the chefs placed fresh salmon steaks into a bed of crushed ice in the display counter. The pizza oven behind her was fired up and ready to go. The flames reflected from the burnished copper up and over the hood. The overall effect was relaxing, the optical equivalent of a sip from a glass of Laphroag whisky. He let the tension leave his shoulders and allowed the ambience in.

A group arrived and sat at the next booth. Three men and two women. Smartly dressed. A business meeting or an afternoon drink to wash the morning down? The woman was aged around thirty, slim with short black hair. She stopped and smiled at him. Jack was taken aback but smiled back politely.

One of the men nudged her into the booth and said to the group, 'Felicity's at it again.'

Ellie looked at him and raised her eyebrows, 'Dad, honestly, I can't take you anywhere.'

'It wasn't me,' Jack protested.

'I know,' Ellie laughed. 'I remember my mate from school, Jacinta Marchant, when she came to ours and said *Your dad's well fit.*'

Jack remembered and thought it was flattering but weird coming from a girl his daughter's age. Helen used to say that women looked at him all the time when they were shopping, but he'd never noticed.

One of the women from the group laughed loudly. It cut through the general hubbub of the restaurant like nails down a blackboard, jarring the rhythm of the room. A few people looked over. The woman laughed again, apparently oblivious.

Attention seeker, Jack thought and tuned back into Ellie.

'How's the training?'

'Yeah, it's interesting, it's early year's development. Some of the vignettes they gave us to work on. Such disturbing behaviour, makes you think you don't know what to think.'

'Don't know what to think. About kids?' Jack asked, nodding his thanks as a different waiter placed a decanter of water and two glasses on the table and poured a little into each glass.

'Yeah, I don't mind working with them, but the thought

of having a toddler of my own,' pausing to sip. 'The good thing would be that if I had one, it could jump the queue for Charlie's.'

Charlie Buckets was the day care centre where Ellie had worked for the last two years. She'd always said she loved her job but didn't want to take her work home with her.

'You and Nate planning for one?' Jack asked tentatively. He'd always piggy backed on Helen's probing of Ellie's personal affairs. He was raising his head above the parapet more now.

'Whenever I've thought about having a baby in the past, I've always imagined Mum there you know?'

It was usually Jack who broached the subject of Helen first. It surprised him that Ellie had this time. Maybe that's progress, he thought.

'What're you having?' Ellie asked, perusing the menu. 'I'm going for the salmon pizza.'

'I'll have the same,' he answered, still mulling over the comment about her mum, wondering if a response was expected.

'You afraid you'll get food envy?' Ellie joked.

'Not at all. I love salmon.'

The waitress arrived with a beer for Jack and a prosecco for Ellie. The woman laughed again. Ellie's eyes met Jack's and she raised her eyebrows.

'Come on, nothing's that funny,' she said.

'Not without a few drinks in you anyway,' Jack replied as they clinked glasses.

Jack savoured the bitter-sweet hops on his tongue and coldness on his throat. He enquired after Nate and they spent a few minutes talking about his work as an estimator at an engineering company.

'I think he wants children.'

There it was again. The expectation.

'What do you want?'

'Yeah,' she fiddled with her sleeves, pulling them over her wrists. 'It's just.'

Jack waited.

'What if it's catching? Mother to daughter?'

'What if what's?'

'Mental illness.'

'What? No? You are half of me too you know.'

'Then I'm really screwed.'

The food arrived and they spent the next few minutes waiting for the vegetables and fries. Jack ordered another beer and Ellie a San Pellegrino.

'I always say I'll never manage all of it,' Ellie said, surveying the food laden table. 'But, I'm happy to say, I always do.'

Jack realised two important statements made by Ellie still hung in the air. He made a mental note to make sure he came back to them before they dried out completely.

'What time's your train?'

'Five-thirty.'

'Plenty of time. Let's space it out, eat like Italians.' Jack suggested, wanting to enjoy the meal before any emotionally demanding conversations got in the way of digestion.

He watched as Ellie cut a large slice of pizza and lifted it to her mouth. The oil dripped over the side and onto her napkin and he had the sudden image of Kay laughing and leaning over, laboriously picking out the tomato pips because Ellie used to hate them. Unlike her mum who would reprimand Ellie saying that fear of food was wrong because so many people were starving.

It was understandable that Ellie had seemed to prefer Kay's company to his, or Helen's. When Helen had been unavailable, both physically and emotionally, Kay naturally stepped in. But after Helen's death, Kay had been preoccupied with a murder investigation and, sometimes uncontactable for days.

For his own reasons Jack had tried numerous times to talk things through with Kay. But she'd shunned him. Her face hard set, speaking words he couldn't process. The change in her had unnerved him, like an episode of the twilight zone. There had been no vestige of the chemistry between them. All he'd valued about her he couldn't access. He'd resented Kay for it. Helen had been his wife. The mother of his child. He was suffering too for Christ's sake. It seemed to Jack that Helen's death hadn't brought him and Kay closer, instead it had created a barrier. The energy which had attracted them, now forced them apart.

Eventually Kay's absence from Ellie's life had forced him to fill in the gaps, step up to the mark as they say. Slowly Ellie had begun to confide in him about her life. They never discussed Helen's death, but they had built some common ground. Kay had inadvertently done him a favour. But he was still navigating a high wire, the burden of his guilt set to topple him.

It had been a shock to see Kay when he'd picked her up from the hospital. The surge of emotions doused him like a freak wave. But the wall was still there, insurmountable. He'd driven away in anger, only to call at her house later to find no car on the drive, no lights on.

Then Joanne Green had contacted him again. *Can we talk about Kay?* He could hear the concern in her voice when she'd asked him if Kay had got home safely from the hospital. He'd been wary, unsure what Kay had disclosed in the therapy sessions. He'd explained she may've gone to the house in Scotland and had immediately regretted it, knowing how angry Kay would be at his disclosure. So, he thought, at least her anger would give him a foot hold.

He'd been unable to pinpoint his own fear at the time but realised later, when he arrived home, Kay was struggling too. Was she having a breakdown? He found it hard to imagine.

Kay had always been the resilient one. But Jack also knew guilt worked like wind erosion, corroding even the hardest rock.

He watched as Ellie dipped her fries into a pink sauce. *Christ*. Love and fear lodged somewhere in his throat. He would never say it to Ellie of course. But he too had wondered whether depression was a genetic thing. What were the implications for his daughters' mental health?

'Your food okay?' Ellie asked.

'What?' Jack realised he'd stalled, lost his appetite. He took another bite and smiled brightly. 'Just savouring it.'

'Have you seen Aunty Kay?'

Jack chewed, giving himself time to think, mind blank as an ungarnished pizza base. He couldn't tell Ellie about picking Kay up from hospital. She'd had enough to deal with.

'Nope, you?'

'Dad, can I say something, and I don't want you to freak?'

Jack stopped, 'Sure, you can say anything. I'm not a freaker. You should know that.'

'Yeah, you don't freak cos I only ever say stuff to you which has a universal rating.'

'I won't freak love,' he gave a small salute. 'Brownies honour.'

'I've been talking to Aunty Kay again.'

Jack raised his eyebrows and nodded.

'Good, that's good. Why would I freak?'

'Because I don't think she's well, she's struggling like mum did.'

Uh-oh. 'What makes you think that?'

'Barbara Dean told her she needed to take some time out and Kay said she thinks Matt set her up. She's solved that murder case and they thank her by forcing her to take a leave. She's really upset but pretending she's not.'

Bloody hell. The words tumbled from her. Each sentence a revelation. Jack tried to keep pace.

Ellie continued. 'You know what she's like, I'm worried. Mum withdrew, remember?'

'Is that why you've been worried about having kids of your own?'

Ellie nodded, not meeting his eyes. 'It's something I think about sometimes.'

'Look Elle. Things happened with your mum. She had a different upbringing to you. Totally different. I think if you were going to be, y'know.'

'Mental?'

Jack shook his head. 'You're very stable. Stronger than you know.'

They ate for a moment until Jack broke the silence. 'So how was it left with Kay?

'I suggested some time at the cottage together the week after next. The thing is, I got the feeling she was already there but didn't want me to know.'

His cheeks reddened at the mention of the cottage like the gradual change on litmus paper, Hoping Ellie hadn't noticed he asked. 'Do you want me to come?'

Ellie smiled. 'I really don't think Kay would appreciate it Dad. I think if I can just spend some time with her again. Like old times.'

Jack saw her smile waiver and the brightness in her eyes replaced by tears. He reached over the table and took her hand.

'It'll do you both good. I know you've missed her.'

A tear ran down her face. She pulled her sleeve down over her hand to wipe it.

'Felt like I'd lost them both you know?'

'I know, me too.'

'Yeah Dad, but you can get another wife. I can't get another Mum.'

Before they left for the station Ellie suggested they picked his car up from home, then called on Kay, she wanted to check out her theory that she wasn't there.

'I don't think it's a good idea,' he said. 'Did she know you were coming into town?'

'No.'

'She must have a reason for not wanting you to know if she's at the cottage. And she won't appreciate it if you just turn up unannounced. Just stick to your arrangement.'

Ellie's train arrived and Jack kissed her goodbye, telling her not to worry about Kay. He strolled home regretting that he'd not said something which might resonate. Being able to pluck the right sentiment from thin air was akin to a super-power for Jack. Helen had always had it. When the situation required, she'd come out with words of wisdom which would leave him standing.

Her way with words had left him with few of his own. It had driven Helen mad in an argument. She would berate him over it. *Why don't you say something? You just stand there, staring into space.* It was true. He usually tried to focus on something just beyond her, a patterned kitchen tile or a small cobweb formed in the neck of a lamp shade. Sure, it was passive aggressive. But he knew, and he believed she knew it too, if he'd fought back there would've been an almighty shit show from which there would've been no way back.

He called it survival.

Chapter Nineteen

—

Dr Joanne Green

Dr Joanne Green is seated at her desk, catching up on her notes and admin. The framed photograph of her son Will, on the junior slopes at Val d'Isere, is on the desk in front of her. He's twelve in the photo, twenty-three now. His hair is darker, face more angular. She keeps the picture because of the expression of joy on his young face. Following some difficult sessions, Joanne looks at this photograph and is immediately filled with hope and love. It helps her to refocus, recalibrate.

She stretches, takes a sip of her coffee and begins the task of providing updates, either to insurance providers– always very short, generalised summaries – or to GPs, more detailed, alerting them to any concerns.

Picking a buff folder up she reads through her notes first, then begins to type.

Dear Dr Sivaraman,

Thank you for referring Miss Kay Harris to me for Cognitive Behavioural Therapy. We have now met on two occasions. I am writing due to my concerns about her.

At her initial assessment session in February, she presented as smartly dressed, reluctant to engage, but attentive. However, today I saw a marked contrast in both her appearance and level of concentration. She appeared unkempt and looked tired, and she reported taking eight co-codamol over twelve hours, for what she described as crippling period pain.

She scores highly across avoidance, intrusive thoughts and hypervigilance, indicating a probable diagnosis for PTSD. She also expresses negative thoughts about herself and blames herself for her sister's suicide. She has been prescribed Sertraline 25mg daily, which, I believe, need to be reviewed and increased.

Kay doesn't self-report any suicidal ideation, but she is reluctant to confide in me yet. Her attendance was a condition of her early return to work and not a choice, which makes engagement difficult.

Kay confirmed that she had recently been advised to take some annual leave by her manager, Superintendent Barbara Dean, because she had noticed signs of fatigue, lack of concentration, and changes to her appearance, which was supported by your referral letter. I'm of the opinion that Kay has used work as an avoidance tactic, and time on her hands is triggering an acute reaction.

Kay fainted during the session; she was unconscious for a maximum of thirty seconds, her blood pressure and pulse low, but all other observations appeared normal. I ensured she attended A&E for an assessment. I also contacted her brother-in-law Jack Ashcroft, and informed him of the situation.

Mr Ashcroft assured me that he wouldn't let her drive, but contacted me later to say she had refused his help and taken her car. He surmised that Kay must be staying at the family holiday home in Scotland, which would make sense, as she is on two weeks' annual leave. He has asked his daughter to visit her during this time.

Due to the use of co-codamol, I did wonder about whether Kay was also experiencing symptoms of pre-menstrual dysphoric disorder, but her responses were too hazy to establish this, or anything else. I have asked her to return in two days when she's feeling better so that we can conduct a further session and assess her more fully.

I will keep you informed. Thank you.

Dr Joanne Green DClinPsy; MBPSs; RMN; BABCP Accred.

When the letter is finished, Joanne reads it back and thinks how difficult it is to convey to the GP the real sense of Kay Harris while trying to keep everything sounding professional.

Joanne has been a therapist long enough to know that the clients who you spend most time thinking about are usually the ones who are in the most trouble, even though they might not admit to it. Intuitively knowing that a client is hiding something is an instinct developed over years. And Joanne wonders, what's the point in twenty-five years of experience if you only pay attention to what clients say? There's something in Joanne's gut which tells her Kay is screaming out for help, while keeping everyone away.

Drumming her fingers on the chair arm, she checks her watch. Her next client is due in half an hour. Standing and stretching, she looks out of the window, contemplating a walk down the leafy avenue to clear her head. Instead she picks her phone up. She's about to put it down again when Barbara answers.

'I was just going to call you.' Barbara says.

'Oh yeah, and the cheque's in the post, I suppose?'

'What? Oh yeah. How can I help?'

'It's nothing really. You know I can't discuss clients, but I was just wondering if you've heard anything from Kay Harris recently?'

'Well, yes, actually, I spoke to her very briefly last night. Is everything OK?'

'How did she sound?'

'To be honest, sarcastic, avoidant, rude. The usual.'

'Hmm.'

'She doesn't let people in easily, not just since her sister died, but forever.'

'Does she have good support around her?'

'Is everything OK?'

Joanne begins to think the call is crossing the confidentiality boundary and begins to back off. 'Yes, fine. I just wanted some independent background on the family situation.'

'Have you spoken to Jack?'

Not letting on that Jack picked Kay up, Joanne says, 'No.'

'He might be your best bet.'

'Yes, sure, I'll call him. I have his number I think.'

'Or you could speak to her niece Ellie. I'd say Kay's closer to her than anyone.'

Joanne returns to her desk and checks through her notes. 'I have her number. I'd have to ask Kay's permission first though.' She's suspicious enough of me, Joanne thinks.

Chapter Twenty

―――

Kay

Last night I fell asleep downstairs, and awoke at about two a.m. convinced I'd just had a completely normal conversation with Helen. It was so real. You know the feeling? That waft of air when someone has just left the room. That's how it was. I got up and searched the house for her. The only room I didn't look in was Ava's because I didn't want to disturb her again.

It's my belief that Helen is sending me messages. I just need to listen for them. The clock stopped yesterday at seven thirty in the evening. It didn't just stop, it stopped with a loud clang of the minute hand. I stared at it for a while, but nothing else happened.

Ava was upstairs. I called to her and asked if she'd heard anything. She came downstairs, frowning, asking what I was talking about, and assuring me she'd not heard anything. She said it must've been the clang of marine bells from outside. She said I should lie down and listen to some relaxing music. She brought me the blanket and covered me, stroking my forehead with cool hands, while I fell asleep listening to Classic Radio.

Chapter Twenty-One

Kay

Friday

Before I leave today my intention is to ask Ava for any other morsels of information which might help me sort out McGrath. Then she can get on with living. Ava gets the 'Pass Go' card Helen should have had. I also need to know I can trust her to keep herself safe. Otherwise, what's it all been for? She comes down to the kitchen looking pale and thin.

'Here, sit.' I pull a hessian-covered kitchen chair out for her, thinking that her bony bum will look like a waffle after ten minutes on that, but it's warmer in the kitchen with the Aga lit. 'Hang on,' I say, and go to fetch a cushion.

My phone rings. What the fuck? It's Joanne Green. More a summoning than a ringing, then.

I've always said that just because someone knocks at your door, it doesn't mean you have to answer it. It's the same with phones. There shouldn't be any guilt about not answering.

I place the cushion on the chair for Ava. She smiles gratefully and sits.

'Hello,' I answer grudgingly.

'Hello, Kay. It's Joanne.'

'Yeah.'

'I'm just making sure you're OK, y'know, after yesterday?'

'Yeah, I'm fine, thanks, much better now.'

'We said we'd re-make the appointment. I know it's a bit of a journey for you, from Scotland.'

Too close, invasive. Spiking hairs on the back of my neck. 'Who said I was in Scotland?'

'Oh, sorry, I should have said. Jack mentioned that you might be-' She says Jack's name as though he's our mutual friend. '-I think it's a great idea.'

That overfamiliar tone I've always associated with used car salesmen grates on me.

'No, I can't, sorry.'

I hear the balloon of her enthusiasm deflating. Then I think of McGrath and my plan. Maybe I can use this to my advantage. 'Just hang on.' I move the phone away from my ear and shuffle some papers around on the table. 'Actually,' I say, returning to the phone. 'If I move a couple of things around, that should be OK.'

'That's great, thank you. Can we say three o'clock today?'

'Sure, yes.'

'Just one more thing, Kay. Sometimes it's useful for the sessions if you bring a family member who can provide some insight from a different perspective. Sometimes family or friends notice things that we don't. Is there anyone in your family who you'd feel comfortable doing that with?'

'Well, most of my family are dead as you know, and my circle of friends is rather lacking in diameter.' I can't seem to help the sarcasm around this woman.

'You have Ellie, your niece, written down as next of kin.'

'No. I mean, she is, but she lives in York. I couldn't ask her.'

'Would it be all right if I phoned her? You can be present when I do. I want to be transparent.'

I think about it for a minute. Joanne's the tenacious sort.

'Let me think about it.'

Chapter Twenty-Two

Ellie

'Just go, Penguin.' It was Nate's pet name for her, ironic because she hated the cold. 'I know you're concerned.'

'I am,' Ellie replied. 'But she's going to be massively pissed off. You know how she is.'

Ellie had just picked up her Aunty Kay's message. She'd tried her number a few times, but it went straight to answerphone. 'She's definitely not home. Dad says he's been twice too. Kay's at the cottage. I'm sure of it.'

'Probably just wants a bit of time on her own.'

'I think she's in trouble somehow. She sounded off, preoccupied. With what happened to Mum, what if...?'

'No, Kay's strong. She's still grieving. We all are.'

'I know, but she's all alone at the cottage. Why? She definitely didn't want me to go up.'

'Have you spoken to Matt?' Nate asked.

'Matt phoned me. He asked if *I'd* spoken to her. He said they'd had a few words and things still weren't right. See, that's what I mean, pushing people away, like Mum did.'

'Well, if you're going, you'd better get gone. Phone me every hour. I'll follow you up tomorrow if you stay.'

Ellie didn't need telling twice. She'd already packed an overnight bag in case her aunt was ill. She'd promised to cover a shift at the after-school club but let them know she couldn't do it. Even if she managed to get home that night, it was a fourteen-hour round trip and she'd be in no fit state.

Ellie thought all this as she searched through the addresses in her sat nav. She'd been to the cottage numerous times, but never on her own. The estimated time of arrival was three o'clock in the afternoon. She selected a Spanish language podcast to listen to, put her flask of coffee in the cup holder, and set off.

Chapter Twenty-Three

Adrian

The hot towel shave had felt so damn good and had left his skin feeling soft and smooth and smelling of sandalwood. He ran his hand over it and imagined how appreciative Lena would be. She was always complaining of having a beard rash caused by his designer stubble and he was keen to minimise any irritations in her life. Especially after meeting her brother Andy.

Andy Melnik spoke good English, despite a dense Ukrainian accent. He was tall, handsome, and wore windowpane check suits like no other man since Pierce Brosnan in his Bond days. He turned heads of both men and women. But he was a low-life bottom-feeder with an alleged natural talent for terrorizing. Adrian could believe it, just being in Melnik's presence made the food in his stomach break down faster.

Lena told him her brother was very pleased she had been invited to the fundraiser that evening. Adrian had tried to dissuade her. It felt like too much responsibility and he didn't want a write up in the M.E.N or Living Edge saying they were a couple. He'd booked a car to pick her up so at least they would arrive separately.

When they first met, he thought that she'd stick around for a bit, get bored and find a younger man. He didn't want another wife. He still had unfinished business with the last one. Wives were time consuming, expensive, and over-rated.

But recently Lena slowed down outside Boodles windows, 'Just to have a little look.' He didn't want 'a little look. He liked it but didn't want to put a ring on it. Neither did he want to be on the receiving end of Andy's displeasure, on the wrong side of bad. He was quite literally between a rock and a hard place. Especially since Andy had begun to inveigle himself into Adrian's business. Which, Adrian believed, had been the plan all along.

As he strode out of Barton Arcade a young couple stopped in front of him to take a photograph. They held the camera aloft and he followed its gaze to the upper floors and the Victorian decorative ironwork and mahogany handrails. He'd never really looked before. It was nice but he preferred the modern glass buildings like those around Spinningfields.

The couple apologised as he stepped around them, at the same time he felt his phone vibrate. The caller was Si.

'Hi.'

'You good?' Si asked.

'Fine. How's it going? Has the eagle landed yet?'

'What?'

'Have you got eyes on the fucking bird?'

As Si filled him in on the details, he stepped into St Ann's square and into a downpour. Grasping its Maplewood handle he opened his automatic umbrella, listening intently as he made his way to the car park.

Chapter Twenty-Four

Kay

Signs for the M56 appear and I feel a sense of relief to be taking some decisive action.

'It's been too long, old friend,' I say. It sounds stupid, I know, but if I spend time talking to myself, I may get a sense of what it's like for other people. Anyway, I like my own company. There are no awkward silences and I laugh at all my jokes.

As I near Manchester my head's full of memories. We were born and brought up in Old Trafford. My dad took us to watch Manchester United on alternate Saturdays before the price of a ticket 'got ridiculous.' Dad always said that, like Cockneys and Bow Bells, you weren't a proper Mancunian unless you lived within hearing distance of the crowd from the Old Trafford stadium.

Helen usually stayed home with Mum when there was a match on. I was relieved. If Helen came, Dad ended up pandering to her, his attention taken away from the game and diverted to Helen's sulking expression. My mum and dad spent so much time trying to decode the enigma of that pout. You'd have thought they were two art critics, contemplating Da Vinci's *La Gioconda*.

Dad taught me how to fish when I was ten, another thing that Helen pulled her face at.

Pickmere comes to mind, the summer of 2006. Dad was unwell. He sat under a tree and dozed while I taught Ellie how to cast from the riverbank. I'd made a picnic of sorts, or Aldi had. Ham sandwiches and cake. I can almost smell the peculiar aroma of tea from a flask, and hear the ripple of the water lapping the bank. The lumpy clods of grass underneath the picnic blanket threatened to topple the cups of juice and tea.

We ended up sitting in the car to eat because Ellie kept being bitten. What was it with her and midges? They seemed to make straight for her. I made mosquito noises and chased her around the car while Dad laughed at us.

According to Professor Brian Cox, we can't travel into the past because time is ordered and chronological. Our universe moves forward, but what happened yesterday, or ten years ago, is protected. It's comforting to think that we are still there, me, Ellie, Dad, in 2006, blithe and carefree, dodging the midges.

Chapter Twenty-Five

Kay

The grass has grown in my small front garden, and I resolve to give it a tidy-up as soon as I've got time. Welcoming noises and mouth-watering smells used to greet me when Dad lived here. Again, the house feels hushed, indifferent.

Dropping my bag onto the hall floor, I walk over the mail and go through to the kitchen. A box of eggs and an opened packet of bacon, darkened and curled up at the edges, is all that is rescuable from the fridge. In the bread bin is a mouldy cob, the colour of a dead toad. I throw little penicillin-covered morsels out of the back door for the birds.

After eating an omelette without tasting it, I stack the dishwasher with the few bits of cutlery I've used and go upstairs to change. The smell of musty perfume wafts around me when I open my wardrobe. The hope that I'll be inspired fades quickly as I view a wall of grey and black fabrics. I'm not sure why I'm disappointed. I chose these outfits. I suppose they reflect that I usually choose clothes that are functional, and I hardly ever wear a heel. You can't chase bad guys in heels. Heels are for chasing good guys.

Pale blue fabric is slightly out of place. A suit Helen gave me a few years ago. Too big for her, too small for me, but I held onto it because it's a Stella McCartney, the only designer item I possess. I have the notion that its presence elevates the value of the rest of the items in there. I pull it out and quickly remove my jeans. The trousers are still slightly tight, but previously the two halves of the zipper just gaped, open-mouthed, prevented from interlocking by the billow of white flesh that was my stomach. Now I breathe in and force it to join. I'm almost jubilant. But the strain of fabric around my crotch gives me a terrible case of camel toe. Really, is there no end to the indignity?

I'm hot now. I pull the trousers off and fling them onto the floor of the wardrobe. The jacket, however, fits nicely if I don't try to fasten it. I try it with a white cotton shirt and blue work trousers. I can feel now that I've lost weight. I can't see it in the mirror, but the pants feel loose around my waist. My hair needs a good cut and colour. For now I tie it back, and slick on a little lipstick. Angling my long mirror backwards a couple of inches takes another nine pounds off. This optical illusion has given me the confidence to get out of an evening on a couple of occasions. OK, I'm ready.

Downstairs, my heart races, and there's coldness in my throat. It's anxiety, I know. I take a breath and try to loosen it up, but it hunkers down.

I make the call, telling myself if it isn't answered after five rings, it's a sign that I shouldn't proceed with this course of action. Magical thinking. It's answered on the fifth ring.

'Hey,' I say. 'It's me, and I'm OK for coffee in town this afternoon.'

When the call ends, I pick my car keys up, tramp back over the unopened post and leave the house.

Chapter Twenty-Six

Kay

It's drizzling by the time I reach Manchester. I pass the cathedral, its gothic spires hazy in the rain. A few wedding guests are huddled together, smoking under a large umbrella, not a vape in sight. I've a sudden craving for a proper cigarette.

Carrying on past the station, I pull into an ancient car repair shop. Its flaking blue sign reads *Harrop & Son. Car Mechanics*. An arrow points to a rusted side door, above which faded blue letters grandly spell out Servicing and Repairs, Reception. There's something nostalgic about the rusting ironwork and flaking paint. I imagine Mr Harrop and his son, proudly hanging the sign, puffing their chests out with aspiration and hope.

I drive on, past another corrugated building, onto a gravelled patch of land. Not for much longer though. There's another apartment block planned for this little plot. You can guarantee it's going to be a glass and concrete monstrosity. The days of baroque buildings like the iconic Lloyds Bank on King Street are over. It's a wine bar now, but the stunning architecture is still intact inside, and if you look up, just inside the doorway is a globe with seven bees, signifying the influence of the city across the seven seas. I've watched people walk in and sit down, with no appreciation of their surroundings, no interest in anything but the happy hour two-for-one cocktail menu with 'Sex on the Beach' and 'Hanky Panky' among the illustrious selection. That anyone should utter those words in that revered space just seems wrong to me.

I spot a white Range Rover and pull up alongside it. An attractive woman in her fifties, smartly dressed with short blonde hair, is behind the wheel. I get out and cross the short distance. Her passenger door swings open and I climb in.

She nods. 'Kay.'

'Maddie.'

Magdalena Moss is my go-to person if I ever need help with anything that might be frowned on in the department, like computer hacking, security software, or the Dark Net.

I don't know if it's reciprocated, but I regard her as a friend first and an asset last. The job I have for her today is so small fry, it should be on a children's menu.

We met about twenty years ago, when I'd been in the force for only a year. I was on foot patrol in Didsbury, wondering what jobs the occupants of the large houses had, and how they could afford the mortgages and heating bills. I noticed smoke coming from the window of a red bricked semi-detached Victorian. There was no response from the doorbell. I radioed for help, then smashed the expensive looking stained glass window, hoping they wouldn't take the cost of a replacement out of my wages if it turned out to be overcooked bacon on the grill.

Inside I found Maddie, coughing and confused. She wouldn't leave; she was trying to get upstairs to her twins. The fire engines arrived and managed to rescue them.

Maddie and I had stayed in touch. That doesn't happen often in this business, but I visited her in hospital, we got on, and it went from there.

Maddie's daughters were deemed to be young prodigies. They are now in their early thirties, and both work in the family property investment business. They live very private lives, with zero social network presence. Maddie is fiercely protective of them.

I've not seen them for several years, but I know that they're capable of hacking the most difficult of security algorithmic combinations without detection.

We lean in and kiss cheeks. A waft of Clive Christian cologne, Maddie's signature smell. I tried it in Harrods once. It smelled oddly of the dentist on me. How can that be? How can we be made of such different stuff?

Maddie places her hand on my arm. 'I'm so sorry about Helen.'

Blood, grit. My stomach flips. I wonder how a painful memory can move so swiftly from arm's length to close and in your face.

'Thanks.'

'I'm sorry I couldn't make the funeral. I was in Japan.'

'I know.'

'Are you OK?'

Thin rain spatters the windscreen. Maddie switches the wipers on. The rhythmic swishing noise is calming.

'In truth, I don't think I'm doing that great.' I wonder why I've suddenly chosen this moment to be honest about my true state. All the prising and poking from a trained professional and I don't give an inch, yet here I am, spilling it like an informant who's just seen the thumbscrews.

'I'm having nightmares. I don't sleep.' I laugh. 'I think Helen might be haunting me.'

Maddie looks concerned. 'What makes you think that?'

'Oh, different things. A feeling more than anything. Maybe it's payback for-' I stop. This is need to know stuff. 'I did a stupid thing.'

The sky has darkened and thunder rumbles in the distance. Maddie puts the air con on, and we both watch a patch of condensation shrink and slowly disappear.

'When I lost Ron, I had all sorts of mixed feelings. Guilt, anger. The grief nearly killed me, but I had the girls.'

'Yeah, Ellie's been great.'

'You see her often?'

'Oh yeah, we're supposed to do some fishing next week.'

'Feelings of guilt can tether you to bad memories and drown out the good stuff,' she says. 'Especially if the person concerned isn't around to talk to about it. It's a typical Catholic reaction, a self-imposed purgatory. I should know. Also, it's only been what, six months?'

'Ten. It was just after my birthday.'

'You know I would never question you about a job,' Maddie says. 'But as a friend I'm suggesting that maybe now isn't the right time, Kay? If you're not feeling quite stable?'

I turn away and look out of the window, vaguely aware of my reflection against the drizzly glass. I'm still here then.

'I'm not saying it won't be done,' Maddie adds.

'I kind of made a promise. I think it'll help me.'

'Well,' she sighs. 'You can change your mind, you know, but okay. Once it's set up, though, I've nothing else to do with it. After that, you're on your own.'

I give her the information she needs. She writes nothing down.

Chapter Twenty-Seven

Ellie

For the last hour Ellie has entertained herself with songs from *The Greatest Showman*. As she pulls the key out of the ignition the sudden silence unnerves her. She looks up at the cottage. The vacant driveway, testament to the fact that her mum isn't here anymore and her aunt isn't home. Unable to recall ever being here alone, she considers putting the car into reverse, and driving straight home. Pressure from her bladder forces a decision. Pulling her phone from her bag she dials her aunt's number again. She opens the car door and places a black trainer-clad foot onto the soft ground.

After a few rings the answerphone comes on.

'Damn. Where the hell are you?' Her voice sounds small in the vast space of garden and surrounding land. She's relieved to feel the air on her face.

A marine bell tolls in the distance, drawing her attention towards the loch. Scanning the shoreline for signs of her aunt, she slings her small backpack over her shoulder. Inside, she drops the bag on the floor and discards her jacket. The house has a character of its own, solidly built, dependable, quirky.

Her black wellies are on the boot rack. Her walking shoes should be there too. She can't remember whether they're here or not; she's driven home in them on a couple of occasions. *Still, I don't think I'll be doing much hill walking in the time I'm here.*

All is quiet. A tartan blanket is thrown haphazardly across the settee, cold embers in the grate. A laptop lies on the dining table and papers scattered around it. Ellie picks one of them up and tries to decipher the scribbled notes. Kay obviously working on something. It doesn't look like she's having much fun with it. Dropping the page onto the table she looks towards the kitchen door. She half expects to see her mum step through, arms wide, welcoming. She's imprinted on the house, it's still hers even though she isn't physically present. Something of her remains.

The thought makes Ellie nervous. Air shifts around her as she climbs the stairs to the bathroom; invisible particles of jasmine register, filling her head with a thousand replays of a time before. On her way back downstairs, she notices that Kay's bedroom door is ajar. Pushing it open she sees that the bed has been slept in. Her aunt has been here. Feeling like an intruder she steps onto the landing again, pulling the door closed. The room opposite is where her grandparents slept. It's now known as the guest room, by far the biggest bedroom and with a view of the mountains. Years ago, Ellie claimed it as her own. A few of her clothes still hang in the wardrobe; a cream dress she'd forgotten all about draws her attention. She holds it up to herself in the mirror. Unable to recall why she left it here, then remembering the small curry stain on the front.

They were supposed to be ruthless in the sorting process, but this was a dress her mum had bought for her and she hadn't been in the right place to give it up, neither could she wear it. Ellie dragged her hand across the fabrics, like wading fingers through water, realizing that everything in the wardrobe was somehow connected to her mum. She'd turned her wardrobe into a mausoleum. *Most of the things here won't even fit me now,* she surmises.

A noise downstairs. She lifts her head, alert. Crossing the landing, she re-enters her aunt's room and looks out of the window. Still only her car on the driveway.

Cautiously she steps out of the room.

'Hello,' she calls, then whispers. 'Shit.' In every scary movie she's ever seen she's always thought that only an idiot would shout 'hello' into a supposedly empty house.

The stairs creak as she descends. Her bag is where she left it, just inside the door, fallen on its side, causing her hairbrush to roll out. Relieved, she picks it up and replaces it, setting the bag upright, then turning to the kitchen. Pots are strewn across the draining board, some washed, some waiting.

'Auntie Kay, you actual slob.'

Ellie runs the hot tap while clearing the kitchen table of bowls and throwing stale bread into the bin. She removes an empty wine bottle. A red circle from its base has bled into the wooden table. Two wine glasses. Why wouldn't she have finished one before starting the other? Frowning, she holds the second wine glass up, wondering who her aunt could possibly have invited in. A man? Surely not?

'Bloody hell, Aunty Kay. If hell hasn't frozen over it's dropped a few degrees at least.' She realises what an insult that is. To be unable to entertain the idea of her aunt bringing a man here and wanting privacy. No wonder she didn't want to be disturbed.

Pots clink together in the sink. She quickly turns the tap off and leaves them soaking.

Realising that she doesn't want to be here when her aunt gets back with whoever she's with, she walks back through to the lounge. A compendium of games catches her eye, jutting out from a stack of old DVDs, the dark blue box, worn edges, so familiar. It hasn't been used for years, but it's something neither she or her dad or Kay could throw out. It seems to belong with the cottage. Removing it would be like tearing out the original coving, or fireplaces, or the stone lintel over the front door.

Lifting the box from the shelf, she sits down on the settee. Facing her is the old armchair. A pair of her mum's shoes poke out from under the fringing. *We must have missed them when we boxed her clothes up*, she thinks absently. As she lifts the compendium lid, the musty smell of the contents, evocative of soft weather days, transports Ellie to a happier time. Mum framed by the glow of the fire, blowing on the dice for luck, before launching them across the board, fingers crossed. They played for pennies. Her grandad used to call Ellie a high roller.

She lifts a small yellowing notepad from its compartment and two miniature pencils roll across the space. The notepad has long since lost its cover, but faded numbers are still visible on the top sheet. Three columns divide the page, three headings written in her mum's squared print: Dad, Mum, and Little Elk. That had been her nickname for a time. Ellie couldn't recall when it had stopped. Maybe she'd been going through her Goth phase and had insisted on something darker.

Ringing drags her back to the present. Nate.

'Hi,' she says, placing the box of games aside. 'Sorry, I should have phoned you. I've just got here.'

'It's fine. You OK?'

'Yeah. It's a bit weird.'

'How's Kay?'

'Not here right now, but it looks like she's not alone. I think she's got someone staying with her. Possibly a man.' Ellie looks at the shoes again and frowns.

'Cool. Who?'

'No idea, but I'm coming home. I've no intention of playing gooseberry.'

'OK, phone me when you're leaving.'

She says goodbye then leans down on the floor and reaches under the chair. Brown leather, low-heeled shoes. Rotating one around in her hand, she examines it, like Prince Charming.

Stamped inside the back of the shoe the number three. Her mum was a six. Aunty Kay is a seven. The shoes belong to someone else.

Chapter Twenty-Eight

———

Kay

Driving from Manchester to Sale takes me about twenty-five minutes. On the way I think about how many sides there are to us all. How we shape-shift to suit our audience, an acceptable composite made up of expectation and reinforcement. I was a sister to Helen – I'm still a sister to Helen – an aunt to Ellie, a cop to Matt, and a patient to Dr Joanne Green. Of all of these, it's the patient I find the most difficult role to adapt to. Being around Doctor Joanne Green makes me feel like I'm going crazy.

Before I press the buzzer on the consulting room door, I hastily apply a little more lipstick and dab some on my cheeks to give me more colour. The door opens and as I climb the stairs, I rub my finger on my lips and pat a little of the transferred lipstick to my cheeks.

Joanne's wearing a green wrap-over dress. She gestures for me to enter.

'Nice jacket,' she says.

Typical, the only compliment I've received in a long time and it's regarding a hand-me-down.

'It belonged to my dead sister.' Analyse that.

When we're seated, she asks how I'm feeling, and whether I want the window open.

'No, thanks. I'm fine.'

Joanne looks hopeful that the rest of our discussion will be as straightforward. She goes through the risk stuff again. I nod.

'Can I ask you to rate your mood from one to ten with ten being good and one being low?'

'Five.'

'What stops it from being a seven?'

'Two,' I answer smartly. If I'd know she was going to ask me sums, I'd have brought a calculator.

'I mean-'

'No, I know what you mean. It's not a seven because I miss my sister, and it's coming up to the first anniversary of her death.'

Believe it or not, I've only just thought of this. At least it's the truth, and it's giving her something to work with.

'Yes, a difficult time. Did you manage to keep a record of the thoughts you're having?'

Shit, does anyone find that useful? I can't think of anything worse than writing my thoughts down and then reading them back. It's bad enough having them in the first place.

'Erm, no I'm afraid I completely forgot.'

Joanne shuffles in her chair, annoyed. She's waggling her foot, another stress cue. I consider fainting again for both our sakes.

'Can I ask you if you have any thoughts about killing yourself?'

Bloody hell, she's more desperate for this to end than I am. 'I have thoughts about suicide because of my sister's suicide.'

Can you give me an example?'

Pain in my jaw, signalling danger. I need to pull back. 'Well, the pain she must have gone through.'

'When you use the word pain, what are you referring to? Emotional? Physical?'

'Both.'

'Do you have any images when you think of that?'

Blood, grit. 'Erm, not really.'

'Would you like water?'

'Yes.'

A few sips quell the rising nausea.

'You know, it might help if you actually talk about the images you get, any flashbacks. Those memories can sometimes get stuck in a kind of loop. They need to be processed. Talking about them can help with that.'

But nothing can help with what drove her to that, what I did. Guilt seizes me. I want to rip my own chest open to let it out. Tears come and I can't stop them. Joanne hands me a box of tissues.

'What's going through your mind right now?' she asks.

'That I miss her.'

'Have you thought about writing to her? It can help you to get things off your chest that you didn't have the chance to say.'

For the first time since I met her, she's said something that resonates, something that I can use. She must see the look of hope in my face and leans forward.

'It will only be between you and Helen. You don't have to show it to me. It won't be easy, of course. Only attempt it when you have the time. And have in mind someone to phone if it gets too much. Phone me if you like.'

Back at the house in Manchester, I'm exhausted and go straight upstairs. Relieved to take off my shoes, I rub my feet and lie down on the bed.

Running over my plan, I set an alarm clock. Then drift into a kind of half-sleep. Helen is with Adrian McGrath; they're laughing about something, like old friends.

I fall deeper, and nothing matters.

Chapter Twenty-Nine

Ellie

Ellie continues to look through the house, attempting to piece together a story which will make sense. As she searches, she runs through the various scenarios.

Maybe Kay left just as I arrived? Went shopping, will be back in the next half hour, wondering what the fuss is about, happy to see me, but deeply insulted.

She'll have an easy explanation about the shoes. And if she finds me here, asking idiotic questions, I know exactly what she'll say. 'I don't need fucking care in the community.' Carried on the grey white noise of the house, she thinks she hears a voice. Head tilted upwards towards the ceiling, tuning in. Only the ticking of the clock, perpetual, lulling, something you only really notice in its absence. *Like Mum,* she thinks.

She walks to the bottom of the stairs. Nothing – a trick of the inner ear, of other senses? Her hand goes to the back of her neck. She's felt uneasy since she stepped into the house, but put it down to her concern about her aunt. Now she feels something else. Once, several years ago, they had let the house out on Airbnb. She remembers her mum saying that she would never do it again. She'd hated the sensation that someone else had occupied the space, leaving their particles forever embedded in the upholstery, in the air. Returning to the kitchen, she boils the kettle and makes a strong coffee.

The aroma goes some way to restoring her composure.

Realizing that she hasn't even set foot into her mum's old bedroom, she climbs the stairs, cup in hand. The attic room is cold as usual, almost misted. She opens one of the skylights to release the condensation and small droplets of water fall onto the carpet.

The bed's made up. She frowns, recalling that she and Kay had stripped it on their last visit, and taken the bedding home to wash. On closer inspection, the sheets appear disturbed. Placing her cup on the dressing table she brings the pillow to her nose. Perfume, or maybe fabric conditioner? The chest of drawers contains a few towels and sheets, nothing significant.

Back downstairs she roots through the coat rack again. Something draws her attention, on the floor, by her feet. A notebook. Was it there before? Ellie bends and picks it up. A burgundy moleskin journal. Opening it, she steps backwards, banging her leg against a kitchen chair, which screeches across the stone floor.

Chapter Thirty

Kay

For the first time in ages I haven't dreamed. My head's fuggy, thoughts dulled, like after a heavy drinking session. It's probably because I'm coming down from the Co-codamol I'm prescribed for period pains. I take them every month, but I've never been so mindless with them before. I think about Joanne Green, and her probing questions about whether I'd ever thought about suicide make me wonder about the Co-codamol. I can see now that I was reckless, as though I was tempting fate. When Helen died, I thought a lot about suicide, about what it would take for me to do something like that. I went back to the car park she'd fallen from and looked over the ledge. Matt was with me. He hates heights; I think he was almost sick just watching me. I insisted that I needed to know the last thing that Helen had seen. Kneeling carefully on the ledge, I looked over the rooftops, at the beauty of the city. The ground below was a clean, concrete canvas where the picture of my sister's body had been painted. To Matt's relief, I climbed down and returned to the car.

Helen had threatened to kill herself many times. In her early teens I'd overheard her threaten it. Trips to A&E followed. Helen returning with an injured air and fresh bandages on her wrists. She'd sleep for days. Funnily enough, these were the days when Mum and Dad were more relaxed. They'd share jokes, order pizza. In that short hiatus, they knew that they would have some peace, a ceasefire. When Helen eventually emerged from her room, battle lines were redrawn, and Mum and Dad bunkered down, ready for the next barrage.

Jack confided to me that he'd seen little evidence of Helen's illness prior to them marrying. Only a few months into their marriage her moods had deteriorated, and during arguments Helen would often run from the house, threatening to throw herself into traffic. Eventually, Jack had stopped chasing after her. On one occasion, he said he'd checked his watch and told her there was a 365 bus due, and if she ran she'd be just in time to chuck herself under it. She didn't of course, and so it had continued. But he'd become more blasé. We all had.

Still feeling leaden-footed, I drag myself downstairs and brew some strong coffee.

My phone's been on charge: four missed calls and two messages from Ellie. She sounds bothered, worried. Fuck me, the responsibility of family. Sighing, I dial, and she answers immediately.

'Aunt *Kay*, where are you?' Yes, stressed.

'Out.' She's not my mother.

'I know.'

Coldness, not the Ellie I know. Wait; she knows I'm out? Heat creeps over me. *Oh no, she's at the cottage.*

'Why are you there?' I ask.

'Because, stupidly, I was worried about you.'

'El, you don't-'

'Is my dad with you?'

'What? No.'

'Why not? Isn't it exciting any more, with Mum out of the way?'

'What're you on about?'

'Mum knew.'

I seem to explode in slow motion. Fragments of my life up

144

to this moment litter the room, suspended, like a Cornelia Parker art installation. *Holy shit, Helen's diary.* Then suddenly the particles reassemble.

'Ellie, you have the wrong end of the stick.'

'I don't think so.'

I'm shaking from my feet up. I slump back onto the bed.

'I'm so sorry. It was-'

'And Mum knew.'

Scorn and blame coat each word. This is shame at a new level. I'm relieved that she can't see me.

'I swear it was finished by-'

'That's what made her ill.'

'What? No, Ellie, she was ill before. You know that.'

How can she have forgotten the years of medication, of talking to me about her concerns for her mum's mental health? No, I'm not having that.

'That diary isn't your business.' I try to sound assertive but the tremor in my voice is a big giveaway. Sinews twist, tighten, like ropes around my neck.

'I've, *we've,* been so worried about you, Kay. I've driven all the way here. And you've been here with *my dad* all the time.'

'No, Ellie, please listen to me.'

'Which explains why you've been acting so weird.'

She's not listening. I can't get her to listen.

'Damn it, Ellie, that's enough.'

'Mum killed herself because of you.'

'Who the hell do you think you're talking to? I don't answer to you. You need to look at your own behaviour.'

'Meaning?'

I almost back down. I know I'm being cruel, but I'm on a short rope. She's reeled me in, now she needs to handle it.

'All the sulks around her, refusals to go shopping, do the mother-daughter things she'd always craved. Always siding with me.' Now she's listening. Jesus, even I didn't know I was harbouring all this, but every word is true. I carry on. 'I never needed you to. You were sly with her, cruel. She knew, and everyone saw it. I'm deeply, deeply ashamed of what I did, it's killing me from the inside out, but don't you *ever* try to blame me for stuff that I already know. Look at yourself and grow up.'

The phone goes dead.

I phone her back. It rings out.

'Fuck!' I shout. 'Fuck, fuck, fuck.'

Chapter Thirty-One

Ellie

Brushing angry tears away, Ellie calls Nate. The sound of his voice triggers a fresh flow.

'I'm on my way home,' she says, as she backs off the long driveway.

'What?'

'I found Mum's journal, the one we thought the hospital had. Well, Aunt Kay had it all along. And guess what, Nate?'

There was silence for a moment. 'Penguin, just slow down, breathe.'

Her blocked nose muffles her words. 'Nate, Aunt Kay and my dad, they had an affair while Mum was in hospital. Mum knew. It's all in her journal.'

She looks down at the diary on the passenger seat, torn pages taped together, enough to be able to decipher her mum's words, her sadness and loneliness.

'Have you spoken to her?'

'Yes. She admitted it. Oh God, Nate,' Ellie whispers. 'She said I was sly and cruel.'

'What? No. Right, just get into town, don't go on the motorway, not the way you're feeling. I'm booking you into The Moness, you remember that one? Just outside Aberfeldy? About a mile from where you are.'

'Yeah, vaguely.'

'Make your way there. If I can't get you a room I'll try some others. Give me two minutes. I'll phone you back. Please stay safe. Remember we've got each other. It will be OK.'

'OK.'

'Just be safe.'

The call ends. Almost immediately it rings again, the display reads Kay. Ellie presses end call. She drives slowly. The road is narrow, with thick hedges and mossy kerbs. An approaching car forces her to slow down and hug the ditch. When she sets off again, the car stalls. For one horrifying moment she imagines herself stuck at the cottage overnight, surrounded by memories that she can't trust. Pulsing waves of disbelief wash over her, making her feel queasy with disgust.

Thankfully, the engine responds, and she sets off. Reluctantly, she acknowledges the wisdom of Nate's suggestion to stay in Aberfeldy.

She turns her attention to her dad, her own father, with her aunt, trying not to picture them together, but it comes anyway. She emits an involuntary 'Ugh.'

Her tears start again as anger builds. The two people closest to her in her life, both traitors to her mum.

Chapter Thirty-Two

Kay

Pacing the room, I'm conflicted. Fear, anger, remorse, are useful descriptors but don't really cover the bubbling stew of turbulence, the disorganised thoughts, and the emotional dyslexia. I consider driving back to the cottage. I've tried Ellie on the landline and on her mobile, but no answer. She's in shock, she needs time to process.

Ava must have seen Ellie's car and is keeping out of the way, watching from a distance. I berate myself for not sorting her out with a mobile phone. I'd thought it safer at the time.

I'm assuming Ellie's left for the drive back to York. I imagine her regaling Nate with salacious tales of infidelity. I consider calling him. Then it suddenly hits me. Jack. Jack needs to know.

'Oh God, what a shit storm.'

Pacing again, my hands shake as I dial his number, heart racing, not in a good way. I'm twelve years old again, fear lodged in my throat, afraid of what will happen next.

Jack answers and I almost put the phone down.

'Kay,' he says. One word and I feel myself crumble. My whole body shudders. I hold my hand over my mouth to stop it saying something unplanned.

I sit down on the bed. 'Jack, Jack, Ellie knows.'

Chapter Thirty-Three

Ellie

Ellie checks into The Moness and is shown to her room. Too tired to bother with the instructions on how to use the shower, she tells the hotel clerk she'll figure it out herself.

After struggling for ten minutes with the water temperature, she finally emerges wearing the hotel bathrobe and lies down on the bed.

She's told Nate that she's OK and doesn't want him to drive down. He finally conceded and said he would see her tomorrow, but his phone would be with him all night.

When the call had finished, she couldn't help thinking that if he'd really loved her, he wouldn't have asked her if she wanted him to drive there. A real man would have taken the decision away from her and insisted. Still, she's too tired to wrestle with the concept of real men and real love. Nate is pretty good overall, but what does anyone really know about anyone?

The journal lies on the bed, she holds it against her. 'Oh Mum,' she whispers. She wonders how her dad and Aunt Kay could have been so cruel and selfish.

Even more than her deception, her aunt's blistering assault plays over and over in her head. Kay admitted the affair, then immediately went on the attack. She's never spoken to Ellie like that before.

What have I done to deserve that? she wonders. What Kay

said wasn't true. Nate knows I'm not sly and cruel. Then she guiltily recalls her fifteenth birthday party. Her mum and Kay had been standing together. Ellie had hugged Kay in front of everyone and thanked her for organizing everything. Kay had covered her oversight and added that Helen had made the beautiful birthday cake. *I had just forgotten. It wasn't deliberate, I explained later, when Aunt Kay had called me out on it.*

And – I didn't go shopping with Mum because we had different tastes and would have ended up arguing. It wasn't true that I always sided with Kay, it was just that I felt she was on her own. Mum had me and Dad. I was being loyal to her, and I thought she recognised that.

Ellie resolves never to speak to her dad or Kay again. She imagines the implications for their future: Dad exiled, never playing with his grandchildren, a bitter, lonely old man. Aunt Kay, alone. Wait, though: if they were both alone, they might get together again.

It's too much to contemplate. She turns the TV on, volume low.

Chapter Thirty-Four

Kay

Phoning Jack was a terrible mistake. I needed an ally, but he turned. He blamed me, said it was what I'd wanted, to break them all up. Sometimes the things people say are so outrageous that it's difficult to give any response. That was how I was. I had so much to say but the words jammed up like the keys on an old typewriter.

Poor Ellie, though. She won't answer the phone to me. I've no idea if she's spoken to Jack yet. I can just see it, though; they'll unite against me. He'll convince her that it was me who wanted to steal Helen's family from her. Helen says as much in her journal.

Matt phoned and I almost answered, but I can't risk it. Something's cut loose. My thoughts are floating around in a gravity-free chamber, detached. I know I should cancel tonight, but then what's it all been for? At least Ava will thank me. Strange, she'll be the only person remaining who I won't have let down.

After reading through McGrath's social media pages, I've discovered that he'll be attending a fund-raising gala in Manchester this evening, something relating to a homeless project of which he's a patron. It's an eight thirty pm start.

Chapter Thirty-Five

Kay

Fir tree branches brush against me as I approach the large double gates of McGrath's house. The confrontations with Ellie and Jack nip sharply at the heels of my concentration.

Checking my watch, I count down the seconds to when Maddie will disable the security systems, then I push at the gate. It opens silently. According to Ava, McGrath should be alone in the house. I've watched for an hour now and there are no other cars parked outside. Anyway, I'm playing it by ear. Risky, I know.

I've precisely thirty minutes to convey my message, then I need to be off the property.

Approaching the double front door, I spot the security cameras, gratefully noting that they don't swivel to track my movement. Within a few moments of ringing the bell, Adrian McGrath stands before me. It seems like a momentous occasion, suddenly to be here in front of the man who to my mind is as responsible for the death of David Foster as Gary Brunswick is. Not to mention the terrorizing of Ava.

McGrath frowns and looks behind me, towards the security gates. 'I thought you were. How did you...?'

I hold my badge up. 'They were open,' I say. 'Must be a fault. Sorry to disturb you, sir, but I just need a few minutes of your time.'

'For what?'

'About Ava.'

McGrath's eyes narrow, a micro-movement. He hesitates, looking me up and down. I resist the urge to pull my hand through my hair. He steps aside to allow me through.

'I'm just on my way out.'

'Thanks. This will only take a moment, then you can get on with your evening.'

McGrath stands before me in the hallway, barefoot, arrogant, hands on hips.

'Well? What about her?'

The high ceiling draws my eye upwards towards a chandelier which drops dramatically through the centre of a curved stairway. It's dizzying and disorientating. I focus on something else. To my left, imposing double doors open into a large expensively dressed room. McGrath walks through and I follow, thinking how much my mum would have loved it, all greys and creams, low lighting. She hated spotlights. McGrath is beside me.

'The building trade must be booming,' I say.

'Look, can we just crack on? I need to get ready.'

'How would you remove stains from sofas like these?'

McGrath looks around. He's wiry, birdlike, with small close-set eyes.

'I wouldn't, I'd throw them out, get new.'

'We live in a disposable world.'

'If you say so.'

'I'll get to the point, Mr McGrath, and let you get on. If you go near Ava again, if you touch her, speak to her, look at her, or send someone else to do your dirty work, it will be a long time before you experience such luxury again. I'm pretty sure, Her Majesty's vast collection of B&Bs aren't big on interior design.'

McGrath pulls his chin in and frowns. He has a dark kind

of energy. I've felt it before.

'You serious?'

'Very.'

He laughs. 'This isn't police business, this is Ava twisting you around her finger, her speciality. Well, that and-'

'Were looking into Brunswick again. Re-opening the case.' A lie but I need to see his reaction.

McGrath rubs his chin and I clock his manicured nails. My fingers curl involuntarily so he can't see mine.

'Look, Detective, what did you say your name is?'

For a second my mind goes blank as a whiteboard. I attempt to convey boredom instead.

'Whatever. I haven't seen Ava for weeks. I've no idea where she is.'

'So you don't have someone looking for her?'

McGrath spreads his arms wide, shoulders raised, the picture of innocence, shallow emotion.

'Aw, come on, this is ridiculous. Who authorised it? I know most of them at the top.'

I'm sure he knows more of them at the bottom. 'I know them all,' I say.

He breaks into a sudden grin. Nose wrinkled and his teeth exposed, it looks more like a snarl. 'Look,' he continues. 'I can get you tickets to this charity event tonight.'

Cunning, manipulative.

He pulls his phone out of his back pocket, then glances at my left hand. 'Bring Ava, if you're that into her.'

Knocking his phone from his hand wasn't part of the plan, but there it goes. It clatters onto the marble floor. McGrath blanches, surprised. So am I. He leaves the phone there, folds his arms, and puts a hand up to his mouth, one finger on his lips, thoughtful. I'm reminded of the selfie, him, and Gary Brunswick. Then an image of David Foster, ten years old, what should have been womb-perfect skin, gashed, mutilated.

'I know who you remind me of. Brienne of Tarth. You know, the big girl from *Game of Thrones*. Bet you get that a lot?'

'And you remind me of the eunuch. No balls.'

He smiles. 'Touché.'

'Sorry, I thought you said this was about my wife? She's a deluded bitch, and she's got you running around after her.'

'Your ex-wife,' I correct.

'She's still bitter, still trying anything to get at me.'

'She's so afraid of you, she tried to kill herself.'

He stops, looks serious, and then grins. 'Again? What did she pretend to do this time?'

Although I'm looking at McGrath, it's David Foster's face I see. His eyes, an innocence of blue. This piece of shit in front of me lied to us. Allowed Brunswick to slice, cut and tear at the flesh of a breathing child.

'Did Brunswick tell you what he did to David Foster?' I ask.

That gets his attention, but he maintains his composure.

'He said it was all a bit of fun, as I remember.'

Bile rises, as I remember his father identifying David's body, sobbing, begging, for five minutes with Brunswick.

McGrath bends to pick his phone up. Instantly, sinews retract, pulling hand into fist, heart into piston. He doesn't see my rage as it surfaces, but it bursts from me like a cannon.

'I'm guessing this isn't official business, so if you want to keep your pension, I suggest you leave, Detective-'

Rage splits the surface. As McGrath straightens up, my foot makes contact.

It's sudden, silent. McGrath's head spins back and he falls. His head hits the marble tiled floor and I hear a noise like the splintering of a hollow eggshell. Blood rushes back, whooshing in my ears. McGrath lies still. I bend down, shouting over the noise in my head.

'Get up.' Fingers on McGrath's neck, I notice my raggy nails as his weak pulse registers.

I pull him into the recovery position. He doesn't make a sound.

'Shit, oh shit.' I check my watch. I've five minutes to get out of the house and clear the grounds, before the security systems are reactivated.

'Daddy?'

I look towards the stairs but see nothing. Rushing forward, I pull the large doors together to hide McGrath's body.

A small boy, about three years old, appears at the bend in the staircase. Blue pyjamas, bare feet. He rubs his eyes with one hand and grips the rail with the other as he descends. Two feet planted jerkily on each step, stop, and start. He hasn't seen me yet. Could this be Josh?

'Daddy?'

Chapter Thirty-Six

Kay

I'm stock still, rooted, my mind an overloaded circuit board. There can't be a child.

He continues down the stairs. Snapping to it, I move towards him, and close the double doors behind me. I offer him a shaking hand.

'Hi, I'm Kay.' I remove my badge. 'Look, I'm a detective.'

I approach him cautiously. Big brown eyes glance over my badge, then towards the doors. 'I'm your babysitter. I'm looking after you tonight while your daddy's out.' Oh shit, he would really need a babysitter if his father was going out. Check my watch. Two minutes left.

'Do you want to play a game?'

Rubbing his eyes, he shakes his head. 'No.'

I'm out of ideas.

'Do you want to see the seaside?'

'Daddy can come?' he asks.

'Yes, definitely.' I take his hand. 'Let's find your bucket and spade and get some warm clothes.'

He lets me take his hand. His legs can't manage the wide stairs, so, making an aeroplane noise, I lift him into my arms.

He's clearly still half asleep. I'm sure that this is Josh, the little boy that Ava said had died. Didn't she?

Reaching the top of the stairs I instinctively make for the

door that's slightly ajar. Bingo.

It's a large room. Josh's bed is against the far wall, its *Toy Story* covers thrown back. The room is lit by two small lamps atop a wooden chest of drawers. Large plantation blinds are open, and the powdery dusk light is at an equal point inside and out. The room is decorated with dark and light blue horizontal stripes. I turn and take a sharp breath in, then realise that I'm looking at a toy stuffed giraffe, at least six feet tall. I stare at it for a moment; its dumb glassy eyes creep me out.

Josh wriggles out of my arms and I let him down gently. My heart's racing. I try to convey calmness with a big smile. 'Where are your socks and shoes?'

He points and I see them. I want to shout and rush around, but it would be counterproductive. On a shelf, large wooden letters spell out his name. Above his bed a framed poster reads DREAM BIG. A small framed photograph on the wall catches my eye. It's McGrath, Ava, and Josh as a baby.

Hurriedly I gather blankets and pillows. I ask him what his favourite toy is. He stares at me, distrusting. Should I just call the emergency services? Fess up? Give up? I feel the energy ebbing from me, and I sit down on the bed. I pull my phone from my pocket and dial Matt's number. It goes to answerphone and I end the call.

Josh walks towards me, bottom lip stuck out. I should just put him back into bed. Tuck him up and leave him with his father. He places something in my lap, a soft, blue felt shark. 'Shark can come,' he says.

I tell myself I'm doing something gallant, reuniting him with his sad mother, saving him from a future with a man who has murderers and psychopaths as friends. A man whom I may just have killed.

Using one of the blankets as a scarf, I carry Josh downstairs. Back in the hallway, I see the house telephone handset. I dial 999, and when someone answers I lower my voice in an

162

attempt at disguise. I provide the address, say there's been an accident, and then I wipe the handset with my sleeve. Glancing back at the double doors, I'm tempted to go and check on McGrath, but I'm out of time and have other priorities.

Out in the fresh air, I feel the warmth of Josh's small body against me. I'm reminded of when Ellie was Josh's age. She loved to be carried. I remember walking around the shops with her, my hip stuck out at an angle, my spine a chiropractor's nightmare. Of course everyone assumed she was mine, and I never corrected them.

His cheek brushes mine as I place him carefully on the back seat, propping him up with the pillow and blankets. He'll be safe enough.

'Daddy come?' he asks.

'Yes, Daddy's coming in Daddy's car.'

I drive away, and as I round the curve in the road a large black Bentley approaches. I turn my head away as it passes. Through the wing mirror I see the Bentley's red brake lights glow. Must be McGrath's driver. I don't have much time

As I drive through town, I glance anxiously at Josh through the rear-view mirror. Streetlights intermittently flash across his face, reflecting off his eyes. He has his mother's eyes.

He looks at the back of my head

'Do you know *The Bear Hunt*?' I ask him.

He doesn't answer, I recite it anyway. 'We're going on a bear hunt, we're going to catch a big one, what a beautiful day, and we're not scared.'

Chapter Thirty-Seven

Maddie

Maddie feels her phone vibrate and excuses herself from the table. Stepping into the reception area, the welcome breeze from the open door offers relief from the unrelenting, ear-jabbing music. She's joined some friends for dinner at The Ivy Restaurant in Spinningfields. It's been a shame to discover that only the name resembles the far more famous, and far more sophisticated, flagship Ivy in London. Blaring music, and more exposed midriff than a Cairo belly dancing club. Maddie knows she'll be making her excuses early and won't be returning.

She listens as her daughter, Isla, explains that they have a problem.

'I'm on my way,' Maddie says, trusting that her friends will understand. She covers the bill for the table, then leaves without saying goodbye.

When she arrives home, she flings her jacket off and goes to the cellar to join her girls. Isla comes to meet her. The movement of air alerts Phoebe and she drops her feet from where they were propped on the desk and stands, pulling her earphones off.

'What happened?' Maddie asks.

'Watch,' Isla says.

She replays the captured video on the monitor. Maddie

watches as Kay comes into view.

'She didn't get out in time. The cameras catch the last three minutes.'

'Is that...?' Maddie asks.

Isla nods. 'Don't think that was part of the plan, was it?'

Maddie watches, rubbing her forehead. 'Oh God, Kay, what were you thinking?'

Chapter Thirty-Eight

Matt

Matt kisses Lucy goodnight and steps out quietly, leaving her bedroom door ajar. Returning downstairs, he hears a wine bottle being opened and looks forward to the evening ahead. A couple of glasses of wine, a bit of bubble gum TV that he can empty his head to. He slides onto a breakfast stool as Caro hands him a glass.

'She's conked out.'

They clink glasses and take a sip.

'It's always like this the first week back at school,' Caro says. 'She'll soon adapt. Make the most of it.'

'Yeah, just have a chilled evening, eh?' He picks his phone up from the breakfast bar. 'Got a missed call from Kay.'

Caro raises her eyebrows. 'You two still not sorted it?'

He stands, shaking his head as he listens. 'She's not answering now.'

As he places it back on the counter-top, it rings again. They exchange a glance. He answers a call from the incident room and realises that his chilled evening will have to go back on ice.

On his way to the scene, Matt calls Barbara. With Kay off for a few more days, he's aware that this could be the opportunity he's been waiting for.

'Ma'am, we have a possible aggravated burglary, also a kidnapping of a three-year-old boy.'

He listens, then ends the call. That name again, three times in the past two weeks. Adrian McGrath attacked and his son kidnapped. He wonders what information Kay had on him, and whether her call earlier related to it.

A stretcher is being lifted into the ambulance as Matt parks his car. Lifting the police barrier, a uniformed officer nods, 'Evening, sir.'

Matt thanks him and continues up the driveway, noting the security cameras as he enters the house. Another officer approaches. Gemma White. They have worked together before, and Matt knows her to be a capable officer.

'Sir,' she says. 'No sign of break in. Forensics are in the front room now. McGrath's driver and babysitter arrived around the same time. They noticed the gate was left open, and when they couldn't get an answer they called us.'

'McGrath?' he asks.

'He's got a head injury, hasn't regained consciousness.'

'Is anything missing?'

She shakes her head. 'Hard to say, nothing appears disturbed.'

'Security firm?'

'They've been contacted.'

'OK, get someone out to them.'

Two officers step aside and reveal a man in his fifties in a black suit, holding a cap, and a young woman of about twenty. They are both seated on a high-backed hall bench.

'Get them to the station and take their statements,' Matt says.

He walks through to the lounge. Evidence markers are placed in a haphazard fashion on the floor. One of the forensic team turns around. It's Ash Girard, the only man Matt knows who can carry off a white forensics suit.

'We've got Mr McGrath's phone. Maybe that will help?' he says, holding a plastic evidence bag aloft.

'The boy's room?' Matt asks.

'This way,' Ash says.

Matt follows him up the wide marble staircase. 'We've not finished in there yet, but no sign of a struggle.'

Chapter Thirty-Nine

Kay

Taking the slip road onto the M61, the enormity of what I've done hits me. Have I really taken a boy away from his home? Did I do it in a dream? The memory of it is still a blur, like a painting, skimmed over with wide sweeps of a wash brush.

Another glance in the mirror confirms it. Josh is fast asleep, his head lolling gently to one side.

I wonder about McGrath, whether he's alive or dead. Am I a murderer now, as well as a kidnapper and adulterer? It occurs to me that ordinary, law-abiding, good people can sometimes do crazy, unlawful things.

'Try telling that to the judge,' I say out loud. Josh stirs and I shut up.

My phone rings. It's Matt, the third time he's called me this evening.

I switch the radio on. Freddie Mercury is singing, *'Too much love will kill you.'*

I doubt it. Loving my job too much was the better part of me. I didn't love my sister enough, myself not at all. It's the lack of it will kill you.

Our parents didn't once tell me or Helen that they loved us. They didn't know how; it hadn't been modelled for them by their parents. They brought us up in the ethos, 'I didn't have it so why should you?' With Ellie, I've actively done the opposite. Whatever influence I've had on her has always been based on the ethos of, 'I didn't have it, so I'll make sure you do.' Maybe that's the problem with her generation.

An image of my mum comes. When I was around eleven, she couldn't wait for the home help and needed the toilet urgently. We struggled and laughed when her wheelchair got jammed in the bathroom door. When she was finally seated on the loo, she asked if I could hand her the toilet roll. As I reached across her, she kissed my arm. Such a tender gesture, in such an incongruous setting, and from a mother who hadn't previously been particularly demonstrative. I've never forgotten it.

I realise that I rarely think of her, but I miss her right now. I want to drive to our family home and let her take us in. She would know what to do. She would make a den for us and trim it with fairy lights, and we could hide in it, and listen to Aunty Ruth, who lost her confidence in Tenerife.

Chapter Forty

Matt

As he returns to the incident room, Matt calls the team in. The urgency is around the kidnapping of the three-year-old, Joshua McGrath. They've provided all news channels with a recent photograph and alerted the airports.

'Who's McGraths next of kin?' Matt asks.

Ashida speaks up. 'We've got Mrs Susan McGrath as his next of kin. She's in her eighties in a nursing home.'

'What about Josh's mum?'

'Ava. They're divorced.' She types on the keyboard. An image of Adrian McGrath appears on the drop-drown screen, next to it a photo of Ava McGrath.

'Apparently, there was a bit of a custody battle for the boy, but Mum lost. Didn't have the same resources that McGrath could put his hands on.'

'We need to find out her last address, her friends, everything. We find her, we'll probably find Josh. We need all traffic cameras around The Avenue coming onto the B5162 at that time.'

Detective Constable Cromer approaches. 'Sir, we have the footage from the house. There's only a few minutes of it. Apparently there was a problem with the feed.'

They watch as a figure comes into view, head down, carrying the boy. The top of his head is visible above the swaddling of blankets. A scarf covers the abductor's head. The person briefly turns, head tilted down, then picks the phone up.

'That's the best image we have, but it's unclear,' Alison says.

'Do we have the recording?' Matt asks.

'Yes, sir. Dispatch logged the call at nineteen oh five.'

They listen. *'Hello, I want to report an incident at The Beeches, The Avenue, Altrincham.'*

'It's a woman,' DI Clive Seymour says. The urge to reply *'No shit Sherlock'* is strong but Matt represses it. Clive is a new recruit and is just finding his place in the team.

'Dispatch reported the voice as a woman's, it could be disguised.' Ashida points out

'Do we have any stats on Ava McGrath?' Matt asks.

'Passport information says she's one point four six metres. Eyes brown, hair black.'

'It's not her,' Matt says.

The detectives look up.

'Show that image from the captured video again.'

Alison brings it up.

'The woman in the video is tall. Look, if we say that doorway is two and a half metres or thereabouts. She clears it by about-' he measures the distance with his hands '-that much. It makes our woman about 1.8 metres, six-foot mark in old money. Ava McGrath would come up to about there.' He points to an approximation of 1.46 metres.

Barbara Dean puts her head around the door and catches Matt's attention. He acknowledges her with a nod.

'OK,' he says. 'We need to bring Ava McGrath in and question her. Any progress on that?'

'Not yet, sir. No answer from her last address.'

'OK.'

'Sir.' Alison approaches. 'The chauffeur said he thought he saw a dark car driven by a woman coming out of The Avenue as he was arriving.'

Matt nods. Something on the periphery is nagging at him.

His phone buzzes and he looks at it briefly. He's asked a freelance police sketch artist, to come in. He's just arrived.

'I need to speak to the chauffeur. Which room?'

'Room three, sir.'

'Thanks.'

The chauffeur is a Somalin immigrant to the UK, has a permit and permanent address, a hard worker, and sends his wages back to his family.

The sketch artist begins with questions about the chauffer's arrival at McGrath's.

'You said that a dark car passed you as you turned into The Avenue?'

'Yes.' he nods.

'I want you to focus on that. Close your eyes if you need to.'

'OK.' He clasps his hands loosely in front on the desk and breathes in.

'The driver would have been to your right?'

The chauffer nods.

'Can you focus in?'

'Yes,' he replies. 'It's a woman, she has a scarf around her head, but her hair is brown and looks curly.'

The artist begins to sketch, and gradually a picture emerges.

Chapter Forty-One

Kay

I've been driving for two hours now and I need to make a judgement call, whether to stop at Happendon Services or just carry on. Josh is still asleep, but I'm worried about him waking up, petrified being in a stranger's car. Would it be better for me to wake him and take him to the toilet? I don't think anyone would bat an eye at a woman carrying a sleepy child to the loo.

But his face might be all over the news by now. That's the first thing I would do if I was running the case. And check all the traffic cameras. I decide to carry on while he's asleep. It's ten fifteen. If I keep going, I could be back at the cottage by midnight, then Josh will be with his mum. I pray that he isn't a light sleeper. I imagine Ava's face, how delighted she'll be to have her son back with her. To know that her ex-husband can't hurt her anymore.

I think about David Foster's dad, discovering that the man who provided Brunswick with an alibi is dead. There will be a price to pay for this I know, but some of it will have been worth it.

Chapter Forty-Two

Matt

Matt phones Kay again, and again it goes straight to answerphone. He's put off speaking to Barbara but can't see any other option now. He's asked DC Cromer to run the make and model of Kay's car, even provided her with the number plate, with instructions to keep it strictly between them.

The first hit on her car was on the B5162, around the corner from McGrath's house, two minutes after the camera footage inside the house. What's more, the image shows a child in the back seat.

Apart from a deep seated hatred of McGrath and the knowledge that she was running searches on his background, Matt has struggled with her motives. The captured video of her with a child, combined with the physical description and the artist's impression, leave him with no choice. He enters the car's number plate onto the ANPR advising traffic police not to stop the vehicle to avoid a chase with a child in the car. Just follow and keep him informed.

Barbara is in her office, door ajar.

'Come straight through, Matt. I've just had the deputy commander on. Any progress?'

Matt closes the door behind him and stands for a moment, head down, unsure.

'Matt?'

He walks to the desk. She watches with concerned expression furrowing her powdered brow.

'Barbara... I'm afraid that the person who attacked McGrath and took Josh may be Kay Harris.' He loosens his tie. The words feel traitorous.

'What?'

'I didn't tell you, a week ago, DC Cromer asked what I wanted to do with the information that Kay had requested on Adrian McGrath. If you remember, McGrath is the man who provided Gary Brunswick with an alibi. McGrath walked away from it, clean as a whistle.'

'She's conducting her own investigation?'

He nods. 'We didn't discuss it; we had a bit of a disagreement.'

'It's hardly evidence.'

'We've just found footage of her with the boy.'

Barbara's slender fingers massage her brow. 'I need to see it. Where is she now?'

'I can't be sure, but I've got reason to believe she's on her way to her cottage in Aberfeldy. DC Cromer is working with Traffic to track the car along those routes.'

'Have we spoken to any of her family?'

'I've tried her niece, Ellie,' he says, as he holds the door open for her. 'No answer yet. We've got someone on the way to her house now.'

Chapter Forty-Three

Ellie

Ellie sits up abruptly and reaches for the hotel phone, aware the sudden high-pitched buzzing is real and not part of a dream.

'Hello.'

'Ellie, it's Matt.'

'Oh.' Disorientated, she looks around for her mobile.

As though he can see her Matt says, 'I've tried your mobile.'

She finds it on the side table. 'Battery's dead. What time is it? Why are you...? Has something happened to Nate?'

'Ellie, please, listen.'

'OK, I'm about to freak out.'

'Kay has abducted a little boy and we believe she's on her way to the cottage.'

Ellie shakes her head. 'Kay did what?'

'Some officers are coming to the hotel to ask you some questions. You need to get up and get dressed.'

'Matt, no... I don't know... what...?'

'Kay's in trouble, Ellie. We don't think the boy's in any immediate danger, but we need your help.'

Completely awake now, she asks, 'Why would she take a child?'

'I can explain later. There's a Detective Inspector Joy Furnham on her way to you now. I'm on my way too. Should be there in about two hours. I've spoken to Nate, he's insisted on driving over. I've told him not to go to the cottage, though.

We need it calm there, and that's where you come in.'

'Jesus Christ, Matt. This is just... I can't take it in.'

'No, I know. Don't go to the cottage until we say so. We're liaising with the Aberfeldy police, so just do what they say. I'll be with you soon. Sit tight.'

Dressing quickly, she puts her phone on charge and orders strong coffee from room service. She dials Nate, who answers on the first ring, and she has time to say 'hi,' as the coffee arrives along with Detective Furnham.

'That's the door, Nate. It's the copper, I think. I'll phone you back.'

'OK, love y-'

Aware of cutting him off, but she's told him they don't have to say 'I love you' every time they speak.

By Ellie's estimate DI Furnham is in her mid-thirties. Long straight brown hair, an open, pretty face clear of make-up. She's wearing a smart black raincoat over dark trousers and shirt with black low-heeled shoes. Ellie is immediately reassured Furnham is someone who knows what she's about, much like her Aunty Kay. Or how her Aunty Kay used to be.

DI Furnham shows her badge. She has a soft Scots accent, as if she's spent time away from the Highlands or was educated elsewhere. She takes a seat in a tan coloured club chair, while Ellie nurses her coffee seated on the bed.

'How would you rate this on Trip Advisor?' DI Furnham asks.

Ellie looks around, noticing it for the first time. 'Oh, it's nice, actually. It was only for the night.'

'And why was that exactly?'

Ellie can almost hear the top popping off the can of worms.

'Because, well, I-' She clears her throat to gather her thoughts. 'Sorry, false start. I'm just trying to get my head around it all, then the parameters change again. It all feels a bit surreal.'

'Sure, I can imagine. DI Anderson has provided me with some background on you and your aunt. Take your time, you're not under oath or anything. These are just informal questions. I'm trying to establish an idea of your relationship. DI Anderson said you were close. Kay treated you like a daughter.'

Yeah, and my dad like her husband.

'I came up yesterday because I was concerned about her. Kay's been weird, not herself. Not answering her phone, distracted. She used to look smart, full of energy, about her job anyway. She started to look dishevelled and tired. I went to the cottage to check she'd not, y'know, followed in my mum's footsteps. Kay wasn't there. She was out kidnapping, according to Matt.'

Ellie leaves out the bit about her mum's diary and Kay and her dad. It's too crude to say out loud. 'I was too tired to drive back. Didn't want to stay at the cottage on my own, too much of Mum there still.'

DI Furnham nods. 'Yes, I'm very sorry about your mum, it must be terribly difficult.'

Usually, when people find out that her mum killed herself, they refer to it as a thing in the past. 'Oh, that must have been terrible,' or 'How difficult that was.' Very rarely did someone bring it into the here and now. Ellie supposed they didn't like it close up. The past was more comfortable.

'It is,' Ellie replies.

They're quiet for a moment. The detective wiggles her feet, stretches her legs out and yawns. 'Oh, excuse me. I've got a two-year-old who has the energy of a hummingbird.'

Ellie yawns too.

'So, you get on well with her, with Kay?'

'Hmm mmm, sure.' Ellie checks her watch. Eleven forty-five; no wonder she feels shattered.

'We're hoping that your good relationship will help us when we go into the house, you know, keep things calm.'

Ellie nods. Her mum's journal is on the side table. Her aunt's hurtful words ricochet around her head.

Chapter Forty-Four

Kay

Pebbles crunch under the wheels as I pull up on the driveway. The cottage looks too dark. I wonder why Ava hasn't left any lights on for me. Please God let her be here.

Josh has slept all the way, but I doubt he'll stay asleep when I move him. I think about waking Ava first, so he has a familiar face. I feel stuck with indecision. 'Just move,' I tell myself.

Getting out of the car, my legs feel weak and my back sore. I stand and stretch. It's so cold out here, I can see my breath. I search through my pockets for the keys as I approach the house. Leaving the front door ajar, I return to the car and open the passenger rear door. Josh is heavy in my arms. He feels dry. I can't remember how old Ellie was when she was out of nappies. I don't think he's wearing one. Damn. I realise how unprepared I am, but it's only a few hours until morning and everything's available a short drive away.

I place him gently on the settee and close the front door. He wakens and looks around, wide-eyed and confused. My heart goes out to him. I want to reassure him that he's safe. I place the blue shark next to him.

'Go back to sleep, my love. You're very safe. Guess what? Your mummy will be here any minute now.'

He takes the shark from me and pulls it to him sharply, then turns his face away, burying it in the blankets.

The room's too cold for a three-year-old.

'Josh, look, I'm going to light the fire. You can watch, but don't go near it, OK?'

Kneeling at the fireplace I scrape out the old ash, then load firelighters and kindling on. The first flames arc and flitter, peacock blue centres eventually glowing orange. Watching them consoles me. I feed it more kindling, then place a small log on top. Sitting back, I feel a tear roll down my cheek. I wipe my face, and turn to see Josh, watching.

I put my fingers near the flames and pull them away quickly, blowing on them. 'Hot,' I say. I pull the fireguard across and sit back on the chair.

Josh's eyes are still on me.

I know that kidnappers are regularly family members and often don't know that they are kidnapping. It can be as simple as forgetting that it's not their turn to pick the child up from school. That excuse is hardly going to wash for me though.

Chapter Forty-Five

Ellie

For the last half an hour Ellie has struggled about whether she should confide in DI Furnham about her falling out with Kay. The detective seems to be the intuitive kind, but she probably assumes that Ellie's edginess is due to the strange circumstances. She has asked Ellie three times how the land lies with her and her aunt. In the end Ellie relents.

'There's something I should maybe tell you,' she says.

DI Furnham's phone buzzes. She answers. 'Yes, OK.' She stands. 'Right, Thunderbirds are go.'

Ellie begins to gather her things.

'Leave that. I've told them to extend your stay another night. Your husband's coming here anyway.'

Two minutes later they're in DI Furnham's car.

'Just shove that onto the back seat.'

Ellie picks up the soft purple dinosaur and tosses it into the back, where it lands in a child seat.

'OK,' DI Furnham says as they pull out. 'Tell me, Ellie, what's on your mind?'

Chapter Forty-Six

Matt

Matt acts cool and unruffled when he alights from the police helicopter, as though he gets to ride in one every day. On the ground he's been joined by a Police Scotland constable who drives him to Kay's cottage.

After parking up a distance from the cottage, two plain clothes officers approach. They inform Matt that they've had eyes on Kay and are certain that she's in the house and has Josh with her. Shortly after, a woman called Josie arrives from child protection services.

Superintendent Dean has been in constant contact and has advised Matt to keep it low key. The local police have agreed to allow him to organise entry to the house, and he's nervously waiting for Ellie to arrive, afraid that if they don't move soon, Police Scotland will be inclined to take over. He's emphasised to them that the boy isn't in any danger from Kay, and he's praying that he's right. It seems incongruous to him that the person who he'd normally turn to for guidance is the one he needs the guidance on.

Chapter Forty-Seven

Kay

Wake Ava, that's the next thing. I'm so exhausted, but I rally myself for the bout of emotion and explanations when Ava is reconciled with her son. Making Josh a drink is probably the priority. Or maybe I can do that once Ava's with him? I don't know. I'm frozen again. What do I do?

As I make my way up the stairs, my phone buzzes. It's Matt again. I switch it to silent.

Approaching the bedroom door, I hear something downstairs, I turn. Josh?

'Kay.'

It's Helen's voice. I could swear it.

'Helen?' I say. I'm at her bedroom door.

'Kay.'

Creaking stairs.

'Kay. Aunty Kay.'

'Ellie?'

God, I was so sure. I've never been disappointed to hear Ellie's voice, but I physically sag, punctured. I hope she hasn't seen. She approaches and holds her hands out to me, uncertainty in her young face.

'What are you doing here?' I ask.

'I thought we needed to talk.'

Helen's diary. I haven't looked for it. I'm guessing that Ellie has it.

'Did you take the journal?' I ask.

'I wasn't snooping. It was on the floor.'

As we're speaking, an instinct tells me something is out of place. I need to get downstairs and check on Josh. It strikes me that Ellie hasn't mentioned him, but she must have seen him.

Ellie holds her ground, blocking my way. She puts her hand on the bannister. I can't read her expression. We stand like this for a moment, then she drops her arm and moves aside.

I'm of a mind to shout to Ava to come out. I wonder why she hasn't been disturbed by the noise. Hearing the front door, I rush downstairs, Ellie close behind me. Matt is in the lounge. Josh has gone. Frantic, I go to the settee, but there's no sign of him, no blanket, no shark. Desperation. I was going to reunite him with his mother. It was to be my redemption. Turning to Matt, loathing gushes like blood from an artery

'He's safe,' Matt says.

It's jarring to see him in my family home. I want to tell him to leave; my mum wouldn't like it. Uninvited particles.

'He was safe before. You don't know what you've done,' I spit, trying to contain myself, trying not to tear at him. Imagine how pleased he must be; he'll make this look like something it isn't, and he'll enjoy it.

He sits. I know all the moves; he's trying to disarm me, staying calm.

'Tell me what I've done, explain it to me,' he says.

'His mother, Ava, is upstairs. She was going to kill herself. I stopped her. Saved her. McGrath, that bastard, was persecuting her. He helped Brunswick, knowing what he'd done to David Foster. Did you see that boy's body? What that monster inflicted on him?' My voice is rising. My body rises and expands with it. 'McGrath let him do that. He put Josh in harm's way too. Why would he do that, Matt? Riddle me that. We need to re-open the case on Brunswick. There's something there we missed.'

'All right Kay, I agree, but McGrath is in intensive care, and you know you can't just take a child.'

Pointing to the stairs, I slow my speech down, enunciating each word. 'I told you. Aren't you listening? I brought him to his mother.'

'She's here?'

'Duh, she's upstairs, asleep, or she was'

'Right, OK, let's speak to her.'

Ellie steps aside as we ascend the stairs again. I'm ahead of Matt. I'll need to warn Ava first, if he'll let me. Reaching the door, I knock. 'Ava. It's me.' I'm praying that I didn't lock it. That wouldn't look good. I can't remember. I turn the handle and push. The door opens and I step inside. The room's cold.

'Ava,' I say, as I approach the bed.

Suddenly the room is illuminated. Matt's hand is on the light switch, Ellie behind him, her face white.

Turning to the bed, I see what they are looking at. It's empty.

I rush to the en-suite and check the shower cubicle and behind the door. I go to the windows. I search under the bed.

'She's paranoid that he's following her. Ellie, when you came here, she must have thought he'd sent you and ran. You scared her.'

I rush over to Matt who instinctively backs away. 'Ava's probably watching and waiting. If you had given me five fucking minutes to settle Josh, she would have returned. I swear to you, Ava McGrath was here.' Pointing to the window. 'She's out there now somewhere, probably lost, probably going to kill herself.' I jab him in the chest. 'And it's your fucking fault, Sherlock.'

Chapter Forty-Eight

Matt

With Kay out of the way they begin a search of the house. Joy Furnham joins them, after Josh has been handed over to child protection services.

Ellie points out Ava's shoes under the settee. They are bagged and tagged along with glasses, bedding and several other items.

'Is there a cellar?' Matt asks.

'Oh God,' Ellie says. 'Yes, I'd forgotten all about it. We never use it. No one likes going down there.'

Matt follows her to the kitchen. She points to a small door in the corner by the dresser.

Signalling to a PC to escort her, Matt leads Ellie out of the kitchen. 'We need to take it from here now, Ellie. You've been a big help. Thanks.'

Reluctantly following the PC, she asks, 'Will Kay be all right?'

'She'll be fine. I'll look after her,' Matt answers.

She turns to DI Furnham. 'Bye.'

'Thanks, Ellie. I'll call by the hotel tomorrow and we can talk about that other thing okay?' DI Furnham answers.

The cellar door opens, the back of it thick with dust and grime. Stairs disappear into blackness. A musty dank smell is released into the kitchen. Matt tries a switch to his left, but nothing happens. Using his phone torch, he steps down, feet crunching on the build-up of muck.

'Hello, I'm Detective Inspector Matt Anderson. Is anyone down here?'

The phone light exposes the white stonework. Old cobwebs drape the walls, like the Spanish moss of the Savannah.

To the right is an alcove, under which leans a wooden clothes horse. A mouldy sheepskin coat lies discarded on the floor. A pair of perished wellies poke out from underneath a small table, upon which an ancient iron mincer stands, abandoned. A rusted bike leans against a black pedal sewing machine. Light hasn't fallen on these objects for many years. They live briefly again, illuminated, expectant, then the beam dims and they fall again into nothingness.

DI Furnham follows behind him. A moment later the light comes on. 'I found a bulb,' she says.

He switches his torch off. 'There's no one down here,' he says.

Following DI Furnham back up the stairs, he brushes himself down, sure that the smell will linger in his nostrils like the stink of a decomposing corpse. 'Don't think anyone's been down there for years,' he says to the forensic team. 'But might be useful to look in the daytime. I think there's an old coal chute, leads outside.'

Matt calls Superintendent Dean, who reluctantly agrees that if Ava hasn't shown up within forty-eight hours, they can consider extending the search to the loch and the grounds.

Chapter Forty-Nine

Allison

Detective Constable Alison Cromer climbs the stairs to number 12A Hartford Mews, Denton, Ava's last known address. She's been waiting to get the nod from the forensic team before entering. Ash sees her and waves her through.

'All done,' he says. 'It looks like there was no doubt about her intentions. Everything's laid out neatly, all bills paid, her passport, driver's licence, phone, and tablet all there. She even left some money for the outstanding electric and gas. There's also this.' He holds up a piece of paper, encapsulated in an evidence bag.

Alison takes it from him, holds the plastic evidence bag taut and reads it out loud, squinting at the small script.

Please take this as my last will and testament. I'm of sound mind and am completely competent.

Tell my son, Josh, that I love him very much and not to be sad. I'm feeling so much better because I see an end in sight. Tell him never, ever to think my decision is his fault. I hope he has a good life.

Please tell my very good friend Aggie, at number eight, that I've left everything to her. Especially make sure she gets the three-piece suite; she's always loved it and it will look lovely in her flat.

Signed. A McGrath.

Ava Louise McGrath [nee Wilson]
Dated 2nd September 2018.

'The writing checks out with her passport and the other notes for bills she's left,' Ash says.

Nodding thoughtfully, Alison adds, 'The date also corresponds with when Kay said she saved Ava.'

When she's finished looking through the flat, Alison calls at number eight.

A lady of advancing years in shearling slippers, black slacks, a lilac jumper, and a slick of light blue eyeshadow on each lid answers the door. Alison holds her badge up and introduces herself.

'Oh,' Aggie says. 'Come in. Is Ava all right?' Her head shakes as she speaks, and Alison wonders if it's a symptom of Parkinson's disease.

'Thank you.' Alison steps into an immaculate cream carpeted front room. Antimacassar's are draped over the back of the matching deep red armchair and settee. It reminds Alison of her gran's house. Her gran used to put a plastic cover on the back of her grandad's chair, because, as she put it, 'He larrups his hair with *Brylcreem.*'

Her grandad was forbidden to sit on the settee in case he stained the headrest with hair oil. Each week, when Father Riley came to bless the holy water at the top of the stairs, her gran would remove the stained antimascassar from the chair, and her grandad would have strict instructions to remain standing for the duration. Or else, her gran warned, she'd have something worth confessing on Sunday for a change.

Aggie gestures for Alison to sit.

'Can I make you a cup of tea, detective? I've got some Earl Grey, or a nice Lady Grey.'

'Oh, Earl Grey would be lovely, yes, thank you.'

Instead of sitting, Alison follows Aggie into the small, neat kitchen. An old-fashioned kitchen unit with sliding glass doors and a pull-down table stands against the near wall. Matching tea coffee and sugar containers are lined up inside, next to a full glass cookie jar.

Alison watches as Aggie fills the kettle. 'Can I do anything to help?'

Aggie waves her away. 'Certainly not, detective. Making a cup of tea for a guest is the only thing I get to do for someone else nowadays.'

Alison smiles. 'Do you see a lot of Ava from number ten?'

As Aggie removes the tea caddy from the shelf, Alison can't be sure if she nods or if it's a mannerism.

'I haven't seen her for nearly three weeks. I knew she might do something like this.'

'Like what?'

Aggie pours the boiling water into the pot. 'I told Ava many, many, times that she could live here with me. Safety in numbers. I have a – well, best you don't know what I have, but if he came around here, I'd bash him all right.'

Surprisingly, an image of Aggie swinging a bat at a trespasser isn't that difficult to conjure up, Alison thinks.

'Where do you think Ava is?' Alison asks, as Aggie places the teacups and the teapot onto a tray and carries it into the lounge area where they both sit down.

'Gone again. She had to keep moving, you see. I've seen him, small, looks a bit like that footballer.'

Not a keen football fan, Alison racks her brains. 'Ryan Giggs?'

'No, little fella.'

'The one with the big ears, does the crisps?' Alison guesses.

'No, oh, I nearly had it then.'

Pouring the tea, Aggie's tremor is more pronounced. She places her left hand over her right to steady it. 'Don't worry. It'll come to me. Anyway, he looks like him.'

'Have you seen him recently?'

'Biscuit?' Aggie offers.

'Yes please.' Alison takes a Hobnob and nibbles it.

Aggie takes a bite of her biscuit and chews, then points the biscuit at Alison. 'Stanley Matthews. The footballer. Before your time, but he looks like him.'

'Is Ava afraid of him?'

'Oh yes, she's a tiny thing. Well, you probably know, very fragile looking, lost more weight recently, I think it was down to him messing her around over access. Obsessed with her, he is. She's all right, isn't she?'

Rising from the chair, Alison considers how to answer, and because of Aggie's kindness and the antimacassars, decides on as close to the truth as she can get.

'I really don't know, Aggie.'

'Oh. Dear God.'

'Were doing everything we can, and you've been a big help. Could I ask one more thing?'

'Of course.'

'Could you look at some photographs?'

Chapter Fifty

Kay

Matt must have pulled some strings, otherwise I'd be in a patrol car. Instead I'm in the back of a black Volvo, accompanied by a detective I've never met before, whose name I can't remember.

I close my eyes on the M74 slip road and open them somewhere on the M56. The scenery has morphed from healthy rural green to sclerotic grey. A metaphor for my life.

Thankfully, we don't return to base. Instead, I'm brought into Harpurhey station and told to wait in an interview room. I'm not cuffed, and I've not had my rights read yet. I know what's coming, though. At least I'm not in a cell.

A young PC offers me a hot drink and food, and a different officer delivers it. Probably taking it in turns to come and have a look. One or the other of them takes up permanent residence outside the room: just procedure.

I fall asleep on the wooden bench. I'm woken for a visit from my solicitor, Patricia Garcia. She's holding a take-out Costa coffee and what looks like a hot panini. I'm not hungry but I accept them both gratefully.

After our discussion, I'm accompanied to the bathroom so I can use the toilet. Washing my hands and splashing my face with water revives me a little, but I still feel only half present. Nothing seems to be touching me. I know I shouldn't be this calm. I'm living in the moment. Forgetting what's gone before, neutral about what's coming.

I return to the interview room and we wait another half an hour. Eventually there is movement and voices outside the door.

Matt enters and sits opposite me.

'How's Josh?' I ask.

He nods. 'Fine. With relatives.'

His voice is gentle, reassuring.

'Good.'

I've that warmth behind my eyes and tingling at the top of the nose: tears threatening. I know Josh was never in any danger from me, but I still feel terrible for exposing him to that stress. Still, it was better than him coming downstairs to find his father dead on the floor.

Matt's struggling too, I can see it. He looks down, straightens his tie, then sighs and rubs his face.

'OK,' he begins. 'DCI Kay Harris, I'm arresting you on the charges of aggravated assault of Adrian McGrath-'

'Oh, he's not dead then?'

'-and the kidnapping of Josh McGrath. You don't have to say anything-' blah blah blah.

After my chat with Patricia, I've agreed to co-operate fully. I see that Matt's nervous. After all, I'm confessing and assessing at the same time. Like a mock-up training exercise. I'm going to hold score cards up for him at the end.

'Interview with myself, Detective Inspector Matthew Anderson. Could you both introduce yourselves please?'

'Patricia Garcia, representing Miss Harris.'

'Kay Harris.' I almost say. 'Detective Chief Inspector, Kay Harris.'

'Time is seven a.m. Thursday ninth September,' Matt says.

He's off the blocks with a question about how I met Ava. I tell him about the building site. He wants an exact description of its location.

'You know,' I say. 'The one on Broad Street.'

Matt gets his phone out and brings a map of Salford Quays up using two fingers to expand it. 'For the purposes of the tape I'm showing DCI Harris the map of the Quays on my phone.'

I notice he still called me DCI Harris.

Leaning over, he shows it to me. As I point to the area of development, a text message flashes up on his screen, from Caro. I see the first few words. *Stay calm, you.*

Then he pulls the phone away.

I continue, 'She was on the fifth floor, I think. She said her husband, I didn't know it was McGrath at that stage, stalked her, beat her, and raped her. She said she'd lost her son too.' That was then, wasn't it? 'I pulled her back from the edge.'

'And she went to the cottage willingly with you?' Matt asks.

'Course she was willing, what do you take me for? Anyway, that's what you wanted isn't it? Me out of the way? Well, you got it, big man.'

He shuffles and twiddles. Matt's a pen twiddler. It always annoyed me when he did it in interviews.

'Have you found Ava yet?' I ask.

Before we left the cottage, I learned that Police Scotland had circulated a photograph of Ava around the area. Also, specialist water rescue teams had been deployed from Perth, alongside police and fire units. I'd suggested that they find the CCTV of me and Ava on Aberfeldy High Street two days before. They stopped and stared at me for a moment, then carried on as if I hadn't spoken. I can't blame them really.

'So, you arrived at the house. What did you do then?' he asks.

I knew he wouldn't answer my question, I was just checking.

'Well, we stayed there. She was scared, understandably very paranoid, convinced he'd send his people for her. I'd made her a promise. McGrath needed to pay anyway.'

'When did you realise that her husband was Adrian McGrath?'

When? Raking through the last few days feels like trying to part water with my hands. I get to a point of clarity, but it immediately backfills. 'I think she told me, the first day.'

'It's just that there's a massive hoarding with McGrath construction written on it.'

I remember now. 'Yes, you're right. But I didn't put the two together.'

'Really?' Matt says. 'We were just talking about him a day or so before. You called him an egg and butter man and said that he should have been hanged for providing Brunswick with an alibi.'

I freeze. I recollect the conversation, but it's the insinuation that worries me. I'm nervous, self-conscious, I try to adopt what I think of as non-criminal posture, hands soft in my lap, good eye contact, but it's harder than it appears. Guilt is in the eye of the beholder. I lean back, cross my arms, something I've seen many a miscreant do to look in control. It doesn't work.

I've always wondered what criminals whisper to their lawyers when I've been on the other side of the desk. Now I know. I turn to my solicitor. 'I need a break.'

Chapter Fifty-One

Kay

'He's saying I planned it,' I'm telling Patricia.

Matt has stepped out of the room and a different PC has kindly brought me a coffee. I've no idea what Patricia makes of what I've told her; she has a real poker face. It's either too much Botox, or she's just very good at poker. I'm distracted by her red lipstick.

'He's saying it's pre-meditated.'

'Your case will be referred to the Independent Office for Police Conduct anyway,' she answers. 'This is just the beginning. If you don't want to answer anything just tell me and we'll break. And don't say anything without me present.'

She pulls her chair closer to me and I get a whiff of tobacco. I remember, she's a smoker. I've rarely met a lawyer who isn't.

'Kay, I need to ask a delicate question.'

Don't you hate it when people do that? I like a challenging question, but there's usually a massive discrepancy between what *delicate* means to the person asking, and what it means to me.

'I've been informed that there have been concerns about your mental state after the suicide of your sister. That you're currently off work because of it, and you're attending psychological therapy.'

As I watch her lips move, I'm suddenly blindsided by the

image of blood, mingled with grit. For once the subject is too delicate.

'Are you OK?' She touches my arm.

'I can't talk about that right now,' I say. 'I need my solicitor. I mean my mother.' My thinking feels blurred, my head foggy, like a beehive infused with smoke. I want to close my eyes and retreat.

Her tone is kind. 'OK,' she says. 'I'm just going to have a quick word with DI Anderson. I think you need rest, and then we need to sort a mental health assessment.'

Chapter Fifty-Two

Matt

Forensics are logging the evidence from Ava's flat when Matt arrives.

'How's Kay?' Ash asks.

'Not great.'

Ash shakes his head. 'Such a mess. At least McGrath survived. I mean, she's not looking at murder or manslaughter.'

Matt exhales and pinches the skin at the top of his nose.

'Anyway,' Ash continues. 'I've logged most of the stuff from the cottage. Police Scotland have been great, very accommodating, realised the delicacy of the *situation*.'

He pronounces *situation* with a Scots accent. Kay would have pulled him up straight away for that.

Ash moves around the room as he talks, rarely looking up at Matt.

'Anything else from McGrath's house?'

'Nope. We've got these from the cottage though.' From a small box Ash removes a plastic evidence bag containing a pair of brown shoes. 'Ava McGrath's DNA's on them. She was there.'

Matt takes the bag.

Ash continues, 'So far it's the only evidence we have, but we're still analysing hair and fibres from her car and house in Manchester.'

Frowning, Matt says, 'According to Kay, Ava used Ellie's old walking boots and coat and a few old jumpers.'

'At least it's not the depth of winter. What'll happen if Ava's not found? Will it add to Kay's charge sheet?' Ash asks.

Matt puffs his cheeks out, exhales slowly and shrugs. 'Jesus, Ash, what a clusterfuck.'

Back in the incident room Matt approaches Sam their specialist cybercrime officer. DC Cromer is seated by her, and they're both focused on the screen. They look up on his approach.

Ali stands and stretches. 'Would anyone like a coffee?' she asks.

Matt nods and rubs his face, momentarily pulling the skin under his eyes, exposing the little pink strips of inner lid. 'I would love a coffee, Ali, thanks.'

She picks Matt's empty mug up from the desk and looks at Sam.

'Love one, ta,' Sam answers.

'Your turn next though Matt,' Alison says. 'And we want doughnuts in the morning.'

'You've been watching too many American cop shows,' Matt says as he pulls a chair up.

Ali moves to the door. '*Bake-Off*, sir,' she says.

Immediately upon discovering that Josh had been taken, and before discovering Kay's involvement, Matt had requested that their cyber specialist Sam urgently access McGrath's computer.

'Anything?' Matt asks.

'Not much I'm afraid. It took a bit of cracking open, but we got there in the end. We haven't found any threatening e-mails or any red flags, but we're still looking. It could take a few days. There are a few e-mails and texts between him and Gary Brunswick though. McGrath has friends in high and low places, and not much in between.'

'What about Kay's? I can't imagine she had any special encryption.'

'One, two, three, four,' Sam answers, as Alison returns with the coffees. 'It's always the first one we try, then family names, then birthdates. Doddle.'

Alison takes a seat and offers a packet of digestives around. Sam takes one but Matt declines.

'Kay's search history, as you'd expect, was McGrath all the way. She searched him, his training centre. His relationship with Brunswick comes up in most of her searches.'

Matt rubs his chin, hating the feel of the sprouting bristles.

Chapter Fifty-Three

Matt

Adrian McGrath is propped up in bed, his face obscured by a tall woman with auburn hair who's leaning over him, removing the foil lid off a carton of fruit. The woman stands back and McGrath comes into view.

Matt produces his badge and introduces himself. The woman is about twenty. Her eyelashes look too thick to be real. She has heavily drawn brows, a trend Matt hopes will have ended by the time Lucy's in her teens.

'Could you excuse us, Miss?'

'Lena,' she answers. 'Of course. I'll get a coffee.' She nods towards McGrath. In return he lifts his fingers in a half-hearted wave.

'How are you?' Matt asks, searching McGrath's face for any injuries.

McGrath slowly lifts his hand to the back of his head and winces. 'Oh, you know, getting there, nothing a lawsuit won't fix.'

'Oh?'

McGrath smiles as he picks up a small plastic fork and pierces a grape. 'Don't worry, I'm messing with you. How is the Detective Chief Inspector by the way? I sincerely hope she receives the help she needs.'

Matt pulls a chair up to the bed and removes his notebook.

'Thank you. Now I just need to clarify a few things if you're up to it of course?'

McGrath smiles and munches on the fruit. He reminds Matt of a hyena.

'Not to be too crude detective, morphine is a wonderful thing, but it does tend to bung you up. I'm on a healthier diet than an orangutan, but nothing's shifting it.'

I can totally understand why Kay would have twatted him one, Matt thinks. 'OK, can you tell me when you last saw your ex-wife, Ava McGrath?'

'Well, as I said, I haven't seen her for about two months. Life moves on, Detective. You should tell your tailor.'

Matt waits, wondering just who this guy has in his pocket.

He continues, 'I let her have Josh for an afternoon.' He waves his fork around and small droplets of juice fall onto the green bedspread. 'Part of the custody agreement.'

'How do you arrange the dates with her?'

McGrath slurps back a piece of melon. 'Phone, text. About that, when do I get my phone back?'

'All in good time.'

'Just a minute. I didn't give you permission to take that or search my home.'

'Sir, we don't need a warrant. It was lifesaving circumstances. We didn't know the extent of your injuries, and your son had been abducted.'

Matt doesn't bother to explain that they've already used their Universal Forensic Extraction Device to access the information on his phone and have hacked into his computer. So far there isn't anything incriminating relating to Ava, but they are still looking.

'It's my business stuff, private.'

'I understand. I'm assuming it's saved to the cloud?'

McGrath looks sheepish and slides his eyes away from Matt's.

Matt continues, 'Ava told DCI Harris that she's afraid of you. She believes that you have people following her, tracking her.'

'Bullshit, delusional.'

'She was about to kill herself when DCI Harris stopped her.'

'I've never touched her.'

'So, no one tracking her?'

'I've got a business to run and a child to look after.'

'Who's Lena?'

'None of your fucking business. That detective threatened me, assaulted me, and abducted my son. So far I haven't been to the press, but if you don't leave me alone I can guarantee that they will be all over you like a bad case of lice. You won't know which bit to scratch next.'

Matt watches as McGrath reaches for the nurse call button, then turns back to him.

'Now please excuse me, I need to shit.'

Chapter Fifty-Four

Alison

Aggie arrives at the station and an officer shows her through to the interview room where Detective Alison Cromer waits. She stands as Aggie enters, wearing a blue rain mac, her hair permed. The customary blue eyeshadow brushed lightly on lids and a dusting of compact powder transports Alison straight back again to time spent with her Grandma. She has to stop herself from leaning over for a kiss on the cheek

Alison offers her a chair and Aggie carefully places her burgundy patent handbag on the table.

'My turn to offer you tea now Aggie.' She signals to the officer who asks if she takes sugar.

'No thank you officer. I'm sweet enough.' Aggie answers, pulling a tissue out from under her sleeve to wipe her nose.

'I've also pushed the boat out and got us a packet of custard creams. Could you bring those with you? Ta,' Alison adds. The officer nods and retreats.

Aggie smiles, pushing the tissue back up her sleeve. 'Isn't that bribery?'

'Depends how much you like custard creams.'

Using the images of friends and associates of McGrath's from Kay's searches, Alison has prepared a photo montage which includes an array of what they refer to as 'fillers.' These are photographs of people with similar features to McGrath but different enough to be able to set them apart. They're aware that Adrian is a public figure and that if Aggie picks him out it won't count for much as evidence. Still, it won't hurt, and it's all part of the ABC. Assume nothing. Believe nothing. Check everything.

When the tea arrives, they chat for a moment about the weather and, while Aggie sips, Alison presents the photographs. 'Just stop me if you see the person you saw outside Ava's.'

Aggie nods.

Alison exhibits the photographs one by one, watching Aggie's reactions closely. When she lays out the one of McGrath, Aggie say's nothing. Alison hides her disappointment and places the next photo down.

'That's him.' Aggie says.

Alison feels a rush of relief. She places her finger on the photo of McGrath believing that Aggie's reaction has just been a little delayed.

'This man?' she asks.

'Oh. That's Adrian McGrath, Ava's ex. I'd know him anywhere. He's a bit of a celebrity around town.'

'Is that the man you saw outside Ava's house?'

'No, that's not him,' she points to the most recent photo. 'Him. That's him. He's the one's always outside. Watching.'

Chapter Fifty-Five

Barbara

Superintendent Barbara Dean has just finished a meeting with Commander Patel. The commander had wanted an update on the search for Ava. News stations across the Highlands have been covering her disappearance. At Patel's request, they're keeping DCI Kay Harris' name out of it, citing Ava as a visitor to the area, but not expanding on that. So far it seems to be working; local press have expressed little interest. However, Barbara knows as soon as they get wind that a detective from the Manchester force is involved, there'll be a no-holds-barred crap shoot. Barbara's planning to tell Matt that the manpower for the search will have to be gradually reduced from tomorrow, and then, unfortunately, it'll be left to 'man walking dog' to find Ava. But for the sake of morale, that can wait.

She makes her way to the incident room. As she enters, she receives immediate attention from the team. Matt jumps up and they confer for a moment before Barbara addresses them.

'As you know, Adrian McGrath recovered consciousness yesterday and has corroborated DCI Harris' story about the assault. He's been informed that his son is safe and will be reunited with him when he's well. Now, I know it's very difficult; Kay is one of our own, a detective who's worked unbelievably hard to put Gary Brunswick away. I can't tell you too much, but she's had a very challenging year, and for whatever reason this has culminated in her arrest for assaulting McGrath and the kidnap of Josh McGrath. We are still searching for Ava McGrath. We believe she may still be alive, although she seems to have vanished into thin air – by all accounts she's very good at that, having spent a long time trying to hide from her ex-husband. The Manchester refuge have confirmed Ava has stayed with them on four occasions.

'There have been no reported sightings so far. But as the case develops and the media become more aware, there will be increased interest. There's already been a story about McGrath by Stefan Laing.'

There's a collective groan from the team.

'Laing was covering some charity event McGrath was supposed to attend on the night of the...' she pauses and regards the nails on her left hand. 'Incident.' She lifts her head again and looks around the room. 'I can't appeal to you strongly enough: this needs to be kept highly confidential. I'm not asking this because I'm trying to cover anything up. DCI Harris will be subject to the rule of law, but it'll provide at least a little dignity for her while we clarify everything. If you have any concerns about this, you can come and speak to me or DI Anderson. Are there any questions?'

Detective Alison Cromer raises her hand and all heads turn her way.

'Ma'am, it's my understanding Ava is genuinely pursued by her ex-husband. As you said, she stayed in the refuge numerous times.'

Ashida spoke next. 'And there's loads of supporting evidence from A&E, treatment for numerous broken bones.'

'Yes, that's true,' Matt agrees.

Alison nods at her colleague and continues. 'Ava has no family we can find, but it seems she's close to her elderly neighbour, Agatha Lavelle. Aggie said that Ava regularly helped her with shopping and kept her company. She said that Ava had only been living at the flat for the last year. Apparently, when she finally left McGrath and went for custody of Josh, she was painted as a drug-taking irresponsible mother, so she lost. She'd discovered McGrath had met someone and was planning to re-marry. Aggie said Ava thought this might mean McGrath had lost interest in her, and she might be able to build a few bridges, see Josh more. But it hadn't made any difference. Aggie said Ava thought she was being followed again. She's positively identified Simon Carter, a known friend and associate of McGraths, as the guy following her.' Alison continues. 'So what if she's right? What if one of McGrath's cronies really has tracked Ava down? What if she didn't run away from the cottage? What if she was taken, and we're all barking up the wrong tree?'

'OK, let's bring Carter in for questioning.' Matt says.

Chapter Fifty-Six

Alison

The ivory wedding dress suits Ava's complexion. She smiles into the camera as a flurry of pink and white confetti flutters around her and alights on her veil like the first fall of snow. McGrath's face is turned away as he speaks to a woman to his left, who wears a wide- brimmed cream hat. He turns back to Ava and says something. She laughs and nods at the lady in the hat. The camera follows them as they make their way through the wedding guests.

'That's Gorton Monastery,' Ashida says. 'I recognise it. It's supposed to be stunning inside.'

The screen goes blank for a moment, then Ava reappears, standing on a balcony, wearing a patterned summer dress.

'Looks like the Italian Riviera,' Ashida says.

'Yeah, Amalfi coast maybe?' Alison replies.

'She looks happy.'

'Honeymooning couples always look like that. Even if they're not feeling it, they have to act it for the camera.'

'Makes you wonder, doesn't it? How did she get it so badly wrong?'

'Sometimes they're wrong from the start, but only one of them knows it.'

'She's really beautiful, isn't she?' Ashida says. 'It shouldn't be difficult to identify her.'

'Yeah.' Alison moves to her own desk as she speaks. 'But the photograph Kay identified her from in her interview was more recent. Shouldn't be too hard though, just take away the wedding dress, the veil.'

'The tan, the glow of health,' adds Ashida. She brings Ava's most recent passport photo up for comparison.

'Then add seven or eight kilograms,' Alison says.

They look at each other, then back at the screen. Ava, thin-faced and pale.

Chapter Fifty-Seven

Matt

When Matt and Clive enter the interview room, they discover Simon Carter accompanied by Riya Campion, a solicitor whose fees would be way out of Matt's league.

There are two cups of water on the desk in front of them. Simon has both elbows on the desk and is resting his head in his hands. Matt apologises for keeping them waiting.

Simon looks up and says, 'I've not had any breakfast yet.'

'Can I get you anything?' Matt asks, affably.

Simon thinks for a moment then answers, 'I wouldn't mind a bag of Quavers.'

Riya maintains an expression of neutrality, as if she's heard it every day. Matt nods to Clive who takes the hint he's on the Quaver run and leaves the room.

Following the PACE interview procedure Matt introduces everyone present and states the date and time.

'Is it okay if I call you Simon?

He nods.

'For the tape please?'

'Oh, sure. Yes.'

Matt opens his document case and removes a photograph of Ava.

'I'm showing Simon a photograph. Do you know this person Simon?'

Simon wiggles his feet under the table, causing a rhythmic upper body sway. Then moves to the side and crosses his legs.

'That's Ava McGrath.'

'Thank you. Can you tell me how you know her?'

The door opens and Clive enters looking flushed.

'Detective Clive Seymour has just entered.' Matt says.

'Sorry,' Clive says. 'The machine only had Monster Munch or Hula Hoops.'

Simon looks as though he's just been asked to choose his favourite child.

'Just give them to him,' Matt instructs.

Clive obeys and Carter looks like he's just landed the jackpot.

'Okay, can we re-commence? I was just asking how you know Ava McGrath.'

Simon prizes open one of the bags of Hula Hoops and puts a couple in his mouth and bites down noisily. Matt reflects that had Kay been asked for Hula Hoops she would have said the machine was out of order and he'd have got a cup of tepid tea, like it or lump it.

'She's Adrian's ex-wife.'

'You're referring to Adrian McGrath?'

'Yes.'

'Can you tell us the last time you saw her?'

Another handful, loud crunching.

'About two weeks ago.'

'And under what circumstances?'

'How do you mean?'

'I'm just asking you where you were when you saw her last, what you were doing. It's not a trick question. We're trying to find her and we think your information might help us.'

Simon manoeuvres himself onto the other buttock.

'You could really help us out here.' Matt adds.

Simon looks at Riya who nods at him. 'I was outside her

house.'

'Why is that?'

'I've been watching out for her.'

He pronounces been as *beed*.

'Watching out, in what way?'

Simon moves around again in his chair. 'I look out for her to make sure she doesn't do anything silly. Adrian worries about her.'

'How do you know Adrian?'

'From school.'

'Wow, you've known each other a long time.'

'He gave me my first job as a bricky on one of his building sites.'

'You owe him a lot.'

'Everything.'

'Look, Simon, I'm not questioning your loyalty at all. It's admirable. But don't you see? You'd be helping Adrian massively if you help us find Ava. After all, weren't you supposed to be looking out for her?'

He looks down at his feet under the table then around the room.

'You could help Adrian to find her,' Matt continues. 'We also have an eye-witness who says you were stalking Ava.'

Simon shakes his head. 'It wasn't stalking.'

'Have you been to Scotland recently?'

'Nope.'

'So, you have never been to a place called Aberfeldy?'

'Abbi what?'

'Aberfeldy, it's in Scotland.

'Never heard of it.'

'We'll need a record of your movements over the last two weeks.'

Simon stares into the empty crisp bag and emits a drawn-out sigh.

'Did you see Ava on September second? It was a Sunday.'

'I don't remember, maybe. Sometimes I fall asleep.' I don't tell Adrian that though, I godda make a living.

'Sure, absolutely. But does that sound right to you? Did Ava want you to be looking out for her?'

A shrug. 'It's for her own good, she's a troubled soul.' He screws the empty bag up and looks around for a bin. There isn't one so he leaves it on the table where it begins to unfurl.

'You don't keep a record, to pass onto Adrian?'

Riya starts to earn her rate and leans over and whispers something.

'I don't write anything down.'

'What's your opinion of Gary Brunswick?'

No hesitation. 'Nonce scum.'

'Why do you think McGrath,' he corrects himself. 'Adrian gave him an alibi?'

'Ask him, I know you all want me to dob him in.'

'Dob him in for what? Is there anything to dob him in for?'

'Well if there isn't, everyone's going to a lot of trouble. And wasting police time.'

Riya raises her eyebrows and purses her lips like she's repressing a smile.

'How do you know Brunswick?'

'He worked with us.'

Matt notes the use of the word *with*, not *for* and asks, 'He worked with you on what?'

'He was in the office.'

'Yes, we know a lot about him, but what did you work *with* him on? When you weren't watching out for Ava?'

'Office stuff, stationary, posting stuff.'

'Okay,' Matt leans back, palms face down on the desk. 'Do you have your phone with you?'

Simon nods.

'For the tape please.'

'Yes,' Simon looks at Riya. 'Don't they need a warrant?'

Riya addresses Matt. 'We have agreed to co-operate in this investigation as my client has not been arrested. And he denies you access to his phone. There is nothing incriminating on it. His phone records will show you that he had regular contact with Mr McGrath as part of his employment.'

Matt changes tack, knowing they can charge Simon within the next 24 hours and seize his phone anyway. 'So, what do you do now Simon? Now that Ava isn't around to watch over?'

'I told you. I work in the office at Ground Up. I do menial stuff. I may have a low I.Q. but I've three kids to feed.'

Chapter Fifty-Eight

Joy

DI Joy Furnham has been supplied with a copy of Ava's wedding video and a collection of the most recent photographs retrieved from her flat.

The Crown Office, Procurator Fiscal Service, and Police Scotland have said they are happy to liaise with Greater Manchester Police, but their policies on sharing CCTV images with an outside agency are complex. For efficiency's sake, Commander Patel has agreed to send Detective Ashida Assante to assist them with the identification and search for Ava.

Ashida arrives at the headquarters, shattered after the long drive, but eager to get on with it, and get back to her boyfriend. After brief introductions she's provided with an ID lanyard and escorted to the investigation room. DI Furnham greets her and shows her to a desk.

Ashida has heard about Joy Furnham from Matt and can see why he has confidence in her. She has a calming influence, and Ashida picks up on the respect she's garnered from the rest of the team.

They examine the selection of headshots they have of Ava.

'Are these the ones Kay Harris identified Ava from?' DI Furnham asks.

'Yes,' Ashida answers. 'We gave her a selection of foils, and she picked Ava out immediately.'

'OK, but she could easily have looked at her online.'

'Yeah, sure.' Ashida feels defensive at the suggestion Kay is lying. 'For what it's worth, DI Furnham, I know DCI Harris. I've worked with her for a while. I'm sure she's telling the truth.'

DI Furnham lowers her voice. 'Please call me Joy, and for what it's worth, I've never met her but I get the feeling DI Anderson feels exactly the same. Now, let's try and prove it, shall we? We've got the headshots of Simon Carter too?'

Ashida nods, feeling better about being away from home.

Joy continues, 'We're looking through the capture from Aberfeldy High Street, using the dates and times we got from Kay. When we've confirmed them, we can look further afield to see where Ava might be now.'

Searching through CCTV from Aberfeldy is a real slog. The use of facial recognition technology as part of the wider biometric technologies is yet to be approved. Instead, 'retrospective' facial search technology, using images from the UK Police National Database, is in use. It's time consuming, but less controversial.

The videos show a town bustling with every specimen of Homo sapiens: the young and old, the weak and strong, all with the shared purpose of damn well enjoying themselves before the sun goes down. Traffic cameras coming in and out of town come under Ashida's keen eyes, and those covering the main through road are under Joy's.

'How long have you been in the force?' Joy asks.

'Three years. Nine months as detective. You?'

'Six.'

'Family?'

'Yeah, somehow I managed to get married and have two kids in between shifts.'

'Good going.'

'You know, Ashida, there's something very intriguing about this case. I mean, Kay Harris has been a copper for over ten years. She has an exemplary record. Yet here she's in Aberfeldy, with a young woman whom she hardly knows. She's attempted to murder the woman's husband and abducted her son, and now the woman is missing.'

Ashida leans in and lowers her voice. 'Kay has had a challenging year. Her sister committed suicide, jumped from a building in Manchester. Kay arrived on the scene, but no one had identified the body, so they couldn't warn her. When she realised it was her sister, she collapsed.'

'Yes, awful. I was brought up to speed by DI Anderson. He felt she returned to work too soon.'

'It was for a big case. Gary Brunswick. We needed all hands on deck.'

'I'm aware of the investigation. You all did good work.'

'Brunswick had an alibi, but Kay was convinced it was him. All the DNA evidence seemed circumstantial, because Brunswick was involved with the junior league football team that David Foster played for. David had been in his house and car. Kay pushed for a warrant, and eventually, when we found photographs of David in Brunswick's possession, he confessed. Kay couldn't forgive herself. She was convinced that David could have been saved if she hadn't been distracted by McGrath's alibi.'

'Ah yes, he's in the detail, isn't he?' Joy says.

'Who?' Ashida asks.

'The devil.'

After thirty minutes of searching Ashida leans forward in her chair. 'I have her.'

Joy wheels her chair over as Ashida enlarges the image and points to a tall woman standing on the pavement. 'That's definitely Kay.'

'What's she doing?' Joy asks.

'She's talking to that guy. Looks like an argument of some kind. It doesn't look like Carter. He's too big for one'

They watch as Kay turns away and walks to the car park.

'According to the time index it's within half an hour of when Kay said she was there, Joy says. 'OK, now let's find Ava.'

Chapter Fifty-Nine

Matt

Following Kay's directions, Matt arrives at the McGrath building site. A couple of the forensic team accompany him, but he's kept it all low key, just a squad car parked unobtrusively nearby and a uniformed officer inside the perimeter. The building entrance has been cordoned off; it's only visible if you step behind the hoarding, for now at least. Matt is doubtful they'll find anything, but he's been trying to get a sense of Kay's thinking. He's had to let Simon Carter go because there was no evidence he was in Aberfeldy and Barbara Dean had insisted.

Joy Furnham has told him about the recent developments between Kay and Ellie. He'd been shocked to learn of her affair with Jack. Kay told him she'd met someone about eighteen months before, but she played it close to her chest. It was Caro who'd noticed the change in her first, even though Matt worked with her every day, too close to see.

'Whose put that sparkle in Kay's eye?' Caro asked.

'What sparkle? Don't be daft. Has she got a sparkle?'

Afterwards he paid more attention, and Caro was right, Kay did look more sparkly. He thought the word was a bit effeminate, but it fitted; he just wouldn't say it out loud.

Then Helen's health really deteriorated and Kay's 'sparkle' dimmed with it. He wondered, if Kay had found love, then why wasn't that person supporting her through a terrible time? Now he knew it was Jack, it all made sense.

He reaches the fifth floor and pauses to catch his breath. The building is just a shell. Disturbed brick dust powders the air; his shoes are covered with it and he imagines he can feel it settling on his chest.

Heights aren't his thing. It's something he and Kay have in common, but for different reasons. He doesn't like flying and is always suspicious of hotel balconies. *If I were ever going to kill myself, it wouldn't be by jumping,* he thinks. *My first choice would be tablets, something less bloody, more peaceful.*

He notices an upturned cement bucket. Walking as near to the perimeter as he can manage without feeling dizzy, he examines the ground.

Ash emerges from the stairwell, breathless and red-faced, in his white overall.

'The cement bucket,' Matt calls.

Ash nods and aims his camera.

Matt signals another disturbed area of brick dust, and Ash clicks away.

Pulling a sheet of paper from his pocket, Matt says, 'I asked Kay to draw it for me, to get a fuller picture.' He squats and looks around. 'So Kay must've been standing here.'

Ash nods and walks closer to the edge than Matt would dare.

Looking across at the Manchester skyline, Ash whistles. 'Great view.'

Matt's phone rings. It's Jacinta, the PC guarding the police barrier. She sounds flustered. Probably the press, Matt thinks. He rises and rubs the white dust from his trousers.

'On my way down,' he says.

Chapter Sixty

Kay

I've been thinking about Ellie. As far as I know she hasn't phoned to see how I am. Even though I've always joked I could count my friends on one finger, the meaning of it has only just hit me. I literally have no one to turn to.

The only person I could possibly phone would be Maddie, but I want to keep her as far away from this as possible. The work she did for me will be the only thing I'll skim over. In fact I'll deny it. I'll make out the camera fault was a pure coincidence. Stranger things have happened.

Patricia Garcia, she of the red lips, has informed me McGrath has recovered. I admit I have mixed feelings. We discuss my plea. I agree to guilty due to diminished responsibility. I'm inclined to agree with her. I've definitely diminished.

Matt enters the room, pale, tired. He looks as though he might have been crying. I hope nothing's happened at home. I want to ask after Caro and Lucy, but the lie of the land has changed so much between us. High walls and deep water we may never be able to cross.

He switches the tape on and clasps his hands together on the desk. I want to reach over and touch them, reassure him that he's doing well, but I can't trust myself not to sound sarcastic, so I keep my mouth shut.

He does all the introductions for the purposes of the tape.

'Have you found Ava?' I ask.

He places a head shot of Ava on the desk and pushes it towards me. 'Can you identify the woman in this photograph?'

I'm exasperated. I've already picked her out from reams of photographs. 'Yes, that's Ava McGrath. Please can you tell me if you've found her?'

'I need to go through the day you met her. Can you talk me through it again?'

It's only procedure, I know, but I'm wary now.

'I left the house at about five thirty. I couldn't sleep. Got to Broad Street at about quarter to six. I noticed something up on the fifth floor.'

'You didn't call the emergency services?'

'No. I didn't think to. I thought it was my imagination, because of...' I look away.

'OK, so, you got to the fifth floor?'

'Yes. Ava was standing right on the edge.'

'You still didn't think to call the emergency services?'

'I...' I can't say it out loud. I thought it was Helen. I thought it was a dream. 'No.' *Keep it simple, stupid.*

'What happened when she saw you?'

'She warned me, said she would jump if I went near her.'

'OK, go on.'

'Like I said. I sat on the floor. I wanted to get her trust.'

Matt waits for me to continue.

'She told me she'd tried everything. Said she felt like he'd put a tracker in her head.'

'Did she use her ex-husband's name?'

'No.'

'So you didn't know who he was.'

'No, absolutely not, no.'

'You only found out her husband was Adrian McGrath when you got to the cottage?'

'Yes. She had nightmares about him coming after her. Look,

I know what you're getting at.'

'Which is?'

'You think I knew all along that she was McGrath's wife. You think I planned to kill him. That I wasn't helping Ava at all. When you find her, she'll tell you. We talked about it at the cottage. He raped her. He took her son from her-' I see David Foster's body on the mortuary slab, and the emotion trips me up. '-And he enabled Brunswick to kill David Foster.'

'That's the real reason, isn't it, Kay?' Matt says.

'What?'

'Revenge for David Foster.'

'Look,' I say, trying to remember what I've already told him. *Don't let him lead you.*

'I've told you, I saved Ava. It seemed the right thing to do. I gave her a safe place. I only found out about McGrath when we discussed it at the cottage. Then I put two and two together, and yes, I admit, I wanted McGrath to pay. I wanted Ava to have a life, to make up for everything I did-.'

Shit. I've gone too far. I'm crying now, I can't stop. My words are sluggish, tear-soaked. Matt has never seen me cry before. I must look like a fool.

Patricia touches my arm. 'We need to take a break, Kay,' she says, turning to Matt. 'This isn't right. We're waiting for the psychological assessment.'

I see Matt's face drop. I know this is a crucial part of the interview for him. I'm cracking open and he doesn't want me to clam up again. I rally and shake my head.

'For the record, please, Kay,' Matt says gently.

Patricia touches my arm again. 'Kay, you shouldn't.'

'Thanks, Patricia. I'm fine to carry on.'

Matt continues. 'You're saying Ava told you about McGrath at the cottage?'

'Yes.'

'Are you sure, Kay?'

'Yes. I remember. Ava said something to me when she was on the ledge. I said I could help her, and she said, *No, you can't.*'

Didn't she? Suddenly the image of Helen comes, blood and grit. Something is very wrong. Ava's on the ledge, Helen is falling. I'm so confused.

Matt leans forward. 'Kay, listen to me. Ava couldn't have told you at the cottage that her husband was Adrian McGrath.'

'What?' Blurred memories scud across my mind, like images from a time-lapse camera.

'Ava was never at the cottage.'

What's he saying? I look at Patricia, but she appears as baffled as me.

'She's out there, Matt,' I say firmly, pointing to the door.

'No, Kay. I'm really sorry. She never made it to the cottage.'

I watch his lips move. His words ricochet around the room. Patricia's lips too, red, her eyebrows creased.

Matt continues. 'Kay, Ava jumped. You didn't save her. We found her body at the construction site this morning. Forensics say she's been dead for two weeks.'

'No, it can't be her.'

'I'm afraid it is, Kay. There's no doubt. She's been identified.'

And I'm sliding away. It's such a relief, just to let go.

Chapter Sixty-One

Kay

Three Months Later

I watch as Gary, a patient with a long grey beard, makes a dash for the exit. Nurses appear from out of nowhere. One called Julie almost collides with me as she rushes past. 'Sorry,' she says as she moves on.

Mesmerised, I watch as Gary fights and struggles against the expert restraining technique. It looks like a take-down in freestyle wrestling. Julie lies across Gary's lower legs, and there's a nurse securing each of his arms.

I've seen the technique used before. I've brought people to this psychiatric unit, under the Police Powers of Safety Section 136. I'd deposit the patient into the care of the nurses and leave, smugly shaking my head on the way out, believing the grace of God had nothing to do with it. People with mental health problems were different from me. I know, not very PC. Or true.

'OK, we're just gonna give you something to relax you, nice and easy, Gary,' the nurse says.

'Get the fuck off me,' he shouts.

His sweatshirt has ridden up and exposed his belly. His panicked eyes cast about from nurse to nurse, then home in on me.

'I need to see her.'

The nurses turn.

My heart thuds. *Fucking crazy people.*

I hurry away.

Gary calls out. 'Hey doctor doctor, can't you see I'm burnin' burnin'?'

I recognise the song. Seventies? Eighties?

Seeking refuge in the day room, I join some of the other patients who are watching a chat show. The song lyric has burrowed into my head, an ear worm. *Can't you see I'm burnin' burnin'?* It rolls around on repeat, while I wait to be called in to see the consultant.

I was admitted to the secure unit three months ago under Section 3 of the Mental Health Act. I'd assaulted Adrian McGrath and taken Josh from his home, and I was believed to be a danger to myself or others. Strangely, I can remember the sequence of events as it unfolded.

However, I've no idea how I managed to convince myself I'd stopped Ava from jumping to her death.

Bernice, my consultant, has explained it to me in psychoanalytic terms. Trauma on top of trauma, Helen's suicide, then David Foster's brutal murder, then Ava's suicide. Like a game of emotional Jenga. The balance of my mind was so disturbed by witnessing another suicide it created an alternate reality. One where I'd saved Ava, thus appointing myself avenging angel.

I understand now how this delusional belief also served to assuage my crippling guilt over my affair with Jack and neglecting Helen when she needed me the most.

It made sense, but I'm still having trouble relating it all to me. Ava was real to me, flesh and blood, present – but an hallucination.

The therapist has suggested I visit the building site and

Ava's grave. She said I should ask a friend to come with me, and a nurse will be there too, just in case I flip out.

I've texted Ellie a few times now, but she hasn't replied or visited me. Out of all the things I've lost, this is the thing which saddens me the most.

Matt has visited me every week, and Barbara Dean apparently came to see me in the first few days, but I was too sedated and don't recall.

Chapter Sixty-Two

Kay

Doctor Bernice Glass is wearing a cream and black patterned dress. She's seated in a high-backed leather chair, hands clasped onto its sturdy arms. She stands as I enter, offers her hand for me to shake and gestures to the chair opposite. Nerves suddenly kick in, and I regret the strong coffee I thoroughly enjoyed only twenty minutes ago. Mouth dry as sandpaper, I take a seat. I notice Bernice's posture and mimic it as closely as possible, hands in my lap, legs crossed, like a *Mastermind* contestant.

'Good morning. How are you doing, Kay?' She swivels her chair around to look at the notes on her computer.

'Good, yeah, getting there, I think.'

'The meds seem to be helping?'

Her voice rises at the end. Her interview technique is so familiar to me now, I know what she expects. She doesn't like it when I'm too sure about my own recovery.

'Yes, better than the last ones.'

'And the therapy seems to be going well. How many sessions now?'

I truly don't know. I've had something called EMDR, where I must watch my therapist's hand as she moves it from left to right (I kid you not) and we discuss Helen's suicide. I've also had numerous sessions of Cognitive Behavioural Therapy, and I'm attending support group sessions.

These combined treatments are the therapy equivalent of Cillit Bang. Think of my mind as an old tile, embedded with the limescale of traumatic thoughts and fungus of delusional beliefs. A couple of spray-downs with this baby and 'bang the dirt is gone.' I'm a fucking *tabula rasa* where Helen is concerned.

'I wish I'd talked before, maybe trusted more in the power of talking,' I say.

'We were hoping the therapy would also help you to recall those last few moments with Ava.'

My last memories of Ava are all at the cottage. I can describe her in detail. The specifics don't change, my story doesn't waver. However, I've accepted that it was a delusion. Ava is dead, she died at the building site. But the memory of her jumping remains concealed, even from me. No matter how much I talk, I always come to a blank wall, unable to describe the moment. It just isn't there. Maybe this is what dementia is like.

'How do you feel about visiting the building site?' Bernice asks. 'It's all part of the treatment protocol. Exposure to the place where Ava died might just help to jump-start the memory.'

'If my brain thinks it's a good idea to protect me from the memory, why would I go against it?'

'Because it's part of the pathology of your illness. The memory hasn't been fully processed.'

'But I've told you,' I sigh, exasperated. I know this isn't a good idea in front of the consultant. My normal personality would probably be considered enough reason to keep me on a section, so I've been at pains to rein my sarcasm and cynicism in. I continue anyway. 'I accept that Ava died, that I had a breakdown. It makes sense to me. I'm no longer delusional or hallucinating. I don't see her any more. I don't have conversations with her. Ava jumped. I didn't save her. Turns out I'm not *all that* after all.' And yes, I do make the inverted comma sign with my fingers.

Bernice appears to take no offence, I'm sure I'm a small-time act compared to other patients she has on her books. She leans forward, clasping her hands in front of her. 'I don't like to hang every symptom on a label, but my diagnosis is major depressive disorder with psychotic features. You have been very poorly, Kay. Perhaps you don't fully realise just how ill you've been?'

She floors me with this comment. All the smart girl responses desert me. I sit back in the chair. 'I do know, and I want to be well too.'

'I want to reduce your meds, but before I do, I think it's worth a visit to the building site and then to Ava's grave. Your review is due in three weeks. If all goes well, we can look at your discharge plan.'

I nod and shrug. I'll do whatever it takes.

Chapter Sixty-Three

Kay

Winter jumpers and a couple of pairs of trousers have been folded neatly in the bottom of my hospital issue wardrobe. Caro very kindly brought a selection of clothes from my house when I was first admitted. She's been a lifesaver, brought me new underwear, and filled a cosmetic bag with moisturisers, cleansers, facial scrub and ylang-ylang shower gel. I have it in my mind to buy her a big bunch of flowers when I'm discharged.

Matt has been a revelation too. I've realised that when you keep people at arm's length and in the dark, they don't flourish. Since I opened up to them, they've filled the space with caring and compassion. Even now, it's still hard for me to accept they might like me, or even admit I want them to. What can I say, I'm an idiot, but I'm working through it.

I pull on one of the jumpers that used to fit snugly. It smells of my house, but has a musty undertone from being in the wardrobe. It hangs loosely on me. With my hair still caught in the neck of the jumper and just my socks on, in the narrow wardrobe mirror, I look unintentionally trendy, like a woman in a high fashion shoot. The image is broken as soon as I pull my trousers and trainers on and free my hair from the jumper. I never wore a lot of make-up before and it feels inappropriate to put any on for the task ahead.

Chapter Sixty-Four

Kay

It's strange to see the building where it all started. The hoarding is still there and seeing the name MCGRATH in large letters robs me of saliva.

Sharma, my key nurse, has accompanied me. Matt's already here in his capacity as SIO, and as my friend, so he's wearing two hats. Two-hat Matt. He walks over and hugs me, something he's only done since I was admitted. I hug him back. He smells of Christmas, old spice and wood smoke.

'You ready?' he asks.

'Sure.'

We start up the stairs, Matt, then me, then Sharma.

When I was last here, summer was in full bloom. The air was as dry as snuff powder and the dust blinked on beams of sunlight. Now it's February, cold and wet. It smells limey and there are damp patches on the walls. The wind whistles through the exposed shell of the building, like a distant boiling kettle.

I stop to catch my breath at level three, then we continue. When we reach level five, the first thing I notice is the yellow cement bucket. I realise Matt must've removed it from evidence to recreate the scene. It doesn't seem like much, but it means my description of the fifth floor was accurate. Walking over to it, I can feel their eyes on me.

'This is where I stopped, when I entered.' Looking up, I point. 'Ava was over there, holding onto the third pillar.'

I can almost see her in her black jacket, her dark eyes full of fear and fury. I feel suddenly hot and pull my jacket off.

Matt walks over to the pillar, but not too near the edge. 'Here?' he asks.

'Yes.'

I feel the energy in the air. I want to leave, but I also want to be off my section and discharged. Sharma must see the doubt in my face and comes to stand next to me. 'You're doing great,' she says, encouragingly.

'Ava was wearing a black leather jacket. It protected her arms when she landed,' I say. I walk over to the point where we both fell. 'She-' I see their expressions and quickly correct myself. '*I* ended up here. I thought Ava was with me.'

Sharma walks to the edge, approximately where Ava stood. 'So, Ava would have been here?'

'Yes.'

'She jumped from this spot?'

'Yes, but I didn't see her. I couldn't testify to it in a court of law.' I'm starting to sound crazy again.

'Did you come and look over the edge?'

'No.' I point to the ground at my feet. 'In my mind she was here. Why would I look over the edge?'

Sharma nods. 'Exactly. I think that's been blocking you. Because you didn't see her body on the ground, you haven't been able to fully process her jumping.'

'So because I didn't see her body...' I start to say, then I remember. I turn around and see the shoes. I walk over and pick one up and hold it to me. It's so small, it fits in the palm of my hand.

'Kay?' Matt says.

'Helen's shoes flew off when she jumped. They were the shoes I'd given her to come home in. They were on the ground where she landed.'

Sharma walks over and lays her hands gently over mine. Tears obscure my vision and my chest hurts. 'They were the only thing Helen ever asked me for, the only thing of mine I could give her. She was always smaller than me. I used to tell her to put weight on, so I could borrow her clothes.'

Sobbing, I crouch down. Sharma kneels, her arm around me. I try to catch my breath. 'I asked if I could have the shoes back. They wouldn't let me.'

Sharma gently rubs my arm and says, 'The shoes were an important connection between you and Helen. Were you hoping that it was the start of something better?'

I nod. 'I hadn't been a good sister.'

'You tried to do a good thing here, Kay, don't lose sight of that.'

Matt joins us and squats down. He looks pale. 'You took Ava's shoes to the cottage, Kay. That's why we believed she was there with you,' he says.

'They must've symbolised something important for you because of Helen,' Sharma adds.

I stand up again and look out towards the edge. I remember now. I'd wondered why Ava had removed her shoes before she'd jumped, but I'd never asked her. I couldn't have asked her, could I?

'I didn't save Ava.'

'No, Kay,' Sharma agrees. 'It's a hard thing to learn: some people can't be saved.'

The wind sweeps through, blowing my hair up off my face, and I shiver as I think about Ava. Her delicate frame, her sense of humour, her bravery. My hope that we would end up as good friends. 'I never even knew her,' I say.

Chapter Sixty-Five

Kay

As the car doors shut the space feels safer, more solid. Maybe it's the proximity of Matt. I've found his presence reassuring over the last few months. I don't get any bullshit from him.

'It's therapeutic to get out and get some fresh air. Christmas passed me by,' I say, buckling my seat belt.

'Saved you a fortune,' Sharma says.

Matt accompanies me back to the hospital and suggests we go for a coffee in the shop on the ground floor. I'm on hourly observations; I'm not suicidal and not a flight risk. I've been in the coffee shop several times on my own now, and I'm allowed to walk around the grounds unaccompanied. Sharma agrees and returns to the ward.

Matt orders the drinks and I find us a free table. He returns a few minutes later with coffee, and two chocolate chip muffins. Once upon a time I would have had a massive struggle with myself over a chocolate muffin, making little deals. If I eat this now, I won't have any dinner later. Or, another favourite, *I'll just eat half of it and leave half.* Amazingly I don't have any such qualms about it now, having completely lost my appetite. The nurses say that's probably a combination of the medication and the hospital food. In truth, the food here doesn't look that bad. I just don't seem to taste anything.

Another revelation is that it doesn't feel as great as I'd

imagined. I look drawn, older. Kate Moss supposedly said nothing tastes as good as skinny feels. She was speaking for those whose fortune and fame is dependent on being thin. A case of hunger pangs all the way to the bank no doubt. I'd give up skinny to be able to enjoy my food again.

However, I'm not so deluded I don't realise that as soon as I'm out of here, I'll probably start bingeing again and regain the lost weight. That's progress, I suppose.

'How's work?' I ask as soon as Matt sits down.

'You know I can't talk about it.'

'Yes, I'm a civilian now.'

'It's not that, Kay, and you know it.'

'I'm joking,' I say, simultaneously disappointed and impressed by his resolution not to discuss work.

'Have you thought about what you'll do when you're discharged?'

'I've thought about advocacy work, you know, supporting people with mental health problems.'

'Who'd have thought?'

'I know, right? I'll be all right financially for a while. I intend to rest, maybe do some fishing, and try to make amends with Ellie.'

Matt avoids my eyes and shifts around in his chair. I can still read him.

'Who else knows about me and Jack?'

'She told DI Furnham in Scotland, and I think Ashida knows. And Caro, obviously.'

'And Barbara Dean?'

Matt nods.

I always thought I'd be mortified by people finding out about my affair, but instead I've the urge to laugh. 'Jesus, I'm white trash-'

'Kay, they don't think that.'

Whether it's the therapy or the medication I can't be sure,

but I feel lighter now it's all out in the open.

Matt still looks worried.

'Matt, I'm joking, really. I'm fine. There's nothing else now. I've no other skeletons, the worst has happened, and I survived. It's all good.'

The discharge process has been tediously slow, but I understand the need for caution.

I've had a total of six overnight leaves. The first periods were just short shopping expeditions with a member of the nursing team. After that, Caro picked me up and I spent a couple of overnights at their house. Caro even came into one of the ward rounds with me and spoke up for me when the consultant asked for feedback on how I'd coped.

The most surprising visit came from Maddie. She phoned the ward and asked if it would be OK to come. I called her back immediately on the number she'd provided.

Glamorous, blonde hair flouncing – she confided that she'd had some extensions put in, as an indulgence for Christmas – she walked on to the ward wearing a camel coat, a white shirt, and beige trousers. I saw other patients observing her. She was a heady reminder of the possibilities of life outside the ward.

Maddie bought me a beautifully wrapped bottle of perfume called *Portrait of a Lady, by Frederic Mallé*. I'd never heard of it. Knowing Maddie, it won't have been cheap.

Quietly, she thanked me for not mentioning her name during the investigation. Quietly, I replied that having a breakdown meant I forgot all sorts of things.

Before she left, she told me if I ever needed any help, or money, I should come to her first. It took everything I had not to cry. Her words stayed with me long after she'd left.

Chapter Sixty-Six

___

Kay

Six weeks later

As I step into my front room for the first time in over five months, the dark blue walls seem oppressive and I wonder whatever possessed me. I've already started to plan a remodel. Lighter walls for sure. Farrow and Ball, maybe Elephant's Breath, or Harwicke Green?

Caro has brought me home and I can hear her filling the kettle. The last time anyone made me a drink in my home was when my dad was alive. I go into the kitchen and watch. It's odd to have someone else search through my cupboards and handle my stuff. I try to remember what food might be lurking to lure my binge eating out of hibernation, but my recall is unreliable, those last few days a blur.

'I bought you some milk and bread, it's on the side.'

'Caro, I can't thank you enough.'

I go to her and wrap my arms around her. I've got so much better at this; hugging people whether they like it or not is so freeing. No longer do I stand awkwardly wondering what the correct etiquette for parting is. I take the lead and go in for the hug.

'Are you staying for a cuppa?' I ask.

'Can't, got to pick Lucy up from her friend's, but I'll pop

round tomorrow, and you're coming to us Sunday, aren't you?'

She looks directly at me, the slight challenge in the fix of her pupils and the blue irises. Moussaka-gate lingers in the air, I can almost smell the aubergine.

'Hmm mmm,' I answer.

'Phone me if you need anything,' she adds lightly, as she checks her bag for keys and phone. Then she's off, in a flurry of Zara and Esteé Lauder.

I take my tea into the lounge. Dark blue walls? I think again. I'm strangely aware of myself in the room. When I sit on the settee, it's like I've mounted an unfamiliar horse. Swinging my legs up, I kick a cushion onto the floor and leave it there, defiantly. Turning the volume up on the TV helps to close up the space, and I wonder how people manage to live in houses with large open rooms and expansive bare windows. I like a room to hold me.

The ceiling has a small damp patch in the shape of Italy. I treated it with stain blocker but it's still there if you know where to look. I focus on it as I think about my future. Having been deemed unfit for duty, I've been discussing my job prospects and I'm considering working as a mental health advocate. I'm trying to stay positive, but the idea of never working in the police force again tears me up.

Denial and grieving processes have been discussed to death regarding Helen, and Ava. But what about me? My identity is so wrapped up in being a cop. I've never envisioned a life as anything else. It was my past, present and future, and I failed. But at least I failed majestically.

Sipping my tea, I consider how different Caro has been. She's like the older sister that Helen never was, and far more assertive than she would have dared be when I was DCI Harris and Matt's superior. I suppose people are going to treat me differently, but I loathe being anyone's cause for concern. Worrying about me: another thing on the list of things for Caro to do, along with picking Lucy up from her dancing lessons. An item for discussion over dinner between Matt and Caro:

'Did you check on Kay today?'

'Whose turn is it?'

'I did it yesterday.'

I've been discharged, and I'm off my section but maintained on medication. A community mental health nurse will come and visit me to make sure I'm keeping up with my meds and haven't got anyone locked in the attic. I make a mental note to modify the wisecracks at my next assessment. Most psychiatrists have no sense of humour, and once you've been sectioned they view banter as a vicious cycle of maladaptive thinking.

The estate agents have been in touch about the cottage and that's on hold for the moment. I haven't told anyone else, but I've a longing, a compulsion you might say, to return there, to see it again, the place where I imagined Ava. Before I do that, I've one more thing to do.

Chapter Sixty-Seven

Matt

Straightening his tie, Matt knocks lightly on the open door of Barbara Dean's office. She waves him in, and he takes a chair.

'Any results?'

She's referring to the NPPF examination for the rank of Detective Chief Inspector, which he sat two weeks previously. Matt's hoping to step into the vacant spot left by Kay.

'Not yet, no.'

'Well, fingers crossed.'

'Thanks.'

'There's been a development.' Barbara says.

'What?'

'Stefan Laing.' She opens her hands out as if she's holding a large story book. 'Our press office informed me that Laing has been asking about Kay again.'

'What about her? Wasn't everything covered at the time?'

'To an extent. But Laing's like a ferret. Once he latches onto a story.'

'You think McGraths fired him up? Told him to go after Kay?' Matt says as he stands. Restless. He's starting to understand that the pressure of being an SIO can tank you up like a high intensity cardio session. 'Kay thinks McGrath owed Brunswick, that giving him an alibi was re-payment. McGrath took a big risk doing that, even though they were mates. And she's still convinced he's being protected by someone,' he adds.

'No Matt. It came down to money. We threw everything we had at finding David Foster and prosecuting Brunswick, McGrath just slipped through the net.'

'What about now? I can break open Lucy's piggy bank if it helps?'

Barbara clasps her hands and rests them on the desk. 'Maybe we could have at the time, but now McGrath will say it's harassment. That we're determined to discredit him because Kay was one of ours.'

'And Kay's just about recovering. This could make her ill again.'

'It's delicate.'

Matt sits down again. Calmer, eager to maintain a professional air. 'Well. I know what Kay would say. Would she have to be called as a witness?'

'We'll avoid that at all costs.'

Matt nods. Unsure if he's just been dismissed or not

'You know if there is a case here it would've been Kay's stepping-stone to superintendent,' Barbara adds.

They share a moment deep in thought.

Matt sighs. 'The irony.'

'Let's open up a low-key investigation into McGrath and let the team know they need to keep it under wraps. Absolutely no contact with Laing.'

Matt nods and rises. 'It'll make their day.'

As soon as he returns to the investigation room, he brings up all reports Laing has written since Kay assaulted McGrath.

The first report covers the Charity event McGrath was supposed to attend on the night he was attacked. The headline reads **Brutal Attack on Local Businessman on the Eve of Charity Event**. Matt realises Laing wouldn't have known about Kay's involvement at this point.

He reads on to the next report **Diminished Responsibility Detective: Guilty of Serious Assault on Businessman and Kidnap of his Three-Year-Old Son.** Two months later; **Suicide Detective.**

Matt speed read through the stories. Lips silently mouthing the words, an old childhood habit. He prints each story off to scrutinise at home.

Chapter Sixty-Eight

Kay

It's a cold February morning. Matt and I traipse past the old church in Marple Bridge. The grey gravel of the path is carpeted by a slippery quilt of moss. We walk a little apart from each other. I puff on my vape with one hand and carry a bunch of pink tulips in the other.

Caro stays a few paces behind us. We look like a Victorian courting couple with their chaperone. Matt trudges along, hands deep in his pockets, his foggy breath on the air. I can sense something's bothering him.

'It's just through there,' he says. He points to a pair of rusted gates.

I don't say that I know the graveyard. This is the church I came to as a child, the school I went to. I don't say I remember the little old out-buildings as the girls' and boys' toilets. Or that on the tarmacked area in front of the main school, I won the high jump and one hundred metres on sports day. And when I was eight years old, my best friend Mari cupped her hand over her mouth and whispered in my ear that girls had something called a period.

Boots squelch on the wet grass as we follow Matt through the worn alleys between the graves. I read the headstones, wondering about the undisturbed dust of the remains they speak of, feeling a pang of guilt that I don't visit Mum, Dad's, or Helen's graves more often. It's not out of a lack of respect, it's just I feel nothing when I'm there. I have an old jumper of my dad's and a cardigan of my mum's. I feel closer to them when I'm holding those than I ever do when I'm at their graveside. With Helen, it feels too hypocritical to stand at her graveside when I couldn't stand by her when she was alive.

Matt points up ahead and we quicken our step.

I catch up with him at a black marble headstone. There's a small wreath of poinsettia and ivy leaning against it. The gold inscription reads:

Ava Louise McGrath
June 12th 1988 to July 12th 2018 aged 30yrs.
Beloved mother, wife and daughter.
Always in our hearts

July 12th was the turning point, the day I went over the edge along with Ava. Although I've accepted what the doctors and Matt have told me, it's still so hard to understand that my mind worked against me and took me so far into crazy.

'I can't pretend that I knew her,' I say. 'But neither can I erase those memories'

'No,' Matt says. 'It must be weird.'

'It really is. I mean, who's to say that the real Ava wasn't just like the Ava I imagined? Does that make sense?'

'Kind of, yeah.'

Staring at the inscription, I'm aware of my feet in my socks, and the cold ground as it permeates up through the soles of my boots. I know it's all real. If there was a map of the graveyard, there would be a small red arrow on it stating 'Kay Harris, You Are Here,' yet I still have that sense of disconnect. I imagine clawing at the clumps of sodden earth with my bare hands until I reach the coffin, wrenching the lid aside and finding it empty save the worms and beetles, munching lazily on the white satin of the lining.

Caro has caught up. She's filled a bottle of water from the tap.

'You think of everything, Caro,' I say, as I take the water. I step onto the mound of earth that is Ava's final resting place and apologise. Somewhere along the way I was taught that it's sacrilegious to step on a grave, but how else are you supposed to put flowers on one?

I empty the flower holder of its pungent contents. Brown water and slimy leaves plop onto the grass. Averting my face from the stench, I pour fresh water into the container and arrange the tulips, and wonder who was here last. McGrath? Josh, maybe? I hope it was Josh.

I remain stooped for a moment. I'm not given to prayer, but I kiss my hand and place it on the headstone and whisper, 'I'm the person who you spent your last moments with, Ava, that counts for something. I wish I'd known you.'

Then I stand back and admire the splash of colour against the black granite.

'Thirty. It's no age, is it?' I say, shaking my head.

'No,' Caro agrees.

I'm not sure what else I'm supposed to do or say.

'You OK?' Matt asks.

I nod as I move away. 'I'm fine really. Thanks, both, for coming.'

'No problem,' Caro says. 'You hungry?'

'Starving my brains out,' I answer.

'Can you give us a minute?' Matt asks Caro. She looks from him to me, knowingly.

'Sure, I'll wait in the car.'

We walk towards the church and he tries the door. Surprisingly, it's open.

'I thought the days of unlocked church doors were over. Too many aggrieved Catholics wanting their money back,' I say, as we enter.

Unwanted proximity to the mothership and the strong smell of incense trigger a thousand memories of kneeling on the wooden pew, bowing my head in silent prayer when all I could think about was how cold I was, or how much my knees hurt. I recall one Sunday, just after my first communion, Mum and Dad sent me and Helen to church on our own. They probably just wanted some time without us squabbling around them. When it came to communion, Helen and I joined the queue. Someone let me go in front, so Helen wasn't next to me anymore. I knelt at the communion rail and Father Riley came along with the Eucharist. 'The body of Christ,' he said, as he laid the host on my tongue. I stayed there and bowed my head and waited, unsure what to do. The next thing I knew, Father Riley was coming around again. He looked a little perplexed, but still placed another wafer on my tongue while the first one was still stuck to the roof of my mouth.

I turned to see that Helen was back at the pew, signalling with her eyes for me to get up. Embarrassed, I returned to the pew, and spent the rest of the service preoccupied with my own stupidity. She taunted me all the way home, saying, 'You've had two bodies of Christ.' She said that was a mortal sin and that she was going to tell Mum. Just before we reached home, I threw up. My vomit was a little white mess of wafer and spittle.

Inside the church the priest is at the altar. He's wearing a grey suit and is changing some of the candles.

'The door was open,' Matt says.

'Good afternoon. Yes, there's a funeral service due.'

We both turn around to leave.

'You're welcome to stay for a bit,' he says. 'They won't be here for another hour.'

'Thanks,' Matt says.

We move towards a pew.

'Is there anything I can help you with?'

'No, we just want a few minutes,' Matt answers.

'Make yourselves at home. God welcomes you.'

'Does God do a flat white?' I say quietly, as we sit.

Matt shakes his head and looks down.

'If you start praying, I'm leaving,' I add.

'Shush. Listen, Kay, I need to talk to you.'

'In the sight of God? It must be bad.'

'It's about McGrath.'

'Oh, is that why you chose consecrated ground?'

'We're opening the case against him using the information you uncovered. I found your notes at the cottage.'

'Oh.' I hold my breath and look at the figure on the cross.

'And Kay,' he continues. He's looking at his shoes and I look down at them too. 'You were right. I think there's something going on with him. I thought it was part of your paranoia.'

A mix of feelings washes over me. I look away from him then up at the curved geometric ribs of the roof and think of all the prayers floating up to them over the last century.

'You're re-opening the case?' I ask.

'A low-key investigation. We're looking at his connections.'

'Just like I said.'

'Just like you said.'

Maybe it's his expression, or the setting. I decide on forgiveness. 'Am I to give evidence?'

'No.' Matt shakes his head emphatically.

'That's a yes then?'

'No, it's a definite no. But your name might be on the news, in the papers again. Barbara asked me to speak to you, ask you what you think.'

'Go for it.'

'You're sure?'

'With everything you've got.'

'What about you? You need to stay well.'

269

'I have a plan of my own,' I say. 'Come on, let's get out of here. The crucified guy's creeping me out.'

'Where's Lucy?' I ask when we get back to their house.

Matt and Caro exchange a glance.

'I'm in here.'

A familiar voice and a giggle from the lounge. Lucy comes through in a turquoise dress, her hair braided like a ballerina's. 'Aunty Kay.'

The last time I saw her was on one of my overnight leave periods. She had a gap between her front teeth that gave her a lisp, and her new best friend was a caterpillar called Puss who she'd housed in a matchbox. She smiles and reveals a full set of pearly shells. There's no trace of the cute lisp, or the caterpillar.

'Ellie's here,' Lucy says, as I stoop down and hug her.

Ellie appears in the doorway. 'Hi,' she says, and smiles fleetingly, then shrugs and looks at her feet. 'It was Matt's idea.'

I look at Matt and Caro.

'We thought it would be a surprise,' Matt says.

'You, well, everyone missed your fortieth birthday,' Caro adds.

They're a formidable double act.

'*Happy birthday*,' Lucy squeals, unaware of any awkwardness.

I walk over to Ellie and hug her. She's wearing a floral perfume, light and fresh. She looks surprised and tenses up, so I hug harder, trying to squeeze out the bad memories.

Lucy taps on my arm. 'We got you a cake, Aunty Kay,' she says, pulling me away.

At the end of the meal Caro lights the candles on a pretty iced birthday cake and Lucy starts singing Happy Birthday. Blowing them out to applause, I thank them. I'm both moved and uncomfortable with the attention. It's highlighting how important Caro and Matt have been, and how I'd underestimated them.

Dinner conversation has been polite and light-hearted. That's what happens when a seven-year-old girl is present.

'Only five candles, Mummy?' Lucy asks, as Caro removes them and slices the cake.

'Yes, because each one stands for ten, and four tens are forty, plus one for good luck because Aunty Kay is forty-one,' Caro explains.

'And we would need a very big cake for forty-one,' Lucy says, nodding, eyes wide in wonder at the thought of it.

'Wait until I'm eighty-one,' I say. 'Imagine how big that cake will have to be.'

'It will be this big,' Lucy says, spreading her arms wide.

'Hey steady on, I said eighty-one, not a hundred and eighty-one.'

Lucy giggles. 'I could eat it all,' she says.

Watching her demolish a huge slice of the cake, I can almost believe her.

Afterwards, Ellie starts clearing the plates and loading the dishwasher.

Matt's phone rings; it's clearly a police-related matter. I feel the old umbilical attachment, pulling me along with him. As he leaves the room to talk more freely, my desire to follow and be involved is overwhelming and painful.

I notice Caro watching me. She smiles sympathetically and ushers Lucy out of the room. 'Come on, let's get your pjs on then you can come back down for a bit.'

I'm sure Caro has contrived this, to give me and Ellie space to talk. I rinse the pans as Ellie stacks the plates.

'Look, I need to say I'm sorry.'

'Kay.' Ellie sighs and stops what she's doing. 'It's over now. It made you ill, and I don't want to lose you as well as Mum.'

You see, this is why I avoid these kinds of conversations.

My facial muscles distort in my effort not to cry. 'I don't want to lose either of us, *any* of us,' I manage to say. 'It was all over with your dad, you know, before.'

'I know, he told me. We don't have to talk about that though.'

'OK.' I'm so relieved, I swallow the tears back and feel my shoulders relax. I pass Ellie the gravy jug, 'great gravy,' I say.

Later, when Lucy has gone to bed, we sit by the fire in the front room, me with a coffee, pretending I'm not craving a glass of the wine everyone else has. The conversation turns inevitably to how I'm planning to spend my time. It's as good an opportunity as any, so I tell them of my intention to rent my house out and move to the cottage in Aberfeldy.

Silence descends, filled with a thousand doubts. Pretending I haven't noticed, I ask Matt to pass me the box of chocolates that's been doing the rounds.

It's Ellie who speaks first. 'You'll be isolated. Do you think that's a good idea when you've been so poorly?'

Everything is delivered in a nutshell with Ellie. Still, she doesn't know about the latest developments. In truth, the McGrath case couldn't have come at a better time. It adds weight to my argument for getting away. Away from the media attention that McGrath's accusations against the police are bound to kick up.

'Well, I'll have the CMHT, and I'll get part-time work as an advocate. And there's a great fishing club. I've always said I'd do that when I retired. And you can all come and visit whenever you want. We could skype.' I lean back and bite into the soft-centred caramel. I think that's everything covered. The chocolate's a bonus.

I wake up in my own bed, having slept through: no disturbed sleep, no nightmares, and no hangover. The meds seem to be doing some good, even though I always feel slightly zoned out. Ellie brought me home last night and stayed in the spare room. I can hear her through the wall; she's either on the phone to Nate, or she's watching something on her laptop.

I lie for a while and think of the past year. I know it's not helpful, ruminating like this. My relapse prevention plan instructs me to get out of bed as soon as possible after I've woken up. Behavioural activation it's called. Moving, doing something, getting dressed, washed, having breakfast. They're all behavioural, they stop the ruminations and the low mood, and the desire to turn over and go back to sleep.

Still, I lie here and think of Ava as the clock ticks, rhythmically, soothing. Matt told me that she died on impact from a broken neck. She was dead even before I'd picked her shoes up and left the construction site. I must say, we had far more lively conversations after she'd jumped than we had before.

On the drive home yesterday, Ellie told me she visits Helen's grave every week. It struck me that I've visited Ava's grave, but not Helen's.

I suppose it's because I have no doubts Helen is dead. I didn't have any enlightening conversations with her after she'd died. Very few before for that matter.

I've made some notes for my next therapy session. What started out as a few scribbles has grown into this account. And it's not quite finished.

I get up and pull my dressing gown on, then go downstairs and make a pot of tea. Little things like this still bring me pleasure. I love a china teapot and a china cup. I've never adorned myself with pretty things, but my home is full of them.

I knock lightly on Ellie's door.

'Hey, come in,' she answers.

Seeing her lying in bed with the laptop propped on her knee and one earphone on, I'm filled with hope for us. Her presence is easy and it's a luxury to have her forgive me. I

hardly deserve it. I swear she's going to have to deal with
extra nice and loving Aunty Kay from now on.

'I didn't wake you did I, Kay?'

I've noticed that she's dropped the 'Aunty.'

'No, it's fine.'

She takes the tea. I sit on the bed with mine and tell her
about the upcoming investigation into McGrath. She nods
her understanding.

'I'm going to paint the front room a more neutral colour
before I rent it out. Come with me, help me pick out the paint.
If you're not doing anything else?'

'Sure,' Ellie says. 'I'll let Nate know. I said I wouldn't be
back until tea-time anyway.'

'Great. No hurry,' I say, casually, feeling like crying out of
gratefulness.

Chapter Sixty-Nine

Kay

Descending the stairs, I smell the drying paint. Three coats of Farrow and Ball Hardwick White have finally eradicated the oppressive dark blue I thought so sophisticated. I open the curtains and the daylight reveals the room as a mellow and welcoming space. I'll almost be sorry to leave it.

My phone rings, I pick it up and listen for a moment, then end the call without speaking. I draw the curtains again and phone Matt.

'It's started,' I say as soon as he answers. 'A flippin' reporter just phoned, asking for comment.'

'Laing?'

'No, some woman from the Stockport Herald or something. I didn't get her name.'

'I was just about to phone you. You made the news this morning. Laing's written a piece about your release.'

'Christ on a bike. Have you spoken to him?'

'In passing. You know the press. They're like the red weed.'

'What should I do, make a statement?' I really don't want to make a statement. I'm just saying words.

'Jesus no.'

The passion of his response startles me.

'Am I missing something?' I ask.

'No, sorry. I agree that you don't want to open a can of worms.'

He's right but he's annoying me by not saying what he means. Since my recovery I've found my critical thinking has receded. I need black and white.

'If he opened this can of worms what would he find?'

'Kay, have you never thought what the charge of diminished responsibility saved you from?'

'What, hanging?'

'No. No one was ever going to charge you with Ava's death.'

'The coroner recorded death by suicide.'

'We only ever had your word for it.'

'It's the truth. There wasn't any forensic evidence I'd ever been near her. Laing knows all of this'

'I know, I know. Look, we don't want him turning any stones over. Just lay low and he'll go away.'

I let everything sink in. Some strands of memory have been triggered. Is Matt worried about what Laing will discover?

'Are you OK?' he asks.

'I'm fine,' I answer, but I don't really feel fine. I'm jittery, pacing. If I were still a detective, I'd have more control, with a team around me and professional advice.

I nip out and pick up the Manchester Evening News. At home, scanning the pages, I find what I'm dreading on page two. It's a feature about my release and Ava's suicide. There's a photo of me with the caption. *'DCI Kay Harris released last month.'* As Matt said, it's written by Stefan Laing. I know him well. Laing is the journalist's equivalent of the spiked pick of a lobster fork. The type who'll scratch around in all the nooks and crannies until he's pulled all the meat from a lawsuit. Gritting my jaw in anger, I rip the newspaper into shreds and throw it away.

It's time to make the move.

Chapter Seventy

Matt

Matt stands in the kitchen area spooning coffee into mugs. He's forgotten who asked for tea and who asked for coffee so he makes three of each and hopes for the best. There's only him and Alison who take sugar anyway so that bit's easy.

When he hands the drinks out a couple of them regard their mugs quizzically, but no-one says anything, particularly when he opens the lid of a large box of Krispy Kreme doughnuts.

'I thought we needed a sugar rush to get us through the last hour,' Matt says as he places the box down. 'Help yourselves.'

In the early days, Matt had felt a draught from the space, just at his 4 o'clock, where Kay usually stood at team meetings. It had taken him a while to adjust to not having her to turn to. She wasn't a show detective like him. When she spoke, she did it with a calm authority. She wasn't bothered about being liked or popular. She was a commitment cop. He'd decided to try to emulate that. He'd become less blasé. Less of a dick, as Kay might say.

'Monsieur, with these Krispy Kreme's you are really spoiling us,' Ashida says with a French accent as she removes a lemon iced circle from the box.

'Okay what do we got?' He refers to the *Link Board*, where all the picture evidence relating to McGrath is pinned. There's a photograph of Simon Carter, Adrian McGrath,

Gary Brunswick, and one of the training Academy McGrath opened called 'Ground Up.'

'We've learned Simon and McGrath went to the same school and we already knew Brunswick worked for McGrath.'

'Carter has a juvenile record for nicking stuff.' Alison says.

'He's small fry. Does McGrath's bidding but nothing which requires an IQ above fifty,' Ashida adds.

'What always bothered DCI Harris,' Matt begins. 'Was why a man like McGrath would want to risk his reputation by giving Brunswick an alibi? There's got to be more to it. McGrath's carefully cultivated his image, he does charity work, helps the nippers out. A proper legend in his own lunchtime.'

He pins two more photographs up on the board. Then steps back.

'Siblings - Lena Melnik and Andretti Melnik. I saw Lena at the hospital attending to McGrath like he was a five-year-old.' He takes a sip of coffee then continues. 'Laing covered the Charity event McGrath was supposed to attend on the night of his assault. Lena Melnik was McGrath's plus one. According to Laing's coverage, she arrived on her own and kept a vacant seat company for a couple of hours before leaving. She didn't turn up at McGrath's house as far as I'm aware.'

'Maybe saw the police and turned around.'

'Who would do that? You'd be knocking the door down.' Clive answers.

'Instinct?' Alison suggests. 'Maybe she thought her brother had something to do with the attack?

Matt has asked Ashida to search the pair on the database and social media. She has filled him in already on her findings. He looks at her and nods.

'So,' she wipes sugar from her fingers and reads from her screen. 'Andretti Melnik. Known to his friends as Andy. Born in the Ukraine 25th August 1984. Came to the UK with his parents and younger sister at the age of twelve and joined an uncle in his restaurant, Paska Palace on Deansgate. He did some driving and odd jobs. They've built up quite a little empire with take-outs and three other restaurants in London, Newcastle, and Birmingham. Parents are still alive and live in Burnage. A respectable couple both retired, Mum was an accountant dad an IT manager. Lena lives with them. Andretti's done a bit of modelling. Hospital records show he got his nose broken in a fight in a nightclub three years ago. He's still a good-looking guy though.'

'If you like that sort of thing,' Clive quips.

Ashida nods, 'And he's got a rep for inflicting cruelty beyond that outlined in his personal development plan.'

'A real company asset. Finances?' Matt asks.

'Are in very good shape. Total assets of around three million. He knows a lot of people, both high and low life's.'

'Dig deeper on that please.' Matt says. 'I'm guessing he's also well connected to a team of expensive lawyers.'

'Can we connect him directly to McGrath or Brunswick?' Alison asks.

'That, detective Cromar, is the correct question.' Matt states. 'I think, we need to go back to the start.'

Chapter Seventy-One

Kay

Have you noticed how some places remain unchanged, no matter how long has passed since you've seen them? The cottage is like that. It appears to exhale when I step through the front door. Despite the disarray caused by the police search, it's untouched, resolute.

The search warrant is propped up on the kitchen table, recording all the items that were removed as evidence. Along with bedding and pots, they've indexed walking boots, coats, hats and Ava's shoes.

I make the fire and offer the warrant to the flames. A memory of Ava returns. I imagined that she'd stopped me from burning Helen's journal. Now I realise that every conversation I had with Ava here was with my own subconscious. Everything I learned about McGrath was from the police database or Facebook. Every decision I made I made alone. Still, her presence is strong. How can that be?

I asked my therapist how it was possible to miss her. After some exploration and probing questions, I realised that if Ava wasn't present, I was providing all the answers. The good news is, that Scrabble score was all mine.

It's difficult to get my head around.

I have a completely new mental health team. I have agreed to continue recording the thoughts and feelings and any dreams I have about Ava. I'm to discuss them with my new therapist, Noreen, who I will meet next week.

Two hours of cleaning and tidying restores the cottage to its former comfort. There's only one room left to do: the attic, which I've been avoiding.

Pushing the door open, I see the small single bed to my left and the chest of drawers next to it. The skylights are tightly shut, but the room remains cold. You'd think this would be the warmest room in the house because heat rises. But the heat doesn't seem able to permeate here. I enter hesitantly, remembering the thoughts I had, that a dead woman was sleeping here, and she was my friend. I confided in her like I've never confided in anyone. It would be embarrassing if it weren't so tragic.

Whistling to myself gives the room an even more ominous feel, so I stop. I make the bed up and lie on it for a moment and look at the ceiling which Helen spent much of her time staring at.

Thinking of Helen, I decide to dress the room as nicely as possible, to integrate it into the rest of the house. I bring a few candles up and pinch some cushions off the settee; it can easily afford it, it's a veritable cushion bank. When I've finished the room looks lush. Downstairs are several photos, waiting to be unpacked. Boxes are stacked upon boxes, but I soon find the one marked PHOTOGRAPHS, HANDLE WITH CARE. I sort through them and come across the album I want, and end up sitting in front of the fire for two hours, reminiscing. There are a few photos of Jack with Helen and Ellie. One with all four of us on it. I consider putting this one in the bedroom, then think it might be inappropriate, especially if Ellie sees it. I decide on one of Mum, Dad, me and Helen, taken at the cottage when I was about eight.

I'd been fishing with dad that day. As a joke, we got three portions of cod and chips from the chippy, to share between us for dinner. Arriving back, I told Mum we were starving, as we hadn't had a bite all day. Mum laughed, but Helen pulled her face and refused to eat. She hated that Mum and Dad had laughed at my joke. Helen would do anything to bring the mood down. Dad ensured that the good humour continued, though. He ignored Helen's mood and put a few chips out for her in the shape of a happy face. I asked Dad to do the same with mine, but he said it wasn't possible, as I was having fish. Helen said that was because I was a fish face. As I remember, no one laughed.

As I'm sorting through the pictures, I wonder why I'm trying to make the room nice. It isn't as if Helen would have done this in memory of me, had the situation been reversed. She would most likely have danced on my grave. If she'd liked dancing.

When I've finished, I step back and survey it. The candles seem to have warmed the room, the cushions make the bed look inviting and the photographs lend colour to the walls. It's a massive improvement. I decide that I'm going to keep it like this, with fresh bedding on the bed and flowers in a vase; to include it with the rest of the house. It's imbued with too much sadness and negative energy; it needs a little love.

I've brought bags of essentials with me, and the new bedding. I'm not a hoarder, so there wasn't a lot of stuff from my house in Manchester to store. I'm happy to pay the estate agent to manage it and monitor the new tenants.

My next-door neighbour, Mr. Henshaw, was a bit concerned that there would be a young couple moving in.

'You're such a quiet neighbour,' he'd said.

Yes, I do cry very quietly.

'And it's been good having a detective living on the close.'

It's the most he's spoken to me in the fifteen years I've lived there. He was friendly with my dad though, and I do tend to keep myself to myself and avoid eye contact with neighbours.

I promised him that if there was any trouble with the tenants, he could personally help to vet the next ones. Which seemed to satisfy his sense of importance and was something he could take to the next Home Watch meeting.

As I'm unpacking my groceries, I realise that the only things I could get the buzz of a proper binge from are a packet of digestive biscuits and a bottle of banana milk. Everything else is food I'd categorise as non-bingeworthy.

Tea bags, too dry.

Bread, a contender with loads of butter.

Toilet roll (see tea bags).

Orange juice, too healthy.

Eggs (see orange juice).

Downstairs the cupboards are stocked, the fire's crackling in the hearth, the radio's on low. I think how this house holds me. It brims with memories, good and bad, which lend it its character. It's the bricks and mortar version of myself. I leave it marinating in its own ambience, while I go upstairs to run a bath.

Soaking in the foamy water, I feel the stress ebbing away. Doubts about being able to settle here have all but dissipated. My mind feels peaceful. I use imagery to picture my brain waves as light undulations. Slowing my breathing, I listen to the plip of water from the tap.

A tiny glow inside me; I can't locate it, but I imagine it like a little pilot light. Hopeful for the future. I make plans. I'm going to do a proper shop tomorrow. I'm not making any promises to myself, but I'm going to try to stick to a shopping list. A binge is a great thing, but the fallout afterwards is bloody awful. I need to protect myself from that, tempting as it is.

Matt, Caro and Lucy are planning to come next weekend. Ellie wanted to come with me today and stay while I settled in. I convinced her it would be better to wait until I've been here for a few weeks. That way I get to establish myself, then her visit is something for me to plan for and to look forward to.

Baking is a thing I've not done for many years; maybe I could pick it up again. I've got the perfect kitchen for it here. Then I remember why I stopped: because I ended up eating most of it myself.

Perpetually lurking in that little repository I call the back of my mind is the possibility that I'm going to binge again.

Sharma often asked me how I'd coped with stress and I'd spewed out the usual stuff, alcohol, humour, isolation, avoidance. Never had I told her about my bingeing. Some things don't bear scrutiny, and besides, I didn't binge all the time I was in hospital. Though had I not been so zonked out, I would have got out and binged somehow. When it comes to binge food, I have the drive and resourcefulness of Steve McQueen in *The Great Escape*.

Sharma had come the closest. She'd touched on how people used alcohol, exercise, and whole array of other things, including food, to cope with stress. Nothing I didn't already know. It had been my opportunity to come clean, but I'd let the moment slide. I'd enough on my plate if you'll pardon the pun.

Food has always been my tranquillizer. Lorazepam or diazepam? Keep 'em. Doughnuts were my thing.

I'd got it so wrong though. I thought hunger was a good thing, it meant that I'd been good, that I could eat what I wanted when I got home. But hunger was really the enemy. Hunger is a red flag. It's deep water, a dangerous undertow, a rapid tide coming in, and I need to take note.

I run more hot water and sink back as the bubbles are replenished. My breasts rise out of the water, islands of shiny flesh. I've been thinking more about sex recently. The absence of it, rather than the desire for it. I'm probably the weight and shape I wished to be for years. I should be out buying new clothes and making the most of my weight loss. Ironically, my libido has deserted me completely. The adage 'use it or lose it' comes to me. I reach down and massage gently between my legs, thinking about Jack. That doesn't work, so I discard the image quickly and refocus. I'm relaxed and floating. My breathing slows. But all I feel is guilt and the urge to wee. I pull myself up and step out, dripping onto the bathmat. I really don't want to live a sexless life. I need to be patient. It'll all come in good time, and hopefully I will too.

Pulling a wide-toothed comb through my wet hair, I wander through to my bedroom. It's cosy and I'm looking forward to climbing between the fresh sheets.

My relapse prevention plan sits on the bedside table. I think about the God-awful things I've dealt with as a senior detective. The challenges I handled, easy as a child's party balloon. Twisting them into identifiable shapes and dispensing with them with a 'Ta da, and now for my next trick.'

Now, I have a list of people to contact. I need to use a thought record, use breathing techniques and mindfulness, take my meds and avoid alcohol, record my menstrual cycle. Oh, and not isolate myself in this cottage, out in the middle of nowhere.

Chapter Seventy-Two

Matt

The reception area at 'Ground Up' had an impressive foyer. Authentic tiled green walls and polished wood panelling. Matt wondered what the original purpose of the building had been. Kay would have loved it, he thought, as a man in a smart blue suit approached.

'Can I help you sir?'

'I'm here to see Mr McGrath,' Matt explained.

'Do you have an appointment?'

He presented his ID. 'By special invitation.'

The man leaned forward on the balls of his feet. 'Yes, of course. Can I ask you to sign in?' Matt complied and was directed towards a large wooden door to his left. 'Just press the intercom.'

A woman answered and after a lot of clicking noises he was buzzed into an expansive room with white walls and a suspended ceiling, embedded with dozens of spotlights. The radio was on low in the background but there was a lot of interference and the announcer's voice faded in and out, competing with a high-pitched intermittent buzzing noise.

To his right was a reception desk, which reminded Matt of the 1970's bar they used to have in the back room of his grandads house. Behind it sat a young woman wearing thick black eyeliner.

'He won't keep you long,' she said, pleasantly.

Towards the rear of the room was a glass partition. Behind which Matt could see the back of about a dozen seated people. Facing the group was a young man with a trendy haircut, proudly brandishing a red pointer pen at a drop-down screen, like it was the best Christmas present ever.

Matt was considering this as a door to his right opened and McGrath appeared, wearing a matching blue houndstooth jacket and waistcoat, dark blue jeans, and tan brogues. Matt begrudgingly acknowledged that the man knew how to dress.

'Good afternoon Detective Inspector Anderson, it's good to meet you under more, upright circumstances.'

It took Matt a moment to grasp the pun, then he realised, McGrath was referring to his hospital visit. He was a twat out of his comfort zone then. Matt wondered what he'd be like on his home turf.

'Yes, thank you for meeting with me at short notice.'

'Shall we go through?'

Matt followed him to his office, noting the predictably large walnut desk holding a laptop and a green two tone 1970's telephone, Matt supposed '70's memorabilia was a 'thing' with McGrath.

McGrath took his seat, rested his elbows on its arms, clasped his hands loosely across his belly, head cocked to one side and considered Matt. It struck Matt that he'd seen the same 'power-posture' on '*House of Cards*,' only delivered more convincingly.

'Can I just offer my condolences, I'm afraid I didn't catch you at the funeral,' Matt began.

'Oh, yes, thank you. Yes, it was all very sad.'

'How's Josh doing?'

'He's doing fine, he'll forget soon enough. Kids are more resilient than we give them credit for. Do you have any detective?'

'Simon Carter said that he was employed by you to follow

Ava.' Matt responded.

McGraths demeanour changed as he caught on to the mood. 'Yes, so it's all been covered,' he replied brusquely. 'What else do you want to know? I was concerned about her mental health. Turns out I was right to be concerned.'

'Did it never occur to you that following her, against her will, was one of the causes of her deteriorating health?' Matt responded.

'Si assured me that he kept it low key.'

'What does Si do now?'

'Basic stuff, records, stationary, stuff like that. He can't think outside the box, you know. In fact, I'd say there was a lot of space inside the box too if you get my meaning?'

'Is he here today?'

'No, it's his day off.'

'He said that he worked with Gary Brunswick. In what capacity exactly?'

McGrath swivelled the chair side to side. Matt thought it a self-comforting behaviour.

'I was wondering when you'd get back to him.'

'You covered for him.'

'This is like déjà vu. I made a mistake, got the days mixed up. I was as horrified as anyone when I found out what he'd done.'

Matt allowed the silence to stretch out, waiting for McGrath to break it.

He did so by asking; 'Are you sure you don't want a drink?'

Ignoring the question Matt asked, 'How do you finance a business like this? Is it public money?'

McGrath removed his jacket and turned to drape it over his chair, revealing a flash of red fabric on the back of his waistcoat. 'I've been in business for many years as you must know, and this is the culmination of those efforts. I'm putting something back into the community.'

'What about private investments?'

McGrath placed his hands on the arms of the chair again and leaned back. 'Funny, you don't strike me as a stocks and shares man,' he answered, sneeringly, but Matt detected he'd hit a nerve.

'Could I have a look around?'

McGrath leaned back in the chair stalling, then relented with a sigh. 'Sure, but I only have a few minutes, perhaps if you'd made an appointment?'

They returned to the main room and Matt noticed the reception desk was now unattended. He walked over to the partitioned area. 'This is where they get trained?' He asked.

The young guy with the haircut looked up at them through the glass.

'Yes, this is where the magic happens. We have a rolling training programme. A maximum of twelve trainees over a period of two months. Part of the training is here, and the rest is on site,' McGrath answered proudly.

'Can I go in?'

McGrath looked reluctant but put his finger to his lips in a 'shush' action and opened the door.

The room was warm and smelled of coffee, concentration, and perspiration. Two thermos flasks sat on a long table alongside a jug of milk. Each trainee had a pad of paper in front of them and were making notes. All heads turned as they entered. Matt nodded.

'So, site safety,' the young man continued, pulling their attention back. 'What are the most important things to remember?'

One of the trainees raised his arm and answered in a strong Eastern European accent. 'Hard hat, boots.'

Matt estimated his age to be around eighteen.

'Good, what else?'

'High viz,' another said.

'Excellent, anything else?'

McGraths mobile rang and he signalled they should leave. Matt followed him into the open space. Relieved to feel the cooler air. He noticed another door to the back of the room and walked towards it.

McGrath ended the call, then asserted. 'Detective Inspector, do you mind?'

Matt turned.

McGrath smiled. 'If there's nothing else? I really need to get on, phone this person back.'

Matt had wanted to poke about a bit, take a few jabs at McGrath, interview one of the trainees, but Barbara had instructed a low-key approach and he'd already pushed it. He didn't want a complaint. So, with a smile, he answered. 'Of course, thank you for your time, very impressive.'

As he returned to the foyer the suited man stood. 'Could I ask you to sign out?'

Matt signed and read through the previous entries, noting that Carter had signed in at 10am. Yet McGrath said it was his day off. There was no signature suggesting he'd left. He asked the concierge. 'How do you ensure everyone signs in and out? What about if you need a break?'

'Oh, I never miss. I have my lunch at the desk. If I need the loo, I ask someone from one of the offices to cover for me.'

'So, this guy,' Matt said, pointing to Carters signature, 'he's still here?'

The man peered at the entry, 'yes,' he nodded. 'He's still here.'

Chapter Seventy-Three

Matt

McGrath had lied again, to his face. Why would he lie about Carter? Matt could tell McGrath was edgy, which could account for a lapse in memory, but he doubted that was the case. He was beginning to fully comprehend Kay's instincts about McGrath

As soon as he returned to the investigation room he began searching through the database again. Something from Kay's previous search niggled at him. At six he called it a day and went home.

When he arrived, Caro was in the kitchen chopping tomatoes. Lucy and Oscar, her school friend, were seated at the kitchen counter drawing. Matt kissed Lucy on the top of her head.

'It's Elsa, the princess in *Frozen*.' Lucy said, holding the paper up.

'That's great Lucy, she looks like you.'

'Oscar's is better though, Daddy,' Lucy answered kindly, smiling at Oscar, who had also painted a picture of the princess. Matt had to agree it was a very good likeness.

'Excellent Osk,' Matt said. 'You got skills.'

He walked over to Caro and kissed her then pulled his jacket off and sat down at the counter with the children.

'It's like he's traced it,' Caro agreed, 'we should get him to sign it. It might be worth a fortune in a few years. When you're a famous artist, Oscar.'

'Or a master forger,' Matt added.

'What's a master forger?' Lucy asked, 'could I be one.'

'No, you're not a master, you'd be a miss forger,' Oscar replied kicking the back of the work counter with grey school socked feet.

'Better not get a taste for it. Once you start,' Caro said, arching one eyebrow at Matt, a warning about the subject matter and innocent ears. 'Now come on, it's ready, wash your hands please.'

Later, when Oscar had been collected by his dad and Lucy had gone to bed. Matt and Caro sat together in the lounge.

'Milk of the Poppy?' Caro asked. It was a joke they shared after watching '*Game of Thrones*.' In the series 'Milk of the Poppy' was an opium-based drink used to treat pain. It had made them laugh and it was now their new name for wine.

'I'll get it,' Matt said.

They chatted for a while about Caro's day and she asked Matt if he wanted to talk. Matt declined and said he felt like he needed to close his eyes and clear his head before he could allow anything else in.

At four in the morning he got up and went downstairs. The concealed strip of light under the kitchen cupboards shone softly on the black counter. Just enough brightness for his sleep dulled head. He flicked the kettle on and made a coffee and sat heavily on a kitchen stool, aware of how exhaustion could feel like illness when it seeped into your bones.

Lucy and Oscar's drawings made him smile. A timely reminder of his life outside of the job. Then he froze. The thing which had been eluding him suddenly glared, bright as a watchman's flashlight. Caro's comment about the pictures on the fridge?

Once you get a taste for it?

On his return to work Matt requested an urgent meeting

with Barbara.

'Okay Matt,' Barbara began. 'I was going to call you in this morning anyway, so this is very timely.'

For a moment Matt thought he was in for a bollocking, but he elbowed the thought aside and leaned forward for emphasis. 'I'm convinced that forgery is the key.' He sat back, then forward again, 'I went over Kay's notes again and that was her hunch. I'd missed it but it's all there on the database. Brunswick had a history of forgery. He wasn't going to let that skill go to waste, was he? That's why McGrath owed him. I don't know whether Carter has taken over, and I don't know what they were forging. But Carter worked closely with Brunswick. When he wasn't following Ava that is.'

Barbara was thoughtful for a moment. 'What about Andretti Melnik?'

Not the response Matt was expecting but he explained, 'I asked detective Cromar to look into his finances. Andretti's sister, Lena, is McGraths girlfriend.'

Barbara frowned, she picked her pen up and made some notes on her desk pad. When she'd finished writing she placed it down carefully. It glinted expensively under the table lamp.

'I've been contacted by the Modern Slavery and Kidnap Unit. Your search for Andretti's finances flagged up on the database.'

'Modern Slavery Unit?' Matt repeated.

'Yes, apparently they have been intelligence gathering for the last four months. Your search vibrated along their web.'

Unsure of the implications Matt asked, 'what does it mean?'

'It means they think Andretti has been infiltrating building companies, trafficking foreign nationals. They want you to stop searching.'

'Oh.' Matt replied, deflated.

'And work with them,' Barbara added. 'The forgery angle is something they have had very few leads on. Also, you need to leave Simon Carter alone. He's their informant.'

'What?'

'He's been promised leniency if he helps.'

'Jesus.'

'It's all good, Matt. Very good work. I'll contact them now and set up a meeting.'

'So, Kay was right?' he uttered. 'Oh man.'

Chapter Seventy-Four

Kay

My new consultant, Dr Frances Calder, is fresh as a lemon, in a dress with a button-down collar. She looks about half my age, but I've learned not to be judgmental about young doctors.

'How was the move?' Dr Calder asks brightly.

'Fairly uneventful. The cottage has been in our family for years, so I know the area.'

'Have you met your key nurse yet?'

'No, I have an appointment with her after this.'

'Ah, good. Now, any sleep problems?'

'No.'

'Did you fill in the form for side effects?'

Digging in my bag I pull out the crumpled paper I completed in the reception area and hand it to her. She reads through and makes some notes on her laptop.

'Could you roll your sleeve up, please, Kay?'

I obey and she does my blood pressure.

'No dizzy spells?'

'Nope.' The cuff tightens.

'Hearing any voices? Seeing people who couldn't be there?'

'No and no.'

The cuff loosens and she removes it, then uses a stethoscope to listen to my heart and chest.

'All fine. You seem to be doing OK on the Olanzapine.'

'Yeah, although I did expect to put weight on with it.'

'With the ODT we found much less weight gain.'

'ODT?'

I hate it when professionals use acronyms, expecting you to know what they mean. I think about my dad. A nurse told him they couldn't give an anaesthetic because of his 'pre-morbid' symptoms. Luckily, I was present and told her Dad didn't have a degree in medical science, so could she explain what pre-morbid meant. It's a frightening term, used in relation to medical conditions – pre-morbid lung function, or pre-morbid heart rate. It's more commonly used in relation to psychological function. As I've come to learn.

'My apologies,' Doctor Calder says. 'It stands for orally disintegrated tablet. It's been found to have far less impact on weight than the standard tablet. Could you jump on the scales for me? We can have a look.'

I hate this bit. Removing my coat and shoes, I consider asking if I can use the loo to empty my bladder first. I remove my watch as Doctor Calder observes.

'It's a Michael Korrs,' I explain, 'heavy links.'

She nods her understanding, skinny thing that she is.

The scales are metric, and I don't have a clue what the numbers mean.

'Height?'

'Six foot,' I answer as I step off and stand under the height chart.

Returning to her notes, she writes down my measurements. I pull my shoes back on and re-clip my watch.

'Your BMI is in the healthy range, nineteen.'

'What's my weight?' I ask.

'Sixty-one kilograms.'

'In old money?'

Frowning, she tilts her head to the side. Understanding dawns, and she searches on her laptop. 'Converts to ten stone and two pounds.'

For once I'm not ashamed.

'All right, I think we can continue with the sertraline and the olanzapine,' she says, tapping on the keyboard.

I start to pull my jacket on. She stops tapping and swivels her chair to face me.

'Is there anything that you'd like to ask me, Kay? We have time if you have any concerns, anything at all?'

It's unexpected and I've not prepared anything. For a nanosecond, I think she can read my mind and knows I've only been taking the meds every other day and missed a few days here and there in error. So far, I've been fine, and I know it's what she would do anyway, to wean me off them. At the first sign of trouble, I'll increase it.

'Erm no, I think I'm OK.'

'Have you seen any of the news coverage?'

'Some of it.'

'They mentioned your name and showed a photograph.'

I've seen the report she's referring too and the light coverage in the Scottish papers, but I'd hardly be recognised from the photograph. Matt said he'd supplied it to reporters deliberately. It's my lanyard photograph, and they were all changed five years ago. Any vanity I might possess is outweighed by my need to maintain my health and privacy.

'Just to reassure you, it's all confidential. No one knows you're in my care, and they never will.'

See, these young doctors can surprise you if you give them a chance. I offer her my hand and we shake. 'Thank you, Doctor Calder,' I say. 'It's been lovely to meet you.'

'Any concerns, contact me, or leave a message with my secretary. I check them regularly. Messages, not secretaries.' she adds, laughing at her own joke.

Chapter Seventy-Five

Kay

Noreen Denbigh is my new mental health nurse here in Aberfeldy. Short, wavy, ginger-biscuit hair and hazel eyes. Petite behind her large desk. Narrow shoulders, small build. Then she stands up; her hips are wide, her legs short and stocky, reminding me of one of those games where the picture is in two halves. You can swap the tops and bottoms of the characters over, so the top half might be a pirate and the bottom half a ballerina. Underneath her purple and green patchwork corduroy pinafore, she's wearing an orange polo neck jumper. Legs are encased in brown tights, potted into a pair of red Mary Jane shoes. I'm hoping her handbag and coat are blue and yellow. I wonder if she's colour blind, like my grandfather was. He was the only boy to present a pink, paper mâché zeppelin to his class, believing he'd painted it battleship grey.

Noreen picks a piece of paper up from the photocopier and waves it in my general direction. 'Your family have lived here for some time, haven't they?'

'Erm, well, we've had the cottage here for over thirty years. It's been a well-loved second home.'

'So, it's a bit of a moot point to ask you if you're settling in.'
'Moot-ish.'

'Well, you're in a lovely spot Kay, right there by the loch.'
'Yes. I'm hoping to get a small boat and do some fishing.'

'Lovely pastime. You'd get on well with my Cameron, he's mad keen.' She hands me the piece of paper and returns to her chair. 'This is our agreement, all outlined for you. I'll come and see you in your home next week, then fortnightly. We'll review at six months. Any side effects from the meds?'

I shake my head. 'I think they're just about right, just been checked by the doc.'

'Great. Early days, but sleeping OK?'

'Yes, I slept really well last night.'

'I've put my mobile number on your copy. If you need anything at all, or you're feeling even the slightest bit unwell, call me. Don't think, 'Ooh it's too late,' or I'll be annoyed, just call me. I might be a bit passive aggressive at first, but by the time we've chatted, I'll have forgiven your intrusion.'

I like this woman. She's a kind of brightly lit, squashed version of me with a Scot's accent.

'Thanks.'

'I run the support group every Wednesday, so hope to see you tomorrow. I'll e-mail the details of other activities. We try and run something every Friday evening, a quiz or something like that. It would be great if you could come.'

'Prizes?' I ask, to appear interested.

Noreen looks at me over imaginary glasses. 'Oh, do we have prizes!' Handing me a pen she indicates where I should sign the form and continues, 'the feel-good factor, followed by smugness if you manage to get a question right.'

I sign and pass the paper back.

'Ta,' she says, and tears a copy off and hands it to me. Then she smiles. 'First prize is you get to keep your sanity. I'm still trying to win that.'

Noreen rises and comes to the door as I'm leaving. She touches my arm lightly. 'You've done a really brave thing, Kay. I admire you, starting over. It takes some courage. For what it's worth, I think you'll be just fine.' She smiles again.

Some people have a feature which redeems their otherwise ordinary features; some people have a presence. Noreen has charisma in spades, and perfect teeth.

The Watermill is quiet, no offers of fifty per cent off for pensioners today. I've spotted the waitress who served me when I imagined I was with Ava. How weird I must have seemed to her. I almost wish I could request the restaurant CCTV and watch myself enacting my bizarre delusion, ordering quiche and chips for two.

A rising giggle surprises me as I think about ordering for Ava again, just to observe the waitress's reaction from a point of sanity. She approaches and the giggle expires. There's not even a glimmer of recognition from her as I order. I realise I must look very different now from how I did then. The weight loss has changed my face. I have cheekbones now, though I'm still hardly Heidi Klum.

After lunch, I stroll down the High Street and call in to the delicatessen. Keeping to my shopping list, I buy cold meat and breads, the only addition a jar of their home-made pickle: delicious, but it's never made it to the binge list, so I'm safe.

The wind has risen when I return to the cottage. It carries with it the distant clang of bells from the fishing boats and the white noise of rolling waves. My hair blows in my face and the car door closes on me before I've had a chance to retrieve my shopping. I pull it open again, lodging it there with my backside.

Clumsily I enter the cottage, the shopping bags digging into my fingers. I drop them on the floor and push the front door shut. Leaves scud across the floor and a door upstairs bangs. It's probably the wind, but I suddenly feel hesitant. When you've been over the edge and not even realised it, it's difficult to know with any certainty when you're not teetering there again. Still, I'm reassured by my check-up and impressed by the team I have around me.

While the storm whistles and whirls around the cottage, I put the shopping away. Dancing to *Kansas City* by The Beatles, I go into the lounge and throw a log on the fire.

It happens so suddenly. The fire continues to spit and wave capriciously, while I'm frozen to the spot. Ava is standing at the foot of the stairs, towel wrapped around her head like a fifties film star.

Chapter Seventy-Six

Kay

Despite her small stature, Noreen fills the cottage with her presence. She huffed in on the wind and immediately took charge. I'm half expecting her to waft sage around, like a shaman. Instead, she puts the kettle on.

'Here,' she says, bringing it through. She hands me the steaming cup and I encase it in my hands like a bowl of soup. Noreen takes the armchair opposite me. Her feet barely touch the floor.

While I waited for her to arrive, I sat with my eyes closed, practising my breathing and mindfulness, filled with doubt, wondering whether I've got so good at putting a front on I've fooled myself and everyone else into believing I'm better. I remember what Helen wrote about Edward Semper deluding everyone, even his psychiatrist.

When I opened my eyes and risked a glance at the stairs, relief flooded through me. It was just a towel I'd left hanging over the bannister. I removed it quickly and considered phoning Noreen, to tell her it was a false alarm. But, in honesty, I was looking forward to her company.

'So, you thought you'd hallucinated?' Noreen says.

I nod towards the stairs. 'I thought Ava was standing there. I was just thrown, petrified to be honest.'

'Nothing since?'

'No.' I stand up and walk to the newel post. Noreen twists

around in her chair, watching. 'I'd left a white towel on here this morning. I meant to put it in the washing basket but was in a bit of a rush and forgot.'

Returning to my seat, I pick my tea up and pull my feet up under me. Feeling calmer and reassured that Noreen came, as she said she would.

'I realised almost immediately but it still shook me up.'

'Was it a memory?'

'Yes, I'd seen her there before.'

'So, it could be classed as the memory of a hallucination, a flashback, of sorts?'

'Yes, I suppose.'

'You said you'd been dancing around the room?'

'Yeah, The Beatles.'

'Do you know how much I encourage the group to move to music? I'm always banging on about it, so good for the soul.'

For a minute I think she might be joking, but she's appraising me, like a proud sergeant major.

'It says a lot about your general mood. If you'd been sitting in the chair, ruminating, it would have put a different slant on it. Also, you could have been a bit dizzy.'

'That's true,' I say. I hadn't considered it before, but I've been feeling like I've just jumped off a spinning roundabout. It's a recognised side effect of reducing the anti-depressants. I hadn't told the doctor because I don't want her interfering with the dosage; I'm managing it myself.

As I rise to go into the kitchen Noreen looks up at me and says, 'Dance, but don't throw yourself about.' Taking a sip of tea, she winks. 'I think it might have been one of The Beatles' too.'

I laugh, feeling lighter, braver. I find the digestive biscuits. I bought them for just such an occasion, and to ensure I don't eat them all myself. Arranging a few on a china plate, I carry them through and offer them to Noreen. She takes one with a 'Ta.'

I help myself and sit back down. 'Sorry to have brought

you all the way out here, Noreen.'

She bites into her biscuit and chews for a moment before answering. 'You saved me from a heated debate with one of my colleagues. I probably shouldn't say it, but she suffers with a constipation of opinions.'

'About what?'

'Well, this afternoon it was a dig at me for having my hair coloured. She said that to dye was a lie and disrespectful to the sisterhood.'

'And you said?'

'In that case, stop bleaching your moustache.'

A laugh bursts from me and I shower the fireguard with tea and biscuit. 'Harsh,' I say, wiping my mouth.

'I know. It was exactly the right time to leave.'

'I really appreciate it. I just needed to be reassured it wasn't another hallucination and I'm not relapsing.'

'By the sound of it, Kay, you've rationalised it all. Also, you didn't have that insight before, did you? You didn't know you were ill. You just accepted Ava was here and couldn't offer yourself any alternative.'

'I still can't get my head around what happened. I was a proper mental case.'

'You wouldn't use a derogatory term like that about someone with a broken leg.'

'I probably would.' I start to think of a derogatory term for someone with a broken leg.

Leaning forward, Noreen shakes her head. She looks serious as she stares into the fire, then back at me. 'Your brain chemistry was broken. It's healing, just like a broken leg would, so you're getting phantom pains.'

I stay quiet for a minute to digest this. Phantom pains. The explanation seems so apt. She's right, I'm healing and might have a few blips.

'You're right,' I say. 'Definitely colour it, it suits you.'

Chapter Seventy-Seven

Kay

Apart from the fact we've all suffered from some sort of mental health issue, to anyone passing the support group could easily pass as a book or film club. I'm only here to see what goes on, and to support Noreen. She's someone I want on my side.

A lady called Alice is talking about her ex-husband's infidelity and the messy divorce, which triggered her depression. It's a bit too close to home for me. However, I listen sympathetically. Then it's Carol's turn. She talks about how her anxiety contributed to losing her high-flying job. I realise I have things in common with a lot of people here.

Noreen manages the group, making sure no one dominates or says anything inappropriate.

As I'm leaving the session, a man of about fifty, hair greying at the temples, comes over to me.

'Hi,' he says.

'Hi.'

'Philip, Phil.' He offers his hand and I shake it.

I recognise him. He told the group his life was near to perfect as you could imagine. His depression came out of nowhere.

'How did you find us?' he asks.

'I followed the yellow brick road,' is the response on the tip of my tongue. I bite it back.

'Good,' I answer.

'Will you be here next week?' he asks.

'Sure,' I answer. 'God willing.' It's a phrase I've never used before. There's something about Philip's shiny face and bright expression, which makes me think he'd appreciate it.

He smiles and gives me a little wave as he walks briskly towards the door. As it swings shut behind him, I swear I hear him say, 'fuck God.'

As I wait for Noreen, a few of the other attendees say 'Goodbye,' and 'Hope to see you next week.' Attendance isn't compulsory, but I think it'll probably be useful to keep coming. I don't feel as much of a nutcase when I'm in the company of people who've been diagnosed as nutcases.

As the group thins out, a woman of about sixty enters. Strips of thin grey hair hang limply from her head and coil up on her jumper-clad shoulders. Brown boots alternately peep out from under a long grey skirt as she strides in. She strikes me as an ex-hippy kind. A believer in the free love movement of the sixties, only for her there were no takers.

'Noreen,' she calls, in a clipped, annoyed tone as she sweeps past.

Noreen's busy, collecting paper cups left behind by the group. She looks up. 'Good morning, Peggy,' she replies.

'I put you down for the clinic on Monday. You've taken your name off,' Peggy says, jabbing a finger at Noreen's chest without actually touching her.

Noreen moves away. 'Good afternoon, Peggy,' she says.

'I'm going to report you.'

I watch, as Noreen drops the paper cups into the bin, then heads for the door towards the rear, which leads to the counselling suites. 'Good night, Peggy,' she says.

I can't help it: I laugh. Peggy swings around, and her irate expression morphs into surprise. She'd clearly assumed I'd left.

'Come through, Kay,' Noreen calls, pushing at the door.

'We'll discuss it at a more appropriate time, Peggy,' I hear her say quietly, as I walk into the therapy room.

Noreen doesn't comment on the exchange, but I'm too nosy to let it go, ex-cop and all that. 'I take it Peggy is the one with the opinion on hair dye?'

Noreen considers me for a moment. 'I should never have mentioned it,' she says. 'It was unprofessional.'

'In my previous life as a non-crazy person, I've been on about three million mandatory training courses, as I'm sure you have. And that, Noreen,' I say, pointing to towards the door, 'looked like Bullying 101 to me.'

Putting the rocky start aside, the one-to-one session goes well. I've discovered that for most of my life, I've craved sistering. I think I took all the mothering and fathering my parents could give. At least they tried to be there for me, but Helen never could. She tried her best to be an absent sister.

This realisation has been helpful to understand my illness. I had unrealistic expectations of what having a sister should be like. It explains, in part, why I might grieve the loss of Ava, someone I never knew.

Noreen suggests I should write a letter to Ava. I did it with Helen and it seemed to help. She said I could give it to Ava, or burn it, or throw it in the loch, whatever felt fitting.

Chapter Seventy-Eight

Kay

The smell of baking sponge is torture. I eat three buns as soon as they come out of the oven. The remainder now reside in a Tupperware container. I know myself well enough not to peek. I've also made a Victoria sponge, which is now covered with a cake dome and a tea towel. Hardly Fort Knox, but at least they can't make eye contact with me anymore.

Checking my diary, I see I'm due on in three days. I can feel it anyway, becoming bloated and irritable. I consider telling Matt not to visit this weekend, but I know how much Lucy's been looking forward to it. Besides, I can always retreat to bed. That's the good thing: I don't have to pretend around them anymore.

Next Friday afternoon, the ladies from the book club – my name for the support group – are coming to the cottage for tea on Noreen's suggestion. She said I had to start somewhere, and then I'd get invited back to theirs.

I told her I wasn't bothered about being invited back. Which earned me a hard stare and a reminder that isolating myself isn't good for my mood.

'Anyway,' she said. 'You get to see inside their houses.'

'OK,' I answered. 'As long as no one uses it as a crafty way to recruit babysitters for their screaming kids.'

I wake up in the night with terrible cramps and know I've started. A hot bath always helps, so I run the water as I swallow a couple of ibuprofens and mark them down, noting the time at one forty-five.

When I've bathed, I fill my hot water bottle and get back into bed. Picking my journal up from the bedside table, I begin the letter to Ava while the painkillers get to work. Three false starts later, I decide just to go with whatever comes.

Dear Ava,

I'm writing to tell you how sorry I'm that I didn't save you. I'm sorry you didn't get to live your life and spend time with your little boy. It wasn't my fault, but I messed up, I was ill.

I've realised now that you didn't want to be saved and I should have respected your wishes.

Instead, I made it all about me. Because of what happened with Helen, I needed you to live. Intent on keeping you safe to make up for her death – and my guilt.

I treated Helen badly, I admit it. But deep inside, if I'm being honest, and I can be in this letter, I still think she deserved it. I tried everything to be her friend when I was younger, but she continually rejected me.

She was cold-hearted, distant and hard. She didn't give Jack the love he needed. Depression had claimed Helen years before, sucked everything from her, like it does. I can't be blamed for that.

I knew from the first day that Helen would destroy Jack, one way or the other. I told him Helen would be the death of him.

Then Ellie came along, and Helen had everything. I'd never really wanted children. My job was my calling. But I did my best to lure Ellie from Helen. It was so easy. Helen didn't have a nurturing bone in her body and Ellie craved a mother figure. Funny how that person was me though. Ellie was drawn to me and I was flattered by it, encouraged it. I moved blindly forward, never imagining.

I saw you disappear over the edge, Ava. I couldn't handle it. I brought you back to life, like Dr Frankenstein. Gave you a personality, a sense of humour, intelligence, shoes! But it was all a delusion, a hallucination, a sickness.

Now I'm on regular medication and feeling much better. I know you were never here. It's a relief to know I didn't actually lock you in the attic. I understand my rationale as Helen was able to kill herself because someone took their eye off her. I was trying to prevent history repeating. And that it was my one hundred and twenty-six Scrabble score, not yours. Even in the depth of my illness, I was still brilliant at board games.

It's a pity, Ava, because I think I created a great friend in you, a sister, better than anything Helen and I ever had, even if you were just a sum of imaginary parts.

I must've fallen asleep. I'm awakened by a noise and realise my journal has fallen onto the floor. Leaning over, I reach for it with my fingertips and lift. My blood stills. The pages I'd written have been ripped from the book's seam and are now in pieces, scattered around the bedcover.

Chapter Seventy-Nine

Kay

Sleep didn't return last night. I came downstairs and switched the TV on and re-stoked the fire. At four-fifteen, I took two paracetamol and noted them down.

A light sabre of blue-sky shines through the narrow gap in the curtains, reflecting off the wall opposite. I pull them open, shielding my eyes. Fresh air is what's needed.

The lapping water of the loch is as calming as any tranquillizer. I perch on an outcrop of rocks and stare at the water as I think about my diary. I recall all those months ago, tearing at the pages of Helen's journal. It's clearly my modus operandi. If I don't like something, I tear it up. Diaries, newspapers, people's lives. What's worrying me is I don't remember doing it this time. Yet I'm supposed to be better.

Noreen's running a social event this evening. I'll run it by her. Thinking of this, I immediately feel lighter. I'm positive Noreen will have a rational explanation for it. It's healthy for me to shelve it until then.

Strolling back along the shore, I try to inhale the beauty of the scenery, breathing it in, relaxing my shoulders, thinking positive thoughts. Reinvigorated, I return to the cottage, switch the oven on and pull my baking paraphernalia out of the cupboards. Chocolate buns are the answer to almost anything.

I arrive at the group room that evening, loaded up with buns and my Victoria sponge. Noreen comes to help me, and we arrange them onto paper plates.

'These look great,' she says.

Alice and Carol and another lady I haven't met have arrived and come over to view the offerings.

'Oh, you can definitely come again,' Carol says.

'I know,' Noreen adds. 'We should make it a compulsory part of the sessions.'

'What is it tonight?' I ask, realizing I have no idea what the plan is.

'Music quiz,' Noreen answers.

'Then we break for coffee and tea, and cakes tonight,' Alice says, smiling at me. 'Thank you, Kay.'

'Then we sit around and chat, whatever people want to do,' Noreen adds.

'Sounds good,' I answer. I'm just happy they didn't say bingo.

I see no sign of Peggy. When I mention her to Carol, she lowers her voice and answers, 'Oh, that one. How did she get a job in the caring profession?'

I'm intrigued. I know I won't leave it there. After the quiz, a small group of us remain behind. Alice, me, Carol, and the other lady whose name is Misha huddle around a table for a post-mortem on the quiz as Noreen chats to people who are leaving. It's not long before the group conversation turns to the absence of Peggy. Carol is the most informed, because Brendan, her son, is a secretary in the community team office, and tells her all the staff gossip.

Apparently, Peggy had been the most senior mental health nurse, running the show for ten years. Then Noreen moved over from her post as a senior nurse on the acute wards. Peggy didn't take it well. To make matters worse, Noreen is more popular, both with the team and with the patients.

Carol says she was one of the patients who asked if she

could move from Peggy's individual sessions, to be added to Noreen's waiting list.

'During one of our sessions, Peggy started using EFT.'

We all exchange confused glances.

'Emotional Freedom Technique,' Carol explains, tapping two fingers against her head, then her nose, her chin and her chest. 'Tapping therapy. This is what she had me doing. All very well, I don't mind trying different things, but she didn't ask me if I wanted to try it. I just really wanted to talk, that's what I find the most helpful. I tried to tell her, but she insisted I carry on with the tapping. Well, I didn't. I stopped going to the sessions and spoke to Doctor Calder. A week after I was on Noreen's list. Peggy doesn't speak to me now if she can help it.'

Licking my finger, I gather up the cake crumbs on my plate, waiting for my moment to catch Noreen alone, to tell her about my diary incident. I see she's free and move away from the group.

'Everything OK?' she asks.

'Could I just have a quiet word?'

'Sure.'

We move to a small table in the corner of the room. I relay the incident with the diary and my worries about doing things in my sleep.

'Have you heard of Occam's Razor?' she asks. 'It means the most obvious explanation is usually the answer.'

'So, I did it, but don't remember?'

'Sure, what else?'

'Well, I was afraid I was losing it again.'

'You haven't changed anything, stopped meds or anything?'

'No. I have just come on, though. I have bad periods. I feel like I've been drained of lifeblood by the vampire Lestat.'

Noreen smiles and nods sympathetically. 'You'd probably been in a deep sleep and forgot. Did you write anything particularly revealing? Something you'd perhaps hidden from yourself and were ashamed of?'

'Yeah, I wrote the letter to Ava.'

'OK, maybe leave the letter for a few days. And get your iron levels checked out with the doc. We can talk about it at our next session in more depth. I can see how it might have frightened you, though.'

'It did,' I admit.

'Haven't you ever made yourself a midnight sandwich? In the morning, you've got mustard on your pyjamas and pickle between your teeth, and you can't even remember getting up and making it?' she asks.

'Yeah, sure, who hasn't?'

'Well, not me, obviously. I'd never do that.'

Chapter Eighty

Kay

Saturday morning is literally a whirl of activity because I still have the dizziness. The pains have notched down to a four and are at least manageable.

I held off from writing anything in my journal last night. Instead, I lay downstairs on the settee and dozed until around two o'clock. Then I had a tussle about whether to go up to bed. Only cold sheets awaited upstairs, and I couldn't be bothered filling a hot water bottle, so I stoked the fire up with logs and had a hot chocolate. Before falling back to sleep, cosy as a dormouse, on the couch.

I prepare Mum and Dad's room for Caro and Matt and the attic room for Lucy. New bedding on the beds and fresh flowers in each room. They all have a stack of fresh, thick towels and I've bought them each a fluffy expensive bathrobe.

Unfortunately, there's an accident on the M74 and they're delayed. They finally arrive at seven in the evening, frazzled from the journey. With only enough energy reserves to show them to their rooms and put a pizza in the oven, I leave them to it. I think they're grateful they don't have to be entertaining for me. The sounds of a family moving around the cottage are comforting, and I sleep easily.

In the morning, Caro comes downstairs and hugs me.

'Kay, it's all so beautiful. Thank you. Thank you for the

bathrobe.' She waves a hand over the breakfast spread. 'This looks delicious.'

'Oh, it's nothing. I eat like this every day.'

'I feel so spoiled.'

'It's the least I can do, Caro. The way you and Matt have looked after me.' I feel myself tearing up and turn away.

'The house is gorgeous. You ever thought of a B&B? You'd be great.'

'If you ignore the fact I hate people and talking.'

She laughs. 'Sheep farmer, then.'

'Wow.' Matt enters. 'This looks great. Look, Lucy, strawberries, your favourite.'

'Sit down. There's croissants on the table,' I say. 'And boiled eggs and toast.'

'Thank you, Aunty Kay,' Lucy says.

Matt nudges her. 'What else?'

'Thank you for the flowers.'

'You're welcome.'

Wiping my hands on a tea towel, I join them, trying to remember the last time anyone sat down at this table to share a family meal.

I sip my tea and nibble at the fruit as I watch, feeling so fortunate to be part of it.

Later we walk around the loch. Matt and I lead the way and Caro and Lucy examine stones and shells along the shoreline.

'You should get a dog,' Matt says.

'Are you kidding? I can only just manage to look after myself.'

'You look like you're doing a good job.'

'You writing a report?'

'Nope, just noticing.'

'Yeah, I'm fine. I have a good key nurse. I went to a social do last night.'

'No!'

'Yeah.'

'Did someone have a gun to your head?'

'No, I just thought it'd be good for me.'

'When have you ever done anything just because it might be good for you?'

'Since I attacked a man and abducted his son and imagined I had his wife locked in the attic.'

'You make it sound like a bad thing,' Matt quips.

I almost laugh. I think he's getting funnier, more relaxed, now he's not my underling.

'I still didn't stay long though,' I add. 'I run out of personality very quickly nowadays.'

'Never, not you,' he says with sincerity.

'That's the nicest thing you've ever said to me.'

I look at him and he looks away.

'You've seen the news stories?' he asks, changing the subject.

'Not actually seen, but I've heard.'

'Watch out for Stefan Laing, he's been sniffing around, trying to find where you are.'

Coldness in my gut. I look around at the mountains and the loch and remember to breathe. What's Laing onto? What might he dig up?

'I don't want you to worry. I just want to forewarn you. I'll do everything from my end.'

'How much does he know?'

'Anything McGrath tells him. Public records.'

'Why does he want to speak to me?'

'He wants to know your side of the story.'

'I won't have to appear in court, will I?'

It's the thing I've dreaded the most, facing people in a courtroom. People who I've worked with for years.

'Don't forget DI Joy Furnham. If you need any help.' He enters her number into my contacts. 'She's a friend, the person to call out here. If Laing comes anywhere near you, we whack a restraining order on him.'

I thank him but the cold knot hasn't thawed.

In the afternoon, on Caro's suggestion, we drive into Aberfeldy and stroll along the path to Tay bridge and over to the Black Watch Memorial.

Glen Lyon café is open, and we find a table just in time for last orders on food. As we chat, we work our way through a cream tea. We all laugh when Matt calls Lucy a tea belly because she drinks so much of it and keeps needing the loo. Caro asks me if I've brought a fishing rod yet, and Matt gently admonishes her, telling her I need to settle in first.

They involve me, but I observe, stand apart. I'm reminded of being around Jack and Helen with Ellie. With Helen, words were like hair-triggers, irrelevant of the occasion, one wrong word from Jack and the evening was over. Or else they were cringingly nice with each other, which was even more unnerving.

I don't see any evidence of it with Matt and Caro. Best behaviour between couples is always impressive to a singleton, though.

The following day Matt asks if we can go for a walk before they make an early start for home.

'I want to tell you how the case is going,' he says.

I wonder if I should cover my ears with my hands and shout over his words.

'I'm telling you this because I want you to know you were right. McGrath is involved with a guy called Andretti Melnik. Nasty piece of work. Melnik is a gangmaster trafficking Foreign Nationals, using forged documents and providing a ready supply of labour at knocked down rates.'

'Labour abuse.'

'It had been staring me, *us,* in the face, Kay, but you were the first one to spot it because guess who was forging the documents?'

'Brunswick,' I answer, though it seems to matter little now.

'Brunswick aided by McGrath. The Modern Slavery and Kidnap Unit had Melnik in their sights for the last four months. The stuff you found on Brunswick, the forgery stuff, was one of the pieces of the puzzle. He was working for McGrath, forging qualifications, work permits, all sorts. The guy McGrath had following Ava was used as a go between.'

'So, are McGrath and the guy in prison?' I ask, for Ava.

'We're still building the case. I'm...'

I cut him off, 'I don't want to know any more.' I say like a loser. What should be music to my ears sounds like someone scraping on a rusty violin.

Matt turns and takes my hands in his. 'I didn't know whether or not to mention it, but I thought you should know you've always been a great detective. The force will be worse off for not having you.'

'Excellent, Matt, now I can tell the newspapers I was only three slices short of a picnic and not the whole loaf.'

Waving goodbye with the sun in my eyes, their car seems to disappear into a white haze.

Turning back towards the house, I realise how exhausted I am, and wonder what possessed me to insist they stay here, when they'd planned to stay in a hotel. The answer is, I was proving a point. I'm not a cop anymore and I drag that shame around, like massive ankle weights on both legs. Learning McGrath could get his just deserts has restored a bit of self-respect. But I can't separate the sweet satisfaction I was right about him from the bitter and salt regret that it's now Matt's case and Matt's glory.

Chapter Eighty-One

Kay

With thoughts about the case swimming around in my head, I lie on the settee. I understand Matt's puffed up because of the case. But I wanted some justice for Ava. I realised this afternoon that the stalking of Ava, the psychological and physical wearing down of another human being, was being overlooked so a bigger fish could be netted. Still, I think Ava will be satisfied, as long as McGrath pays.

I'm just in that comfortable state between a doze and sleep when the house phone rings. I answer it, thinking it might be Matt, unable to get me on my mobile. It's Stefan Laing. I ask him where he got my number. He tells me it's a public record. It isn't, it's ex-directory.

In my most authoritative voice, I tell him I'll get a restraining order if he attempts to contact me again. Then I call Matt. He promises he'll sort it out.

'Don't worry, Kay,' he says. 'I'll be on it first thing tomorrow. Remember you can call Joy.'

But I don't want to call Joy. I don't know Joy. I have an appointment tomorrow with Noreen; I'll talk to her.

I try my breathing techniques, but they don't work. I'm a sitting target for Laing. I need to keep my wits.

Chapter Eighty-Two

Matt

Matt crossed from the Corporation street tram line and onto the pedestrianised area, outside Selfridges. Most of this area was part of the re-build initiated after the IRA bombing in 1996. He remembered, not just because his whole street felt the reverberations two miles away, but because it was the weekend that Russia and Germany were supposed to play in the Euro championship at Old Trafford. He was only fifteen at the time, but he recalled hearing people say that the blast was the catalyst for the regeneration of the City, turning it into the modern British 'powerhouse' it is today.

It was a busy time of day and full of the diversity that is the hallmark of major cities. Shoppers criss-crossed the area, many held take-out coffee. A girl in a black beanie ate what looked like a cheese toastie from a cardboard envelope and Matt imagined she was Lucy in a few years-time, hanging out with her friends, going to bars and clubs.

He spotted Stefan Laing, seated outside Salvi's; an Italian restaurant situated at the old Corn Exchange building. As he neared he caught the aroma of freshly roasting coffee beans as it wafted out from the mouth of the open door. Like the café had coffee breath

The reason Laing was outside in the finger-numbing cold became apparent when he lit up a cigarette. He rose and shook Matt's hand.

'Matt.'

'Stefan.'

Up close Stefan looked about fifty, though Matt had no idea of his age. He had very pale skin, dark hair and blue eyes, trimmed with very dark lashes. He was wearing a black overcoat and had a newspaper protruding from one of the pockets. Black boots stuck out from under the frayed bottom of his jeans.

'Hope you don't mind being outside? Stefan asked, holding his smoking cig up. 'It's in the job description'.

'Go ahead,' Matt answered as they both sat down. 'I've shared space with people who have far worse habits.'

The waiter arrived out and passed them a laminated menu.

'Just black coffee for me,' Stefan said.

Matt ordered an Americano with hot milk and the waiter left.

After taking a deep drag Stefan crushed the stub out in the metal ashtray. It scraped along the table with each prod.

'So, detective, what can you do for me?' he emitted a stream of smoke from both nostrils.

The combined aromas of cigarette fumes and coffee reminded Matt of continental holidays.

'Off the record?' he asked.

'Of course.' Stefan answered. He opened his coat to reveal a navy-blue jumper then peered into each sleeve like a magician. 'I got no strings.'

'Right, well you've probably guessed then. It's about Kay Harris.'

'Ah, yes. Detective Chief Inspector Harris.'

'Please, can you leave her for now? Kay's just getting back on her feet. She's fragile.'

'Sure, sure. I get that. But it's like me saying to you, can you not investigate my mate? He's killed someone but he's just getting over an illness.'

The coffee arrived and they both thanked the waiter.

When he'd gone Matt said, 'Kay hasn't killed anyone.'

'You sure?'

'What? Course I'm sure. Ava McGrath took her own life. There's nothing to suggest any foul play. And we both know what happened with McGrath.'

'I'm not talking about Ava McGrath. I'm talking about Kay's sister Helen.'

Matt shook his head, 'And we were getting along so well. I was ready to put this on expenses.'

'Matt, look, I understand and of course, I'll respect Kay's privacy, seeing as you're asking.' He sipped his coffee and Matt followed suit. 'But haven't you ever thought it's a bit of a co-inky-dink? The same detective, involved in two suicides? Doesn't it activate the sleuth juices?'

Matt leaned forward earnestly, inadvertently rocking the table. Coffee spilled into his saucer and Stefan gripped the edge of the table to steady it. 'No, it was all very clear. Tragic, but clear, and there's no evidence,' Matt said, dabbing the spill with a thin serviette.

'Sometimes no evidence is the evidence.'

'Come again?'

'On the grounds of public well-being I requested to view the CCTV tape from the car park where Kay's sister jumped, and guess what? No joy.'

'And that means?'

'I don't know, that's why I asked for the tapes. Did you ever see them?'

'Of course,' Matt lied.

Stefan looked into his eyes and Matt was reminded of 'The Terminator', conducting some detailed kinetic study, designed to detect deception.

Matt looked away stating, 'it's as Kay said.'

Stefan rummaged around in his pocket and removed another cigarette from the pack.

'Cool as a mountain Stream.' The memory came to Matt. It was the slogan for Menthol cigarettes his grandma used to smoke back in the day. They were advertised as being a healthy alternative to other cigarettes.

'You didn't finish the last one,' Matt pointed out.

'All the bad stuffs near the filter so I keep away from it. I'm on a health kick,' Stefan added, wryly.

Matt smiled. 'You and me both.'

Stefan lit his cig and put the lighter back in his pocket as another couple sat down at the table across from them. Over at the Printworks an advert for 'Misguided' flashed up, brightening the grey air around it, then it slid away, replaced by another promoting energy drinks.

'They have the best buffalo mozzarella here you know, imported from the Campania region, you won't get it anywhere else in Manchester,' Stefan said.

'You come here often?'

'You flirting with me detective?'

'If that's what it takes.'

'What else have you got?'

'A man could be insulted. '

The waiter approached and asked if they would like anything else. Stefan ordered another coffee. Matt followed suit just to be polite, then asked the waiter for a take-out of the mozzarella. The waiter obliged and brought a small box of it to the table when he delivered the drinks.

'For you,' Matt said and pushed the box towards Stefan, who nodded appreciatively.

'Also,' Matt added. 'We're building a case on something now, something big. If you leave Kay alone, I'll give you first

dibs on it.'
  'McGrath?'
  'Might be.'
  'Well, to be honest you had me at the mozzarella.'

As they parted company Matt hoped Laing would be true to his word, and he would be able to deliver on his. Not just because working with Modern Slavery would be a feather in his cap, but because of his concern for Kay. He'd looked for the tapes Laing referred to and he was right. They had never been logged. Matt was unsure what it meant but couldn't shift the feeling Kay would know exactly what it was Laing suspected.

Chapter Eighty-Three

Kay

Sleep last night reminded me of a date I'd been stood up on. The hopeful anticipation, the clock-watching, the denial and then the sinking realisation sleep just isn't that into me. I almost called Noreen, but thought better of it, knowing I have an appointment with her today.

When I arrive at the centre there's a woman on the desk who I have not seen before, and I have to explain why I'm here. I watch her rifling through the diary, turning pages back and forth. I have the urge to lean over the counter and grab it from her.

'What name was it again?'

'It was, and still is, Kay Harris.'

'And your appointment is with?'

'I just told you all of this. My name is Kay Harris, my appointment is with Noreen Denbigh.'

She turns the pages again, then goes to the computer.

'Ah, yes, Miss Harris. Sorry, I was looking for K, you're an H,' she says.

'And you're an ass,' I say, under my breath.

I try my breathing, breathe in black, breathe out pink, and think nice thoughts.

'I'm sorry, Miss Harris, but Noreen isn't here today.'

The woman smiles at me, as though she's just told me

they've run out of tea bags.

'Sorry?'

'It's OK, I think Peggy Ryan can see you. If you'd like, that is?'

'What? I'm here for a therapy session. You can't just swap mid-therapy.'

'Yes, I quite understand.'

She clearly doesn't. With the same vacuous expression, she continues. 'Only I'm not sure when Noreen will be back.'

'What's wrong? Is she ill?'

'I'm afraid I can't tell you, Miss Harris. I'm really sorry. I've been trying to get hold of everyone she was seeing in her clinic today. She said she'd e-mailed everyone.'

'Well, I didn't get it.'

Reluctantly I break eye contact with her in order to locate my phone and check my e-mails. It's there sent at seven-thirty this morning.

Apologies all, I've had a family emergency and will be in touch shortly. Noreen x

I bristle a little because it's not a personal message to me. A family emergency, though. I suppose it was good of her even to take time out to send a message.

Deflated, I apologise. 'Sorry, yes. I have it, I just hadn't seen it.'

'You have an appointment with Doctor Calder tomorrow. Shall I see if she can see you today?'

'Oh, no. Thank you though for your help. I'll wait until tomorrow. Noreen might be back then anyway.'

The receptionist smiles again. 'Hopefully, yes.'

I leave the clinic and wander around the village. It's a misty wet day. Tree boughs hang low, laden with the dainty pit-pat of drizzle. It's a day to be indoors.

Returning to the cottage I stoke the fire and go into the

kitchen. Two Danish pastries remain from yesterday's breakfast. I eat them, along with a packet of chocolate biscuits, two *pains-au-chocolat* and a packet of gummy bears which Lucy left.

When I've finished, I'm disgusted with myself and my lack of willpower. I've been here before; I'm 'off script' as actors say when they know their lines by heart. I throw the wrappers onto the fire and sit, clutching the folds of my stomach. There's not as much to grasp but there's enough to justify some self-disgust. I should make myself sick. Instead, I put my coat back on and go out for a walk. I worry about Noreen's family problems and regret for my binge whirl around my gut like a butter churn.

I almost call Noreen but shove my phone back in my pocket and trudge head down, seeing nothing but my feet on the shore.

Why would I have seen Peggy Ryan? Does it mean Noreen isn't coming back?

There's no way I would have Peggy Ryan as a therapist. Especially after witnessing the way she spoke to Noreen. I wonder whether Noreen's sudden family problems are actually something to do with Peggy. I couldn't be so traitorous, to swap from Noreen to Peggy.

There's a pathway running along the hillock about thirty feet above me. It dips down to twenty feet and rises again. Passing by the dip, I look up. There's a man wearing green wellies and a green waterproof coat, walking briskly along, arms swinging. I stop dead in my tracks and feel my boots start to bed themselves in the sand and rock. From where I am, I can discern that he's about forty, hair greying at the temples. He comes out of the dip and we're parallel. Further along he's momentarily obscured by a thicket. He turns his head slightly. I don't know if he's seen me, I move closer to the drop, out of his eyeline. Then I turn back for home, checking behind me all the way. From a distance the man resembled Stefan Laing.

Breathless and shaking, I reach the cottage and slam the door shut, then draw the curtains. Hands shaking, I scroll down my contacts for Joy Furnham's number. I find it but hesitate. I would be her superior if I was still in the force, but she knows me only as an ex-detective who kidnapped a child.

Instead, I call Matt, trying to slow my breathing. I inhale black and exhale green.

Matt eventually answers.

'Kay? Everything all right?'

'Matt, I think I've just seen Laing.'

'Why, where are you?'

'I'm at the cottage and was out walking. He's here, Matt. He's found me.'

'I don't think so, Kay, he promised he wouldn't, but I'll call him this morning.'

'Why not call him right this minute?'

'I have just stepped out of a debriefing Kay. I can't tell you anything, except this debriefing wouldn't be happening if it wasn't for you.'

The investigation is his world now. I have member of the public problems. 'I bloody hate this. When will it be done?'

'In the next half hour but I can tell you it's not him. Call Joy. She's literally around the corner.'

'Matt, will you stop telling me to call Joy? Don't you know I absolutely hate having to call *you* for help? I have never yet relied on a man to bail me out. And what's Joy gonna think anyway? What a ball-ache, having to babysit the crazy woman. No, I'll call her in my own good time.' Or not.

'Sorry, Kay, I do know, but she offered and I'm not around the corner anymore,' Matt says calmly.

'Matt...'

'OK, I'll sort it Kay, sit tight and I'll get back to you.'

My breath is slowing, but the stomach flips are still going on, and the damn dizziness. 'OK thanks,' I manage to say. 'Just find out where the scumbag is.'

'And Kay? Do call Joy if you-'

I end the call. 'Killjoy,' I say.

Pacing, pacing, and pacing, around the dining table, into the kitchen. I go up to my bedroom and look out of the window, then up to the attic. I look at the landscape on the wall. The painting of the loch reminds me of the threat I face from Laing.

Downstairs again, I pull the curtains aside and peek out, imagining him clicking away with his zoom lens, capturing my pale face peering out stupidly through the paisley curtains. The headline:

DISGRACED DETECTIVE WITNESSES TWO SUICIDES. NOW IN HIDING.

My heart is going to thump out of my chest if I don't get a grip. I'm expecting a knock at the door any minute. I can't stand the wait. I phone Noreen's number. It goes straight to answerphone, so I leave a lame message. 'Hi Noreen, hope everything is OK?'

It's clear I'm calling for myself, not because I'm worried about her. Fifteen minutes later, Noreen phones me back.

'Hi, is that Kay Harris?' She sounds different, so formal.

'Yeah, hi, Noreen.'

'Sorry, this isn't Noreen. I'm Paula, her daughter. I have her phone. Are you one of her patients?'

'Yes, I'm a new one.'

'Mum's in hospital. She was poorly last night. I'm not supposed to tell you anything, sorry. She's given me strict instructions not to worry anyone.'

I'm not sure what to say. 'I hope it's nothing serious?' I'm fishing but Paula doesn't bite.

'I'm sure she'll be fine,' she answers. 'I know she feels bad about not being able to do her clinic. She said everyone will get a letter, explaining the alternative arrangements.'

'Could I visit her?' I ask.

'Well, she needs to rest right now. Wait until she contacts you herself and take it from there.'

'OK, thank you. Please give her my regards.' I end the call and feel bereft.

I wrap up on the settee and watch an old Bette Davis film called *Jezebel*, with a pot of tea and some biscuits. Reading my record of medication, I realise I've got out of sync with recording the olanzapine. I can't remember whether it's my day to miss or take one. I decide to miss and angrily throw the record onto the floor.

Matt calls me at four. 'It can't be Laing,' he says. 'He's been in court this morning.'

'You spoke to him?'

Someone else is on the line, saying, '*You kidnapped a three-year-old.*'

'Wait, did you hear that?'

'On the phone, yeah,' Matt answers.

'You heard it?'

'I spoke to him twice now.'

The voice again: '*He's lying.*'

I'm stock still, breathing on hold.

'*I'm lying, Kay.*'

'What?'

'Knowing you like I do; I checked the list. He definitely signed in.'

'Matt, someone else is listening.'

'What?'

'Someone just said *You kidnapped a three-year-old.*'

'What?'

There's complete silence. I listen closely, eyes wide, everything receptive to the slightest sound.

'No one said that, Kay. You must have misheard me.'

'No, Matt. I think someone's bugged the phone.'

Silence again.

'Kay.'

'I need to get off the phone Matt.'

When the call has finished, I tentatively open the curtains and peer out. Maybe Matt is lying? Why would he lie? Maybe Barbara Dean has told him to put listening devices on the phone? But why?

Shaking my arms and loosening my shoulders, I put the radio on and rummage in the cupboards. I find a tin of carrot and coriander soup and eat it at the kitchen table, breaking chunks of bread from a soda farl and mopping the soup up with it like a hermit. I feel adrift and remind myself I have my appointment with Doctor Calder tomorrow. She'll be better informed about when Noreen's likely to be back.

Chapter Eighty-Four

Matt

Matt returns to the investigation room, concern about Kay jabbing at his concentration.

When the meeting's over, he asks Ashida if he can borrow her phone and tries Kay's number.

He's not surprised when she doesn't answer, so he texts her from it.

Hi, Kay, it's Matt. I've borrowed Ashida's phone. No one else will have her number. Can you call me back on this? I'm here all day.

'If that rings and it's a number you don't recognise, pass it to me, will you?' he says to her. 'Sorry, I know it's a pain, but it's important.'

Ashida nods her understanding. 'Sure thing.'

Stepping into the corridor, Matt calls Joy Furnham.

'Hey, how's it going?' Joy asks.

'I need a big favour is how it's going.'

'OK.'

'I've talked to you about Kay Harris. She's just moved back there.'

'Yeah, I've not had a chance yet-'

'It's fine. I'm worried about her though. I just got a call

from her and she thought my phone might be bugged.'

'Ah. Is it?'

'No,' he says emphatically. 'I don't think so. There's this reporter, Stefan Laing, Kay's got it in her head he's after her, might have followed her there.'

'Could he have done?'

'He's actually not a bad guy. I've told him Kay's not well. He agreed to give her privacy. She thought she'd seen him, even though he's here in Manchester. That's when she said the phone was bugged.'

'What can I do?'

'Kay said she liked her key nurse, but I didn't get her name. I thought maybe she could just call on her. Make sure she's safe.'

'No problem, I'll call at the community centre and have a chat. I'll go and see Kay myself if need be.'

'Joy, thank you. I owe you.'

'You owe me four big ones now. You free to babysit? I'll cover your travel expenses.'

Chapter Eighty-Five

Kay

My phone rang before, a number I didn't recognise. It spooked me, so I've switched it off.

Sitting with my back to the cellar door, I can feel a draught around my feet. The coal chute is down there, the cottage's only weak spot. We installed a metal grille cover, many years ago. It may have perished, and I haven't been down there for a while. It's a possible route of access.

Scraping the chair across the floor, I stand up and turn the cellar door handle. Relief: it's locked. Poking around in the kitchen drawer, I worry the key might have been one of the things itemised on the warrant list. Thankfully, it's there, a piece of blu-tak and a pink and white striped cake candle from a long-forgotten birthday stuck to it.

I insert the key into the lock and the door creaks open like the soundtrack from a horror movie. The musty smell rises to greet me; its tendrils lasso my ankles. I flick the switch, but visibility is still poor, the weak light subdued by the crypt black.

Reaching the bottom of the stairs, my eyes adjust. I can vaguely make out various shapes. The air is so still, nothing seems to permeate. I can't even hear the radio. I can vaguely make out the area where the coal chute is. It appears to be intact.

Clearly, no one is here. The absence of anything is the most unnerving thing. This subterranean space sits silent, uncomplaining. Is it waiting for something, biding time? My old fishing rod is propped against the wall, covered in mildew. I almost reach for it but stop myself. This was its final resting place. I decide to leave it undisturbed. I wonder if the cellar called me to witness the things I left behind.

Emerging again into the bright kitchen, I hear a noise which seems to come from above. At the foot of the stairs I listen. Treading softly, I ascend.

The rooms on the first landing are clear and the air still. Rounding the next landing, I can see the attic door's ajar. I swallow hard, mouth sapped of moisture. I enter, wary as a stalked deer. I stop, breath caught in my throat. I re-made the bed with fresh linen after Lucy went home. Now the covers are awry. The pillow appears indented, as though someone has rested their head on it.

'Ava?' I say. 'Is that you?'

There's the lightest kiss of air on my face.

An involuntary noise escapes me, and a visceral instinct tells me to get out. I step back, and stumble. Trying to right myself, I twist around and reach for the bannister, but it's moving away from me. As I fall backwards down the stairs, arms flailing, I think, *so this is how it feels*.

Chapter Eighty-Six

Joy

DI Joy Furnham enters the community centre and presses the bell for attention. A woman of about thirty comes to the window. Joy knows her as Gaynor Fields. She's divorced; her husband left her with two young children. Joy considers her a contender for her list of potential babysitters.

Gaynor smiles as she slides the window aside. 'Hi, Joy. Please be here to arrest me, so I can spend the night in a quiet cell and get some sleep.'

'Have you committed a crime?'

'Not yet.'

'Let me know when you do, I'll do everything in my power to ensure you get a long sentence.'

'Thank you.'

'Could you do me a favour, please? Tell me who the team are who see Kay Harris at Tay Cottage.'

'Sure.' Gaynor checks the computer. 'It's Noreen Denbigh, but she's off poorly. I think Peggy Ryan is covering. Her consultant is Doctor Calder.'

'Are any of them in?'

'Yes, I'll call Peggy for you.'

'Thanks.'

Five minutes later Joy is in Peggy's office. She relays the concerns Matt has about Kay. 'I had a call from a colleague.

He's worried about her.'

'Oh, okay, I'll go and visit her,' Peggy answers.

'She's been very ill. You might need to take the doctor with you when you assess her, be on the safe side. Or I could check on her?' Joy offers.

'Thank you, Joy. I think I know the procedure by now. Miss Harris should have been a client of mine anyway. I'm sure Noreen will appreciate it if I can take some of the caseload off her.'

Joy senses resistance from Peggy. She considers her for a moment, then gets up to leave. 'I'm sure you know what you're doing,' she says. Digging into her wallet, she pulls out her card. 'Could you call me on this number as soon as you've checked on her, please? Today, if possible?'

Peggy takes the card. 'Of course. Leave it with me.'

As she waves goodbye to Gaynor, Joy's still trying to work out Peggy's angle. She gets the impression Peggy Ryan might be a bit of a control freak. Definitely not babysitting material.

Chapter Eighty-Seven

Kay

I land on my back with my legs almost toppling me over into a roll. With my neck at a painful angle, I manage to grab the bottom of the stair rail and halt my fall. My body's too long to stretch out on the landing. I lie for a moment, trying to get my breath back, seeing the stairs and ceiling from an inverted angle. The ceiling pendant appears to be rising rigidly out of the floor. A white face looks down at me over the bannister, then it's gone. Coriander and carrot rise and burn my throat as I try to assimilate the information. I'm seeing things; disorientated.

It's like being underwater and trying to figure out which direction to turn to reach the surface. Very slowly, I allow my legs to roll to the side. My back complains, so I stop for a moment, then continue, crying out in pain as I come upright. I try to assess the damage, and stand, very slowly. I seem to be all right, apart from some grazes. Luckily, there's a thick carpet at the turn in the stairs. I sit down and put my head in my hands, wondering what just happened? Why was I so afraid? Then I remember.

Tears come and I don't bother to stop them. I run a bath and pour some Epsom salts under the flowing water. Of course no one else slept in the attic bed. There's no one else here. It's me. I've always been drawn to the room.

I find the olanzapine and take one. Clearly, I need it. I had convinced myself I was cured. Seems I have a long way to go.

Nine o'clock and I'm in bed. I leave the window ajar and listen to the sounds of the evening drawing in and practise my breathing techniques.

I need to write.

Beginning on a positive note, I write about how well the weekend went. Then I write that tomorrow I'm going to buy a fishing rod. I write in a hurry, eager to get to the crux of my worries. Stefan Laing. He's probably the one who's bugged Matt's phone. It's a worry, especially without my new friend Noreen around to bounce things off.

I allow myself to fully express my fears. Apart from the horror of being exposed by Laing, the next most awful thing is losing Noreen as a therapist. I've bonded with her in a way I never could with Joanne Green. I think Peggy has something to do with Noreen's absence. It's her fault Noreen may be lost to me.

I'm learning to write without censoring myself. I continue.

The first time I felt loss like this was at school, when my best friend Ann fell out with me. She quickly found a new best friend, Julie Ashworth. For a while I had no one to sit with at break times or walk home with. We used to spend hours on the phone, Ann, and me, even though we'd talked all day.

Everyone had their own cliques at school, and it was hard to break into them. Even Helen, my own sister, ignored me. So that Ann and her new friend couldn't see what a loser I was, I grieved alone in the school toilets. I told my mum, but she just shrugged. Parents rarely grasp the depth of the heartbreak and loneliness their children suffer at school. In those days I didn't know about suicide or self-harm. I don't recall knowing of anyone my age who killed themselves. There was no social media back then. Maybe if I'd known about self-harming, I would've given it a go, instead of bingeing.

I wonder about Noreen, whether she's still in touch with school friends. I know so little about her. I didn't once ask her a question about herself. It came as a surprise to me that she had a daughter. How self-absorbed have I become, that I imagined Noreen only existed to administer to others?

I take some painkillers for my grazed back, and eventually sleep.

I dream that I'm upstairs in the attic with Noreen and Peggy on the bed, playing cards. They both look up at me, but it's Peggy who gets up. She's smiling and I think she's going to invite me in. Instead she slams the door in my face.

I awake with a gasp.

Wrapping myself in my quilt, I hurry downstairs and blow on the dying embers in the grate. Shivering, I rub my hands together, then run them up and down my arms. Sitting on the settee, I watch the fire as it catches. Loneliness is always heightened in the middle of the night, but nightmares when you're alone are the worst thing. There's no one to comfort you, to tuck you in and make soothing noises. I'm sick of self-soothing. It's all I've ever done. If I didn't bother self-soothing, what would become of me?

I lie down and cry, for my mum and dad, for Ellie, for Jack, for Helen, for Ava, for Noreen. I almost heave with the force of the sobs. I feel so lost and alone.

Chapter Eighty-Eight

Kay

When morning comes, I feel like I have a bad cold. My head's fuggy and I can't grasp my thoughts. Then a wave of nausea hits. I want to cry again, but can't seem to keep my footing anymore. Everything seemed to be going well, but my mood is chopping and changing. I look up at the clock. It's only ten to five, though it feels later.

I decided last night to return to Manchester. I'm going to face the music; whatever Laing's discovered. I have Matt, Caro, and Lucy there. It's easier for Ellie to visit, and vice versa. Coming here was a bad idea. I have become paranoid. I am not sleeping, and no one here cares about me.

I drag myself into the kitchen and look for something to eat. There are a few strawberries left from the weekend, and some other bits of fruit. I make a fresh fruit salad. I wash it, leave it to drain in the colander, then go upstairs, have a quick wash and pull an old jumper over my pyjamas.

Back downstairs I stoke the fire, then hear the crunch of tyres on the gravel. I open the front door, smiling, hoping it's Noreen.

Maybe I'll stay?

It's a blue car I don't recognise. A woman with long thin grey hair emerges. Peggy Ryan. She's seen me, so I can't pretend to be out. Grabbing her crocheted bag from the front seat, she slams the car door shut and approaches.

'Hello there,' she calls.

'Morning,' I answer, retreating into the kitchen.

She follows and wipes her feet on the doormat. 'Can I come in?'

'As long as you're not a vampire,' I say from the kitchen door. 'I'm in here.'

Peggy follows me through. She's wearing a loose-fitting cream and brown striped cheesecloth dress.

'I'm just checking you're alright. You heard about Noreen?' she asks.

'No,' I answer, so she's forced to tell me. I might learn something more.

'She's not well, unfortunately. Don't know yet when she'll be back.'

I turn my back on her and slice a banana. 'Who will be my therapist?'

'We don't know yet. There's me, of course. Or Ben Grainger. He's a man, obviously. We were concerned because you didn't make your appointment this morning with Doctor Calder.'

'What?'

'At eleven-'

Studying the clock, it dawns on me I mistakenly read the time as ten to five not twenty-five past ten. But the clock hasn't been right since I replaced the batteries.

'I was going to come last night, then I saw your appointment with the doctor this morning and thought I'd catch you then.'

'Goodness, I'm sorry. I slept through,' I say.

You stupid bitch, I wasted my time coming here.

The voice comes at me in surround-sound. Still, I can't be sure whether it's inside my head or not.

'Not to worry. How are you doing?' Peggy asks.

I watch her mouth as she speaks, noticing the hairs on her upper lip, short and stubby, white as the bristles of a toothbrush.

'You think you've wasted your time?' I ask, aware of the danger. I'm on my own ground, though. She's almost as tall as me, but she won't be as strong.

'Not at all.'

She smiles. Can I trust it? What game is she playing? She's watching me closely. I move to the chopping board.

'How is Noreen?' I ask. I keep my back to her, so she can't see my agitation.

Noreen's fine. She just can't stand you. You kidnapped a three-year-old boy. You're evil.

It's Peggy's voice, but higher pitched, accusatory, spiteful. Why is she doing this?

'Well, it's confidential, but she'll be home very soon, I hope.'

Tears run down my face. I slice strawberries.

Blood mingled with grit.

What's happening to me?

I know what you did, Kay. You killed your own sister and you've not been able to live with it.

'It's not true,' I answer. The strawberry juice stains my fingers.

Now that reporter is onto you. He's found you out.

'Oh, I'm sure it is. She'll be back in no time.'

You were there, weren't you? You pushed her, then made out you were in the area. You used your position to collect the CCTV, made sure it all got lost, no evidence.

'No, no, no!'

I turn around and see Peggy on her phone. Who is she calling? She's telling them what I've done. Staring directly at me, she speaks.

You're the best liar of all of us.

I turn back and continue chopping, but the red pulp makes me retch.

'Oh, my dear girl, it will be fine. Come on now.' She approaches me. I turn, and she appears to register my anguish, my terror.

'What is it?' she asks.

Everyone here knows you're mad. As if Ava McGrath would ever have been a friend of yours.

Then I see *her* terror. Her mouth forms a perfect circle. Her eyes almost mirror it, grey eyebrows arching. She staggers back, clutching her stomach where the knife is embedded. Blood seeps through her fingers.

'None of it is true!' I shout.

I feel something leaving me, energy evaporating through my pores.

Peggy gasps, clutching at the knife, hands slippery with blood. I watch as she sinks to her knees, then keels over onto her side like a tired dog, mouth agape, glasses askew.

After a few minutes she lies still, clutching the wooden knife handle which protrudes like Excalibur through the mess of red soaked cheesecloth.

Blood leaks out onto the stone floor. It reaches my feet and I step away from it.

'Ava was the best of us,' I say.

I wrap her in my quilt, along with her handbag. Hauling her body down the cellar stairs, I flinch each time her head hits the edge of a step. I pull a piece of tarpaulin over her and remove the light bulb. Whoever she called; I didn't hear her give an address. It doesn't matter anyway. I've got her phone. I can always chuck it into the loch.

For now, I move her car around the back of the house, to where it won't be visible.

Cleaning blood up is a messy business. It's started to congeal and glistens like a perfect royal icing. It gets everywhere, in all the nooks and crannies. I'm not kidding myself. I know that even an average forensics technician will find it with a quick spray of Luminol.

Scraping the slime of strawberries and banana from the chopping board and into the bin, I heave, tasting bile.

Whatever happens now, is out of my hands. It looks like I'm staying, though. I can't leave now.

I climb the stairs to the attic. Pausing at the door, I knock very gently. Nothing, I knock again. Nothing. Dejected, I try again.

Noises from within. A small voice answers. 'Yes?'

'It's me, Kay.'

'Come in.'

Opening the door, I feel a surge of relief and love. Ava is there, sitting on the bed, reading. I gasp, rushing over to her. I kneel on the floor and she leans forward and embraces me.

'Where did you go? I ask, sobbing, feeling jubilant, elated.

'Nowhere,' she answers, as she strokes my hair. 'I've been here all the time.'

Epilogue

Kay

Three years later

Of course I agree to go back. I feel very calm about it. I've felt like this for a couple of years now. The hustle and hum of life is still happening around me but I'm in a contented place, like a cat napping in a sheltered corner of the garden.

Ellie has finally made her peace with her Dad, so it followed that forgiving me had been part of that treaty. Following discussion with them both earlier this year, we all agreed selling the cottage was the right thing to do. Ellie is expecting another child, having given birth to a daughter, Amelia, two years ago. I think the money from the sale could be better spent on a bigger home for their growing family, and it's what Helen would have wanted.

As part of my treatment plan I had an injection every month.It's been gradually reduced by the doctor. I've been free of it for almost six months now and I'm doing fine. I've come to understand myself and more importantly, accept my vulnerabilities.

In the Piazza Navona in Rome there is a statue sculped by Bernini called 'The Fountain of Four Rivers.' Each of the rivers is represented by a muscular personification. One of the figures, 'Nile' is covering his eyes with a lifted arm.

Rumour has it that Bernini fashioned it to shield Nile's eyes from the facing building, which had been designed by his loathed arch-rival Borromini. The sculpture of Neptune resonates with me. It's solid, immovable, but it's also fallible, shielding itself from the ugliness of the world. I've been doing the same for years, covering my eyes, playing peek a boo while projecting an image of strength.

I'm learning to see now. To keep my eyes open. I have a list of 'red flags' to look out for that would be the first indication of relapse, but I believe that if I continue as I am the risk of one is unlikely.

'Isn't there any medication where expanding in all directions isn't a side effect?' I ask Dr Glass after I have stepped off the scales at my quarterly check-up.

'The one you were prescribed had the least and you will lose the weight now you're no longer on it. But isn't a little increase in weight a small price to pay?'

Skinny people say stuff like that all the time.

'Would I rather be psychotic and thin than sane and fat? Is that what you're asking?' I turn the snow globe on her desk upside down and absently watch the flakes settle on the pretty Swiss scene. 'Come to think of it, you don't see many fat serial killers, do you?'

'How do you feel about going back to the cottage?' she asks, swerving the direction of the conversation. 'Do you still want to do it?'

'I'm interested to see it. I need to say goodbye.'

'Well, you know I support that. I think you're well enough and being involved in the sale may help the healing process.'

'Go on, say it.'

'What.'

'The C word. Closure.'

For the first two hours of the journey Ellie and Jack and I have mostly chatted about the progress of Ellie's pregnancy, and baby Amelia, who is at home with Nate today. The rest of the conversation is just gossip and overspill. Any topics concerning Helen are still cautiously steered around like hairpin bends, but we are getting there slowly, reuniting as a family, building back trust, healing.

Jack pulls in at Bothwell Services and we grab a coffee and freshen up. When we're back on the M74 it feels like we're all more comfortable within the confines of the car. I can only see the back of Ellie's head from my seat in the rear, but I catch glimpses of her reflection in the side mirror. Her pretty, heart-shaped face is fuller now she's in her second trimester. Her eyes sweep back and forth, scanning the passing scenery. Now and then she closes them and leans back into the headrest.

Jack is focused and in control. His hands are firm on the steering wheel, shirtsleeves rolled up. Sunlight from the late August sun catches the dial on his watch and the reflection bounces around the roof of the car.

I observe him through the rear-view mirror, deep brown eyes hidden behind his aviators. I can't read his expression, but his body language tells me he's relaxed. Finally, I feel content enough to rest my eyes and allow the scene to carry on without me having to attend to it.

I still dream of Helen sometimes, but the nightmarish quality has long gone. Instead, when I wake, the memory of her lingers then floats away like straw on the wind.

Three years ago, I was taken by ambulance from the cottage and sectioned because I was deemed a danger to myself and to someone else. It was Peggy, but it could have been anyone. Peggy just got caught in the cross hairs of my psychosis. There in the kitchen she'd observed my distress and had the foresight to call the emergency services. They'd arrived in time to save us both.

I've little recollection of it, but I'm told once they had gained access, they found me in the attic, terrified, my speech garbled and incoherent. I was thankful for that.

I spent a year in a secure unit before I was able to stand trial. I was found not guilty by reason of diminished responsibility and I spent a year on a community treatment order.

I've never laid eyes on Peggy or the cottage since then, but I have written to thank her for getting me help and to tell her I'm sorry for my actions and any pain I caused, and that I'm recovered. I waited for a postcard, but Peggy didn't write back. How rude.

Matt has arranged for Joy Furnham to call and let Peggy know I will be in the area overnight, just so she doesn't hear it from anyone else and freak out. I have the notoriety of Michael Myers in Aberfeldy.

Matt is now a DCI. His work with the Modern Slavery Unit paid off and they dismantled the whole supply chain from the transfer of illegal immigrants to the forged work documents. 'Ground Up' had been a legitimate front used by Melnik, and McGrath had got in over his head with the forgeries. McGrath is now residing in one of Her Majesty's holiday homes and Josh is being cared for by an aunty.

Occasionally Matt calls by to run something past me on a case he's working on. So, I have become a kind of a consultant, but with no pay, and no glory. I once suggested that I could work as a private investigator. I know it's a long shot with my history, but he didn't have to find it quite so funny. Still, I'm currently enjoying my work as an advocate's assistant for the local mental health trust. It's really opened my eyes. We discuss denial and I tell them a little of my history. When they learn I'm now off medication I see the hope it gives them for their own recovery. Each telling of my story reinforces hope for myself too. Sometimes I wonder what I would have made of me if I'd ever attended one of these groups as a patient. I can just see me, wiggling my feet, checking my watch and puffing dismissively at comments made by other members. God what an absolute self-righteous arse I was.

Lulled by the motion of the car I must have fallen asleep. When I open my eyes again the roads are green-walled and winding. I know this place, but I'm a stranger here. I could connect to it, plug myself in, but I don't. It's just scenery.

We approach the cottage and I deliberately don't look at it until I'm out of the car.

When I do it appears smaller than I remember, which might be an optical illusion, because the trees around the back and the side have flourished and overshadow it. Branches brush against the roof tiles and scrabble at the upper window on the left. But the cottage remains unblinking and passive.

There's another car on the driveway, a white four-by-four. My heart beats faster.

'You OK?' Jack asks.

'Fine,' I answer.

The door of the white car opens, and a leg encased in yellow and brown striped tights appears, followed by another one. Then an auburn topped head pokes out, and Noreen shuffles forward off the high driver's seat and plants two red ankle booted feet onto terra-firma.

I was informed that because I was walking into an untested situation, Noreen would be on hand as the mental health contingent, but I hadn't been prepared for the surge of emotion triggered by seeing her again. I learned that her illness turned out to be gallstones, thankfully she made a full recovery. She smiles at me and I walk towards her. Ellie and Jack stay where they are and watch. We hug and speak simultaneously.

'Hi, Kay, good to see you,'

'Hi, Noreen.'

Jack introduces himself and shakes Noreen's hand, but Ellie goes in for the hug. Good for her.

'You look well, Kay,' Noreen says.

I feel shy under her scrutiny. I know I have changed.

'You too. Love your tights. Aren't your legs hot?'

'To be fair, without them I still look like I'm wearing tights, purple ones, my legs are so veined.'

I laugh, and we both turn at the sound of Ellie opening the door of the cottage.

'You coming?' I ask.

'I'll wait here. You go on. You know where I am.'

'But you're coming back to the hotel for dinner with us, right?'

'Of course. I've already looked at the menu online. There's a monkfish with my name on it.'

The cottage has been cleared of most of the furniture, and our belongings are in storage. It smells of soot and dusty carpet. The room looks so different. It's hard to relate this empty space to the wellspring where I was nurtured as a child. Where, as an adult, I fell in love with Jack, then went out of my mind with guilt.

'You okay?' Jack asks again, coming towards me.

I do a kind of physical scan of my body. Nothing goes off, no bleeps, no buzzers. I nod. 'Hmm hmm.'

I can hear running water in the kitchen. The house pulls me in, and I walk forward. Jack follows. I keep my eyes away from the floor and on Ellie, who's filling the kettle.

'Do you think Noreen would like a cuppa?' Ellie asks as she flicks the kettle on.

'I'll ask her,' Jack says, turning around, happy to have something to do.

I drop my gaze. The pine table remains, and there's a large, unfamiliar rug covering the stone floor where I last saw Peggy.

I waver a little and pull my gaze up. The sound of the heating kettle kicks in, reviving the paused heart of the kitchen.

'This must be very weird for you,' Ellie says, turning to me.

'And you. The last time you were here was when-'

Jack interrupts as he re-enters. 'Yes please, two sugars if you've got it.'

Ellie puts teabags into four mugs and pours the water. She produces a carton of milk and a small packet of sugar from her shopper.

'You thought of everything,' I say impressed.

She delves further and produces a packet of shortbread.

'Be prepared,' she jokes, pre-empting the inevitable comment from Jack about her days as a girl guide and the motto.

Jack picks up his and Noreen's mugs. 'I'll take these out' he says. 'I told her to come in, but she said she didn't want you to feel crowded. I'm going to join her if you've no objection?'

I nod. 'Sure.'

Ellie holds the front door open for her dad. 'I'll stay, if you don't mind?' she says. I know they've already agreed that I'm not to be alone in here.

I take a biscuit and my mug of tea and head upstairs.

'I'll give you a minute,' Ellie adds.

My bedroom has been cleared and there's a clean rectangle of carpet where my bed once stood. I stand in it, sip my tea, and look around. The branches brush against the window and create a dappled effect on the opposite wall. A reel of images flickers through my mind.

Mum and Dad re-papering the room. Me and Helen scribbling our names and poems by Emily Bronte on the bare plaster, imagining whoever came after us would uncover these treasures and wonder if the Bronte sisters had ever lived here. Awaking as a child to the smell of a cooked breakfast. Dad asking everyone for the crispy rind off their bacon because it was the best bit. The regular sound of a slamming bedroom door as Helen stomped into her room.

Me and Jack.

Me and Ava.

I hear a car on the gravel outside and see a silver Ford Focus pull up. A woman in her thirties gets out and is met by Jack. I dunk the biscuit in my tea as I watch them shake hands. The woman opens the boot of her car and removes a for sale sign. I assume this is Sharon, the estate agent. I crack the window open and hear Jack say it's inconvenient for her to come inside. She looks up at the window and I step back. When I look again, Jack's helping her to plant the sign. He tells her he'll drop the house keys off in the morning. The wind has got up and whips her hair around her face as she gets back into her car. Then she reverses down the drive and is gone.

I go up the next flight of stairs, treading carefully, remembering the last time I did this. I turn the handle to the attic room.

Sharon will have to put a fan heater on in here before any prospective buyers view it. It's still so cold.

During a conference call Sharon said she was confident it would sell quickly. The 'history attached to the house,' as she delicately put it, had diminished, and besides, no one had died.

I don't know what I expected to feel. Sadness? Nostalgia? Fear? But I feel nothing. Nada.

I remember visiting the funeral home after Dad died. He was all shiny and clean, waxy like a mannequin in Burton's window, dressed in his best navy suit, nice hanky in his pocket, a Windsor knot in his tie. But the sense of him, the spirit, what you'd describe as the essence of the man, had left the building. It feels like that now, especially in this room. There's nothing of Helen here. The memories I have of her and Mum and Dad are within me, not these walls.

The rest of it was madness.

I've seen enough. I close the door behind me and make my way downstairs. Ellie comes from the kitchen.

Catherine Wimpeney

'I'm ready to go if you are,' I say.

'If you're sure?' she answers and takes my empty mug from me. 'You think it helped?' she calls back, as she returns to the kitchen.

'Definitely.' I answer as I roam the lounge. I lean against the fireplace and touch the hard, cold stone.

Ellie wanders past with her shopper. 'I've turned the water off.'

'OK,' I nod.

I tell her I'll be out in a minute. She hesitates, then nods. I look around once more at the place which gave me the best and the worst memories of my life.

I follow Ellie out and see Jack leaning casually against the car, chatting to Noreen. His relaxed manner puts people immediately at ease. I know we have a way to go. Ellie is getting comfortable with leaving us on our own in a room and I can feel the dynamic changing. I can see the day when I'll have what I wanted all along.

I recall the first few weeks after my admission. I emerged slowly from the initial wallop of medication, and despite the numerous hours of probing questions, it became clear some of my memories had gone, particularly those about Helen.

The truth? It's been lost in all the treatments, in all the talking, the writing, and the medication. The truth about Helen's death is between the lines somewhere. I don't go there. I try to focus on what's real, not the blank spaces.

Jack lifts his head and smiles at me, and Noreen and Ellie turn and watch as he approaches. He reaches me and puts his hand on my arm.

'Ready?' he asks.

'Ready,' I answer, and pull the cottage door closed behind me.

Noreen waves to me as she starts her engine. 'See you there,' she calls from her open window.

Ellie climbs into the back seat.

'Your turn for the front,' she says to me, and pushes her shopper and handbag into the vacant child seat. When we're all belted up Jack reverses down the drive. It appears to me like the cottage is withdrawing, shrinking away from us, then he puts the car into first and drives away.

Ellie calls Nate and thrusts the phone between the front seats so Jack and I can hear Amelia's babbles in the background. We all laugh, when she shouts 'Mama!' and I feel a surge of well-being at the possibilities opening up before me.

Truth is overrated. What would be the point? Who would it help?

I have never said it out loud.

Not to a living soul.

Acknowledgements

First and last to my amazing husband Ian, who always has my back. We are an effective team.

To my son Adam, who has inherited the creative gene and then some. His encouragement, support and astute insights helped me to keep momentum when I was flagging, (at least once a day). To my talented step-daughter Emma Brereton, for her excellent PR and marketing skills. Every author needs an Emma.

To my brother Martin, for all the help with plot twists, which we regularly thrashed out in front of a roaring fire, over lashings of tea in a New Mills country pub. To South Manchester Writers Workshop who helped me believe I could do this from day one. To my first editor Lynn Patrick, who taught me some hard truths about the correct use of the comma. To James and Tom at Northodox Press for believing in my novel, and for representing Northern crime writers. Finally, to my cat Jonesy, a master at relaxation and indifference. I am in awe.

NORTHODOX
PRESS

HOME OF NORTHERN VOICES

 FACEBOOK.COM/NORTHODOXPRESS

 TWITER.COM/NORTHODOXPRESS

 INSTAGRAM.COM/NORTHODOXPRESS

 NORTHODOX.CO.UK

SUBMISSIONS ARE OPEN!

WRITER &
DEBUT AUTHOR   [ ]

NOVELS &
SHORT FICTION   [ ]

FROM OR LIVING
IN THE NORTH   [ ]

Lightning Source UK Ltd.
Milton Keynes UK
UKHW010214311021
393098UK00002B/393